Praises for *Stealing Wishes* by Shannon Yarbrough

"I like to feel humanity, and in *Stealing Wishes*, we get that, we more than get that."

-Cheryl Anne Gardner, author of *Logos*

"I should have known that I would end up liking the main character as a person, and that the plot would drive the story. I should have anticipated the subtle philosophy sprinkled throughout the book and the smart writing style that pulled me along with the narrative. I should have known all of that but I let my preconceptions of "gay romance" sway my decision and that's a shame."

-Dan Marvin, author of *Briefs for the Reading Room*

"The theme of the book is universal, as we all contemplate at one time or other what love is, and struggle with the intricacies of relationships, whether gay, hetero, or both."

-LK Gardner-Griffie, author of the *Misfit McCabe* series

"*Stealing Wishes* is a smart, enjoyable novel whose memorable setting and quirky characters stay with you beyond the last page. It provides real insight into gay life in a Midwestern town with warmth, wry humor, and a deft touch."

-Mark Zero, author of *Give the Drummer Some*

Are You Sitting Down?

Also by Shannon Yarbrough:

Stealing Wishes

The Other Side of What

Are You Sitting Down?

Shannon Yarbrough

Are You Sitting Down?

ISBN: 978-0-984-23833-0

Printed in the United States of America

10 9 8 7 6 5 4 3 2 1

Cover Art: "Abandoned Chair" by Sally Ashbrook
www.sallyashbrook.com

A happy family is but an early heaven.

-George Bernard Shaw

To my brother and my sister.

I may be taller, but I will always look up to you.

Prologue

A severe headache woke me from my dreams. I dabbed at my tongue with my fingers, thinking I tasted copper. Maybe it was just the wine we'd had with supper—*But wait!*—Lorraine and I had not shared a bottle of wine in years. I sat up in bed and did not know where I was. I did not recognize the aging beautiful woman sleeping soundly beside me. She was nuzzled into my arm like she knew me. I pulled myself from her grasp, threw back the sheets, and put my feet on the floor. My sudden movement woke her.

"Frank, honey, what's wrong?"

She knew my name.

"Where am I?" I asked.

"What do you mean? Frank, what's wrong?"

"I feel sick...don't know...what..."

I tried to stand but suddenly felt light-headed. My left arm ached like it wasn't there. I reached up to rub my temples but I couldn't feel my face. As my sight began to fade in and out, the woman beside me got up and walked around to my side of the bed. She knelt down in front of me and looked deep into my face.

"Frank, are you okay?"

"Who….are….you?" I uttered. Inside my head I knew she was my wife, but I had no control over the words coming out of my mouth.

A tear fell down her face. She ran to the dresser and picked up the phone.

"Hello, this is Lorraine White. I'm at 48 Main Street in Dogwood. It's my husband. I think he's having a stroke or a heart attack. Yes, please send an ambulance. Please hurry," she managed to say through heavy sobs, dropping the phone on the floor.

I had lain back down on the bed clutching my numb hand. My ears clogged up like I had gone under water. Lorraine's voice was suddenly muffled. I watched her drop the phone and rush back over to the bed. She sat down next to me and pushed sweaty strands of hair from my forehead. She took my gimp hand and squeezed it. I could feel it again, there in hers. As I tried to steady my breathing, I concentrated on her lips mouthing muted words of comfort and love but I could not hear them. It was one of those blurry moments in a movie when someone has just opened their eyes to find a loved one standing over them, only nothing was coming into clear focus for me now.

I studied the wet wrinkles beneath her eyes. I needed to tell her good-bye. I wanted to tell her I loved her and to take care of the kids, but the photo on my nightstand proved they were all old enough to take care of her now. I knew in my heart that she was my wife and that those young people in the photograph were my kids; this was my family. My dear wife. My loving family. But the ruptured blood vessel, the lack of oxygen to my brain, blocked all of my comprehension.

"She's going to be okay. She won't be alone," a voice said to me from somewhere in the room. It was a voice I knew, but had not heard in a very long time. Looking at Lorraine's face, I knew she had not heard it. I was either imagining it or it was only a voice for me.

"Tell her I love her," I said back to the voice, but I said it inside my head because my lips still would not move. "Tell Lorraine I love her."

"She knows you love her. The kids know too. They will be okay without you. It's time to go, Frank."

Had I only known this evening would be the last time I kissed Lorraine and laid down beside her for what should have been just another routine night of peaceful sleep, I don't think I would have gone to bed at all.

By now, Lorraine was crying out in agony. The phone screamed a busy signal behind her from being left off the receiver. She crawled across the floor on her hands and knees and picked it up. She madly pressed the buttons, calling someone again.

"Martin! It's Mom. Are you sitting down?"

I stopped fighting and let my eyes close, and when I opened them again I was standing with my mother and father who had both died long ago. They were smiling at me like they had not seen me in years. They hadn't. I felt the need to look back and see Lorraine just one more time, but something wouldn't let me. My parents took me by the hand and we faded away.

Beautiful white light surrounded me and I didn't hurt anymore, and I knew it was the end of days when our stories— Lorraine and mine and the kids—had happy endings. Or was it only the beginning?

Travis

"What happened to your goat?"

Mom had asked me to stop at Four Points Grocery on the way home to Dogwood to pick up her ham. She'd left it there two days ago to be smoked. It was a service Mr. Greer, the owner and sole employee for as long as I could remember, offered during the holiday season.

"What'd ya say? You Lorraine's boy, ain't cha?" Mr. Greer was hard of hearing.

"Yes sir, I am. I asked what happened to your goat."

"I got her ham ready. Be right back."

Mr. Greer lived in a small farm house behind the grocery in a grove of trees surrounded by an old rickety fence. He kept a black pygmy goat tied to the fence during the warmer months. As a child, I always looked for the goat when we drove by going to and from school. Sometimes Mom would stop in for a fill-up or just for a bag of ice. I'd sit in the car and through the window I'd watch the goat nibble shoots of grass as far away as his leash would let him.

Four Points Grocery was the only convenience store from here to the town of Ruby Dregs, which was only five miles away. To the few hundred people who lived in Dogwood and kept Mr. Greer in business, they preferred not having to "go to town" just for a dozen eggs or to buy a stamp. Veterans played checkers in the corner atop a pickle barrel. Mr. Greer still sold penny candy and cold drinks in glass bottles.

The highway had been paved and painted with a dotted line years ago, but you almost expected to see horse-drawn wagons in his parking lot. It was as if someone had put a glass dome over the place to preserve it just the way it was. It was the way it'd always been. Although there was snow on the ground now and the goat was probably keeping warm in Mr. Greer's barn, I was sincerely interested in that grass-eating childhood landmark of mine.

"Here's that ham," Mr. Greer said, returning from the back room. "What else did you need?"

The cowbell on the door clanged behind me. I turned to see some local farmer coming in, clad head to toe in camouflage. He knocked his snow-caked boots against the threshold.

"Jeb, I got that goat all wrapped up for ya. Right there on the counter," Mr. Greer called out.

Jeb didn't say a word. The floorboards creaked beneath his pot-belly weight. He picked up the mound of white butcher paper wrapped in twine, laid two wrinkled twenty-dollar bills on the counter, and walked back out into the snow.

"Was that your little black goat?" I asked wide-eyed and confused.

"Sy? Naw, old Sy died bout two summers ago. Laid him to rest on that hill where he always liked to graze. Lots of folks miss him. They put a big write-up about it in the paper."

"I'm sorry. I would have liked to have read that." I made a mental note to ask my mom about the article. It seemed trite, but I was somehow interested in the life of that goat who had grazed serenely in the distance of the gas station for so many years.

"Old Sy was twenty years old. Goat dat old no good for eatin'. Meat too tough. Jeb there is an ole goat farmer. He knows. That goat he brought in sure was tender. You like Billy goat, boy?"

"No, sir. Only if they are in a petting zoo."

Mr. Greer laughed a toothless chuckle that was more like a whistle.

"That's a purty ham ya Momma got there. You like ham?"

"Not really."

"Turkey?"

"Now you're talking, but we have that at Thanksgiving. We always have ham for Christmas."

"Ah, I got a turkey you'd like. Deep-fried. How 'bout that?"

"No, that's okay. Thank you," I said.

Mr. Greer was already fishing a sample out and handing it to me on a paper napkin. I took the white meat from his callused fingers. The turkey's encrusted skin melted in my mouth like butter. The dry meat and kick of spices reminded me why I liked Thanksgiving better. I couldn't resist. I paid Mr. Greer for smoking the ham and then bought the turkey as well. Between Jeb and me, Mr. Greer had made eighty dollars. Something told me his modest living made him feel like a rich man that day. After all, the man still sold pickled eggs for a nickel out of large five-gallon jars of brine.

He helped me to the car with the turkey and ham although I told him he didn't have to. I wished him a Merry Christmas, and then offered my hand so that he wouldn't fall on the slushy pavement while going back inside. He smelled strongly of tobacco and whiskey. He always did. He stood at the door of the grocery with a heavy dentureless frown on his face and watched me like a parent who was sad to see his loved ones go when the holidays were over.

I looked up the hill and was sad to see one of my faint childhood memories replaced with a wooden cross and some faded silk flowers half-buried in the snow that I hadn't seen there before. It's odd how our eyes trick us sometimes because we are so accustomed to seeing the same things in the same places everyday; and when it's been so long and they suddenly aren't there anymore, it's hard to see what replaced them. The sound of a car pulling up behind me broke my thought. I turned to make sure I was not in its way.

"Merry Christmas, Travis," the driver called out the window as it rolled down.

I recognized the wispy falsetto voice immediately. It was Justin's father.

"Merry Christmas, Mr. Black," I said leaning down to his window to speak to him as he put the car in park.

"When did you get into town?" he asked.

"I actually just arrived. I haven't even been home yet. Mom called and asked me to pick up the ham on the way in."

He glanced over at my car out of the corner of his eye. The wrapped gifts in the passenger seat assured him I wasn't lying. Something deep inside him wanted to find Justin sitting there. I longed for the same sometimes.

"Nobody smokes 'em like old Greer, eh? I see your mother each week at church. Lorraine looks good," he said, looking back up at me.

"She's doing very well, sir. What about Mrs. Black?"

"She has her ups and downs. Some days are better than others. Tomorrow won't be a good one. The holidays never are. You should stop in and see her. Visit with us a while."

"I just might do that." This was a lie.

I had not seen the Blacks since Justin's funeral. They had made it a point to tell me several times that they didn't hold me responsible for not getting Justin back to them soon enough. In the hospital that day, on the phone, at the funeral home, even in a birthday card the following year, they constantly reminded me it wasn't my fault.

It *wasn't* my fault.

Standing in the cemetery on that last day of summer, Mr. Black had looked so uncomfortable in the black suit he'd outgrown. It was probably the same suit he'd worn to his wedding years before. Tufts on the shoulders left from the hanger told me he'd slipped it on right from storage. A faint brownish-gray ring of dust encircled the collar, where it had been left exposed outside the garment bag in the attic or in the back of his closet untouched for so many years. I remember his face was pale and blotchy, like someone had kicked him really hard.

The cool wind that rustled the first autumn leaves from the trees blew Mrs. Black's handkerchief from her hand. It flitted through the air like a white downy feather then landed in the hole in the ground there between us, slipping off Justin's coffin and disappearing in the fresh dirt beneath. Everyone looked at her for a response. Mr. Black touched her arm and she gave a nod to just leave it. She buried her face in his side and cried out. Everyone winced with sorrow. I was accustomed to the sound of her weeping since I'd heard a lot of it for more than two days now, but one never becomes comfortable with the sound of a mother's pain. Lorraine, my own mother, took my hand in hers without looking at me. She felt my pain too.

I didn't mean to distance myself from them after that. It wasn't intentional. With Justin gone, I also needed to mourn and then find a way to fill the empty void in my life where he had been. After spending nearly ten years of your life with someone, a part of you dies with them or just goes missing. There are no pictures of broken hearts or your sanity on the back of milk cartons like the ones of lost children they once put there.

Justin had been quite remote with his parents. He didn't visit them as often as I visited mine. He took his reasons to the grave. I figured his parents blamed me, but they always hugged my neck when we did go to see them. Inside my head, I imagined it was just his mother being hospitable. In her head, she probably gritted her teeth and loathed the day Justin had met me. And Justin always made me go with him to see them. He never wanted time alone with his family.

And now that he was gone, I couldn't be there for them. I couldn't answer their questions or be the last living entity to connect them to their son. When he was living, their house was a shrine to him. School photos from every year decorated the walls in numerical order. The trophies he'd won running track or playing piano recitals still adorned the mantel. I had my photos and souvenirs too, now tucked away for rainy days. I knew Justin would understand. It was easier to think his parents despised me because I knew their son better than they did.

That was two summers ago when I lost my lover and my best friend, and without even knowing it, I lost a part of my childhood too. Sy the goat.

"Is your mother having a big dinner tonight?" Mr. Black asked.

"Yes sir, the whole family should be there. It's the first time in a long time since Pop died."

"Your brothers and sisters?"

"Yep, all five of us."

"Justin always wanted a sibling," Mr. Black said. The glazy look in his eyes told me he was fading away to grab hold of some distant recollection of a better day.

"What about you and Mrs. Black? Any plans for Christmas?" I asked, changing the subject to bring him back.

"No plans. Just us. If you find the time, please come by and see us. Will you?" He pleaded.

"I'll certainly try," I said looking away to avoid the hope in his eyes. I glanced at my car and then looked down the long empty stretch of highway like a weary traveler with miles to go, but my mother lived within walking distance from Greer's.

"Tell your mother Merry Christmas from the Blacks."

Justin had always hated their last name, mainly because in a small town like Ruby Dregs "the blacks" was also used to reference the African Americans, who mainly lived on Forrest Avenue. There were no colored people living in Dogwood, but when a family of them showed up one morning at the Baptist church because the preacher had invited them, "the blacks are here" is what everyone whispered in Sunday school. Justin once told me a wooden plaque reading "The Blacks" hung on the side of their home below the mailbox till he conveniently buried it in the backyard one summer while in grade school. His father had blamed "the blacks" for stealing it.

With my last name being White, it didn't help much. It never made Justin mad but it was good material for a joke whenever he started talking about it. "Whites and Blacks shouldn't date one another," he'd say in a twangy voice while imitating his mother. We never put our name on the outside of the house, though, because Mom would have thought a sign reading "The Whites" was tacky. I'd have to agree with her.

Mr. Black shook my hand after opening his car door. I stepped back and got into my own car and watched him disappear inside the grocery. He had always been a big man, but it looked like he'd put on even more weight. Walking looked tedious, and he had to steady himself against the door handle just to climb the three small steps to get inside.

The sweet smell of the ham and turkey lingered in the car, reminding me of home. I was glad I was almost there. I closed my eyes tight to erase the thought of tears. Fishing my keys out of my pocket, I hurriedly started the car to drive away before Mr. Black came out.

* * * *

My mother's entire yard was a garden. It disappeared in the winter beneath the South's heavy ice and snow, but grew back almost effortlessly every spring. Mother pampered large ferns, poppies, roses, lilies, daffodils, and every kind of bloom imaginable as long as the warm weather would let her. The month of December sprouted a garden of lights and plastic Christmas people. A life-size Santa waved to passersby where the birdbath had been. Neon blue icicle lights hung from the gutters. A plastic baby Jesus lay in the rose bed with an entourage of colorful nativity characters that all lit up at night. With the Christ child in one corner and ole Saint Nick in the other, Justin had laughed at the Las Vegas-like menagerie the first time he saw it.

"Is Lorraine a baptist or a methodist?" he asked.

"Which has the better bake sale?" I replied.

Justin had always called my mother by her first name. She never corrected him. She was Lorraine to all of her old friends in town. I liked the idea that he was an old friend too. There was a time long ago when she would not have been so accepting of him because she was not accepting of me, but I had yet to meet Justin back then. Few boyfriends graced the White family holidays until Mom asked me once if I'd like to bring someone along.

"I'm afraid the family might scare them away," I joked, but I was secretly glad she had asked.

My younger brother brought a different girl every year, and no one ever asked twice what happened to the last one. It seemed to be routine, and expected, that he never dated the same girl for more than a year. My older brother and sister were both married. Even my younger sister had a steady boyfriend in high school that ate dinner with us once. I was tired of appearing to be the only single man at the family table. I was tired of having to forget about my special someone for a day, kissing them good-bye before the 150-mile journey back home, exchanging gifts with them the night before or the day after.

I indeed had my own personal life, and then there was my family. But I was old enough now that I was ready for both of them to stop being so personal and separate. Thanks to my Mom, they converged. There was Robert that first year, then Rodney the next. (At first, I seemed to have developed my younger brother's dating habits.) Billy was only a friend I invited who otherwise would have spent Christmas alone that year, but Mom insisted on asking how he was doing every time we spoke on the phone for a while after. Then I met Justin.

Surprisingly, we'd gone to high school together right here in Ruby Dregs. He was a year behind me, and although we were both closeted, questioning teenagers we never once spoke to each other. We had different friends, played different sports, and joined different clubs. I moved to Memphis for college; Justin attended the local community college after he graduated.

Six years would pass and I was home for a week's vacation visiting Mom. I bumped into Justin one night at a community theater production. I didn't recognize him from high school, but he later told me he had recognized me. Our eyes met and locked in that chilling stare that two people like us share, when no words and no introductions are necessary. We immediately knew the one thing we had in common. We both slept with men.

He was seated several rows behind me. I could feel the weight of his hazel eyes on the back of my head, so much that I wanted to turn around and look back at him. I didn't. At intermission I stood up to stretch and faced the back of the auditorium, nodding to the familiar yet nameless faces I had not seen in years. Justin's seat was empty. He had rushed out to smoke, and hoped I'd come out looking for him. But he had no words to share with me, and smoked half a pack anxiously hoping I'd come speak to him first. But I was a chicken too and didn't go looking for him.

The lights flickered signaling the start of the second act. He rushed back in and just as I was about to sit back down, our eyes met again. Justin smiled an awkward smile; he later told me he was just glad I was still there. I gave a nod as if I knew who he was. I wanted to know. Gutsy, he waited for me at the back of the auditorium when the show was over. I stayed seated to let the crowd thin out, somehow knowing he'd be there looking for me. I wanted him to be, and had secretly wished for it through the second act. My wish came true.

"Did you go to RD?" Justin asked, pulling away from the wall where he'd been leaning. Ruby Dregs was also the name of the local high school.

"Yeah. Class of '93. You?"

"Class of '94."

"Really?"

"I'm Justin. Justin Black," he said offering a trembling hand for me to shake.

"I'm Travis—"

"Travis White?" he asked, interrupting me.

"Yeah," I said. His hand was cold and clammy when I shook it, but I didn't want to let go.

We went for coffee that night at the Pancake House. After community college, Justin had worked odd local retail jobs. He was currently the manager of a wicker imports store that had just opened here two years ago. Although this was his hometown, he wasn't happy here. He lived at home with his parents. He'd never had a boyfriend. He needed to escape.

It would be six months before that happened. He stayed with me every weekend in Memphis when he didn't have to work. I showed him the city. He liked it. He wanted to be here with me on a regular basis. I wanted him here. To my surprise, he secretly started looking for a job. When he found one, he surprised me over dinner one night by asking if he could move in with me. My studio was too small for us, so we looked for a larger apartment. Our first place. Together.

We often shared a laugh about our last names being opposites. Black and White. We dressed as salt and pepper shakers one year for a Halloween party. But secretly, it worried me. I was afraid as a couple, we'd be total opposites too after Justin moved in with me. I knew what it was like to be a young man finally free of the chains of a close-minded small town and new to the city. It changes you. You rush into things just to experience them. You break hearts and get yours broken. You turn your back on regrets. I'd had six years to myself in the city to get past all that, but Justin was different and he constantly reminded me of that. And he was right.

He never once turned his back on me.

* * * *

My mother was a tall lady, as tall as me at six-three. She was elegantly thin with straight, shoulder-length frosted hair that she parted down the middle. Her black thick-rimmed glasses and Roman nose gave her a boyish look in the face, like a clumsy cartoon bird. We'd tried to get her to swap the rims for something a little daintier. She hated the word *dainty* and refused to be associated with it. She only wore the glasses for reading, and since she read often the glasses were usually on her face even when there wasn't a book in front of her.

She almost always wore black. Her closet consisted of nothing but black pants, black jeans, and long black skirts. Her tops were always white blouses, white turtle-necks, or maybe a white sweater with hints of silver. She'd accent it with a red scarf or a vest, and some shiny jewelry. Today, she had on black fitted pants and a white turtle-neck covered in small bunches of holly.

"Hello darling," she called from the front door. I had just driven up and parked my car behind hers and was opening the back door to unload the food.

"Merry Christmas!" I called out, busy with the ham.

"Merry Christmas to you, doll. Do you need some help? Let me get my shoes."

She disappeared inside and came back out in a hurry, bustling down the steps. Mom had a way of just hurriedly reacting to situations, not giving you a chance to answer. At thirty-five years of age, I was quite accustomed to just saving my breath. She opened the passenger's door and began filling her arms with the wrapped boxes.

"Are these all for me? You shouldn't have. What'd you get your brothers and sisters?"

I have four siblings: an older brother and sister, and a younger brother and sister. I was right in the middle, the dividing point between traditional conforming generations and the not so compliant ones. My older brother and sister were each married with children. I was gay. My younger brother was a recovering addict who'd lost a girlfriend to drugs. My younger sister also "ran around with the wrong crowd," to quote my mother.

"Are they here yet?" I asked.

I knew they weren't because there were only two cars in the driveway, mine and Mom's. But by asking she'd give me the updates on all of them and when they were expected to get here.

"You are the first to arrive, my dear. Ellen and the two kids will be here shortly."

"What about Mark?" I asked.

Ellen was the oldest sister. Mark was Ellen's husband. They had a young daughter and a son. Mom seemed startled when I said his name.

"He won't be here this year," she said in a heavy whisper as if someone might hear us.

"Is something wrong?" I asked.

"Ask your sister."

I left it at that. I knew their marriage had been on the rocks, but had not heard the latest. Since I was the only one who lived out of town, I was usually the last to know about anything.

"Martin and Marline and the kids will be along later," Mom said.

Martin was my older brother. Marline was his wife. They had a boy and a girl also.

"What about Sebastian?" I asked.

Sebastian was my younger brother.

"He should be here by mid-afternoon."

"Is he seeing anyone?"

"Oh no, not since what happened with Lind. Clare should be here any minute with Jake, though."

Jake was my younger sister's son. He was two. My sister just turned twenty-two, still quite the baby herself, and unwed. Jake's father was *a black* man named Andre. No one in the family had ever met him. Clare had told me Andre didn't even know about Jake, and she preferred it that way.

Although Jake definitely brought attention to our family, it wasn't the first time the White family had been the center of church pew gossip. My mother took it very well, and tried very hard not to make Jake seem like, quite literally, *the black* sheep of the family.

"I'm sure Andre is a very pleasant person, and I see nothing wrong with interracial relationships. It's not my choice, but I do know one thing. A black man and a white lady sure do make a pretty baby," Mom told me once.

My mom is not a racist. I think she was more accepting of Jake than when she found out I was gay, but then again, Jake is her grandchild. There's a reason to be proud. There's a baby shower to throw and cute little outfits to buy. There's a nursery to paint and a name to pick out.

Although Clare would have no part in any of that, my mother was at least allowed to dream of it. No mother throws a party when her son announces he sleeps with men. They weep, maybe because they really wanted grandchildren. And so there's Jake.

"What time is dinner?" I asked.

"Six-ish."

"Why so late?"

"It's Christmas Eve. Why do you care? Got somewhere better to be?"

"Maybe," I said slyly, just trying to be funny.

"Go early this afternoon if you want," she said in a sincere tone. She knew I was talking about visiting Justin's grave.

Mom always wanted to prolong everything around the holidays. When we all lived at home, we never ate that late any other day. She always tried to make Christmas different. She would want to eat at six or seven, and then assume we'd all want to sit around and talk while we let our food digest. She tried to make us wait until eight to open gifts.

"At least wait till it gets dark outside," she'd say.

In reality, Sebastian would arrive around four, starving and ready to eat. All the food would have been long prepared by then, but Mom would keep it tucked in the oven and under the broiler. She'd stand at the stove and stir a pot of beans, guarding the stove and busying herself with nothing. Ellen and Clare would offer to help, but she wouldn't let them. Anything to delay dinner while Sebastian and Martin watched a football game.

After an hour of Sebastian's complaining, she'd empty the stove in ten minutes, laying out a buffet bar of hot food. We'd all grab a paper plate and get in line and then sit down to eat and be done in thirty minutes, except for Mom. She'd help the grandkids put food on their plates and make their drinks. She'd pass out napkins and refill our glasses with iced tea. She'd wait until everyone had a plate before fixing her own. Then, she'd purposely eat slowly.

"Does anyone want dessert?" Mom would chime.

"No!" We'd all say in unison.

"Let's have dessert after we open gifts," one of my nieces or nephews would suggest, trying to drop a hint.

By six, Mom would give in and the gifts would be passed out. When we were all young and lived at home, Mom had the duty of sitting on the floor and passing out the gifts to each of the five kids. She'd attempt to make us take turns, letting Clare go first because she was the youngest, making everyone pay attention and watch. Martin and Sebastian were never patient, and usually had secretly peeled the paper off one of their own gifts before it was their turn.

With all manners aside and now five small grandchildren present, Mom preferred to take photos. She let Ellen and Clare pass out gifts. Sebastian would watch from the kitchen while nibbling on leftovers. Martin and Marline would keep the kids from fighting over toys. I'd entertain Jake and watch empty space grow underneath the Christmas tree. Piles of crinkled and torn paper and bows would fill the rest of the room. The grown-ups would all grab a trash bag and help pick it up after each kid had a turn running and jumping into the red and green mess, and maybe after Sebastian took a turn, too.

Paper plates and plastic cups overflowed the trash can. An

Elvis or Liberace Christmas CD was drowned out from the squeals of children and roar of mechanical toys. Sebastian would be the first to leave. Martin would fall asleep on the sofa while Ellen, Clare, and I helped Mom clean up the kitchen. We'd all sit and chat over pecan pie and coffee. After his nap, Martin and Ellen would collect the kids and toys for their drive home to prepare for Santa's arrival. Clare would be the last to leave unless she was staying over. I always spent the night at Mom's.

This was the White Family Christmas.

No matter who else attended with us each year, the rest of the holiday never changed. It'd been that way for quite some time. Predictable. Long-established. Traditional.

Although I was alone now, something told me this year would be different. There was nothing odd about Mom to make me think this. Her house and yard were the same, as if she'd given immaculate attention to making it look exactly like it did every year before. It had been a while since we all spent any time together—Mom and all five kids—but there was no reason to think this year would be unalike from years passed.

It still felt unusual, almost as if Mom was keeping something from me. Like an anxious child guessing at a gift under the tree based on the shape of its colorfully wrapped box, I hoped I was right and no surprises were in store.

Mr. Black

Like some predator lurking in an alley-way, I stood just out of view of the front door to Greer's Grocery so Travis could not see me once I had stepped inside. He wasn't even looking in my direction after I had finished talking to him, but I admired him with a bit of desire in my eyes as he got into his car and drove away.

As his car disappeared out of sight, I turned away and forgot about Travis. I looked around the grocery having forgotten momentarily why I had even stopped by, a lapse in my senses thanks to old age. The smell of meat in the stale air and the sight of cheap candy on the counter quickly reminded me.

I put a nickel and a penny in the metal bowl on the counter and then helped myself to only five pieces of black licorice. Mr. Greer had always used the honesty system with the penny candy on the counter. As a teenager, I had taken advantage of the old man by paying for only two or three pieces but usually taking four or five. For the last ten years or so, I'd been silently paying him back by regularly leaving a penny or two more.

"Any gizzards today?" I asked Mr. Greer loudly because I

knew he didn't hear well.

"Just took a batch out the fryer. How many you want? I'll bring 'em over to ya."

"Six, please."

I walked over to the ice cooler and took a bottle of root beer. I popped the cap with the bottle opener mounted on the side of the cooler. The familiar clink of the bottle top falling into the well on the cooler was so relaxing. My root beer bubbled over and dripped onto my hand and the floor.

"Shit!"

I grabbed some napkins from the nearby table to wipe off the sticky bottle. I licked my hand, and then guzzled the fizzy cola to appease my thirst. The loud rap of the bottle smacking the table as I sat it down startled me. I hadn't meant to sit it down so harshly. I looked over at Mr. Greer to apologize, but he had not heard the noise. Hank Williams was playing on the radio.

"Here you go, Manny. Careful now. They still hot," Mr. Greer said walking over to the table. He sat the small cardboard tray down in front of me and then stepped back and waited for my approval.

Four Points Grocery was the only place around where you could still get fried chicken gizzards. I looked down at the crispy brown pieces of meat sitting in the wax paper and licked my lips.

"Hot mustard?" he asked.

"Sure. Why not?" I said. I tucked a paper napkin into the front of my shirt and spread it out for a bib.

Mr. Greer returned with a small paper cup of hot mustard for dipping. I thanked him, but he didn't hear me as he walked away to tend to things behind the counter. The gizzards were extremely hot, but the callused tips of my fingers were rather immune to the blistering sting, as many times as I'd eaten these by now. However, my tongue was not. I guzzled the rest of the root beer, and then blew out as if I was whistling, to cool my mouth. Flakes of crust spit out across the table and fell onto the napkin on my chest. I wiped the table with my sleeve and then retrieved another root beer from the cooler. A bell from outside announced that someone had pulled up to one of the gas pumps.

"Pump two is on," Mr. Greer yelled into a microphone. His garbled voice echoed from the speaker on the outside of the building.

"Thank you," a polite voice yelled back.

These were the extremely proverbial sounds of my daily trek to the grocery for midday snacks of gizzards or tater logs. My bulging belly pushed up against the table was proof enough of my loyalty. I had always made the occasional stop for a weekend snack for me and Helen and a tank of gas. It wasn't until Justin passed away that stopping here became more frequent. At first, coming here was just an escape from Helen's monotonous crying. Long after the crying stopped, Helen spent her time either sleeping most of the day or bitching at me when I was around. Coming here cured the latter.

Seeing Travis outside was like a hard smack across the face, like that old gag in black and white movies where someone steps on a loose board in the floor and it flies up and pops them in the nose. Looking at me, he winced like someone does when they see someone in pain in a hospital. I had not seen that look of sorrow since Justin's funeral. I don't blame him. I wrinkled my nose at the sight of myself in a mirror. There are no mirrors in our old house that I even fit into. Luckily, I had no hair to comb. I held my teeth in my hand to brush them. The facial hair gene had skipped me growing up so I didn't have to shave. It'd been years since I'd seen my own face, about two years to be exact. The look in Travis's eyes told me I hadn't missed out on anything.

Travis still looked as charming and supple as the day Justin had first introduced him to us. Helen had never cared much for the boy, shunning him for taking Justin away from her. She selfishly knew Justin deserved a better life than here with us, but she had preferred that Travis had been a female. Instead, he was a constant reminder of yet another disappointment in Helen's life that she cursed God for.

"Why me, Lord!" were three words I should have carved on her gravestone as an epitaph if she goes before me. She had screamed them practically every day for since we'd been married: for every job I'd lost, every argument we'd had, and every bill we had to ask her father to cover. Having her only child announce that he was gay, and on the same day he told us he was moving out to be with his boyfriend in the city, topped the list. It became just another frustration she would have swept under the rug when company came over. But company never came so the things that caused her stress lay out in the open like yesterday's newspaper or the pile of junk mail gathering on the dining room table which neither of us ever threw out.

She was a tough old gal. She married me right before Vietnam purely out of necessity for the both of us. I could draw a bigger check. She'd have good benefits and not have to work. It got her Bible-thumping parents off her back. Stupid me had a vasectomy long before the war, and even before I'd met Helen. I never told her. A reversal was imaginary back then. Everything was fine until her thirtieth birthday when she told me she wanted a baby.

I bought the ejaculate of some kid in a trashy public toilet. I'd started going there several years after we married, not attracted to Helen and unsatisfied by our almost non-existent love-making. Back then, instead of hot pickles and beef jerky at Mr. Greer's grocery, I bought boy favors from street hustlers in the park. I rushed home and pushed the sticky substance between her legs with my fingers that night and prayed. Helen was accustomed to me crying when I orgasmed, so tears shed that night were no different. I cried again a month later when she told me our prayers had been answered.

"What about AIDS?" Helen screamed the night Justin sat us down and said he had something he needed to tell us.

AIDS. Something that had never crossed my mind all those

nights I'd made trips to the park, slumped between the legs of some punk kid in the back seat of my car. If I had contracted some disease by going there, it would remain a secret like everything else had in my life.

"Why me, Lord?" Helen bawled.

For the first time, Justin looked at me for an answer. Like always, I didn't have one.

I wanted to somehow blame myself for some homosexual attribute Justin had inherited from his father's genes, but then I remembered he wasn't of my own flesh and blood. I still blamed myself. It was God's punishment from where the seed had come from, and what I'd done to get it. If so, God continued to scold us by what Justin *had* inherited from his mother.

The gene for cancer.

Justin had begun suffering with migraines about five years after meeting Travis. Once Travis learned of Helen's battle with cancer, he urged Justin to go see a doctor. X-rays revealed a pebble-sized tumor near the back of his head. It was easily removed. I drove Helen to the Memphis hospital to visit Justin in recovery. He had made the nurses shave his head completely bald instead of just a patch on the back where the surgery would take place. We joked about how much he looked like me. He laughed, but on the inside I knew he resented that joke. We stayed three days in Memphis at the motel directly across the street from the hospital. Travis had offered to put us up, but Justin said the apartment wasn't big enough for three.

Doctors were confident the tumor was not cancerous, but there was no guarantee of remission. Brain cancer returned four years later, and took our son the following summer. Justin was too young to have made any prior plans for his death, and the cancer took him so quickly. He refused to think of making arrangements. He had high hopes he'd make it through.

We all did.

Travis told us that Justin had once expressed interest in being cremated. With no legal document holding us to that,

Helen demanded that her son have a "proper burial." I don't know why I asked Travis to come along to help pick out a coffin. Helen had already changed the burial clothes he'd picked out for Justin. She put him in a suit. Justin wore a tie to work, but I don't remember ever seeing him in a suit since the day he graduated high school.

Travis had brought a polo and jeans, Justin's signature choice of attire. Travis also picked out a mahogany rosewood casket. It was way out of our budget, but he offered to pay half. Helen refused. She wanted a cheaper model with sky-blue inlays and shiny handles. I sweated bullets when I wrote the check. Travis pulled me aside later when we'd taken Helen home. He asked if I could take him to a bank.

"Which one?" I asked.

"Any bank. How about yours? Where do you bank?"

"Citizens National."

"Take me there," he said.

I waited behind him in line for a teller. I was going to sit down but he asked me to go through the line with him. He'd already filled out his check and deposit slip in the car. When we reached the teller, he pulled me in front of him and handed me the check. It was made out to me.

"Deposit it," he demanded.

"I can't do that, Travis," I said looking at him with shock when I saw the amount. It was enough to cover the entire check I'd written at the funeral home.

"You will. You knew that check would bounce, but you wrote it anyway even after I offered to help. Now, Helen isn't here and can't stop me. I knew you'd either rip it up or spend it frivolously. That's why we are both standing here."

"Is there a problem?" the teller asked with concern.

"I don't have my checks with me. I don't know my account number," I said, throwing out excuses.

"I'm sure this nice teller can look it up for you. Can we have a blank deposit slip, please?" Justin said.

After making the deposit, we sat in the car in front of the

bank and said nothing. I just sat behind the wheel feeling violated. Helen never touched the accounts, but I was still afraid she'd find out.

"That was more than enough, Travis."

"The rest is to cover his headstone. Take Helen to Stuart's Monuments when all of this is over."

"Are you mad about the clothes? The casket?"

"No…" he said with a long sigh. He'd been staring at the floorboard. He lifted his head and looked out across the old downtown court square. There was magic in his eyes as if he was reliving a hundred sunsets. "Those things aren't the Justin I know. It's your Justin, or at least the Justin you want to remember."

The Justin I wanted to remember had never been born. He died in my late teenage years just before the war, with a doctor's incision and the snip of my vasa deferentia. The unspoken words lingered at the back of my throat. They dried my mouth like cotton. I stopped at Greer's on the way home for a root beer to wash them back down. I had never told anyone. I certainly couldn't tell Travis now, although it might explain a lot or it might not explain anything at all.

Rather than make things more complicated, I buried those secrets with my son. *I'm not your son*, Justin called out in my head from beyond the grave. He'd haunt me. He'd died and gone to heaven and some angel had whispered in his ear the truth about what I'd done. He'd come back to haunt me. I just knew he'd cut the brakes on my car on my way home from work or punch me in the chest until I had a heart attack. I could never be so fortunate. Having to walk this earth without him on it was my punishment. No matter how distant he became when he was living, he was still the hope that held the Black family together.

Helen left all of Justin's pictures and trophies on the wall, an everyday reminder of better days. We crumbled, and Justin hung there on the wall to bear witness to every minute of it. His toothy first and second-grade smiles were now like the gnashing of teeth out of anger. In a fit of rage after a fistful of pills and a bottle of bourbon, Helen had more than once smashed the pictures from the wall. She'd lay in the floor in a smatter of glass with her bleeding fists and cry out.

"Why me, Lord!"

God wasn't listening.

I'd stopped going to church shortly after Justin passed. About a year later, I started back. It was just another way to escape the confines of the house. The congregation rarely spoke to me. I might as well have been a demon sitting on the back pew.

I was.

The preacher still shook my hand every morning at the end of the sermon when we all filed out. I always waited until everyone had passed by. I'd gained so much weight that maneuvering myself out from between the narrow pews could be quite embarrassing.

Lorraine had stopped to say hi once. She was the one smiling face I had left, always greeting me cordially and saying it was nice to see me. I had not seen Travis since Justin's funeral. I always asked Lorraine about him.

"He's fine. Travis is fine." That's all she'd say. That's all she needed to.

A lady coughed into her hand outside as she pumped gas. The quick white smoke of her car exhaust blew by the window, lost against the piles of snow. I could hear the rotary clicks of the numbers changing on the old gas pump. She stepped back to the driver's seat and sat down with the car door open. She put black mittens on and then fidgeted with a baby in a car seat in the back. I pulled the greasy napkin bib from my shirt and crumpled it in my hand as I watched her through the window. She looked very familiar. I'd seen her around town carrying a black man's baby.

The pump clicked off when the tank was full. The lady crawled back out of the car to put the nozzle back. There was a snap of electricity when she touched the nozzle. A whoosh of orange flame licked at her. She screamed, breaking me from my perverted trance. The baby in the back seat shuddered awake and joined in.

"Mr. Greer! Mr. Greer!" I yelled.

Her immediate reaction was to get back in the car, either to drive away or to get the baby out. Some defense mechanism or rush of adrenaline stopped her from doing that. She took off the mittens and threw them in the car. Trying to avoid the flames, she managed to pull the nozzle out of the car. She tossed it onto the ground. Droplets of gasoline continued to feed the rising flame. Luckily, there were no flames coming out of the gas tank on the car.

She kicked at the flames, and eventually got a foot under the hose. With her leg, she scooted the nozzle into the pile of snow the plows had pushed up next to the pump when clearing the lot. The flame went out. Mr. Greer had just made it out the door and down the steps. The lady leaned against the car in tears. He patted her arm. I couldn't hear what he was saying to her. She took his arm and he helped her inside.

"I'm okay. I just need a gallon of milk," I heard her say over the cowbell clanging on the door as they came inside.

She looked at me with strange eyes, probably wondering why I had not come to her aid. I bit my lip and looked back out the window to avoid her glance. She'd left the screaming baby in the car. I tried to be like some chameleonic animal blending into its surroundings, but felt more like a fat helpless pig at some county fair trough with people gawking over its size.

"Thank you, Mr. Greer. I'm so sorry," she said paying for the gas and the milk.

"As long as you are okay, Clare, that's all that matters. You be careful out there," Mr. Greer said.

He followed her back outside to the car. He tapped on the back window and played peek-o-boo with the crying baby. The lady waved good-bye and drove away. Mr. Greer shook the snow from the nozzle and examined it. He put the nozzle back in the cradle and waddled back inside.

"Them White kids sho is trouble," he said, shaking his head.

"Who was that?" I asked with a dumb look on my face over the whole thing that had just happened.

"Clare White, Lorraine's youngest girl. You know she got a mixed baby? Her brother was just in here. He's a queer."

Mr. Greer didn't give me a chance to respond. He disappeared into the back whistling to the song on the radio. I had nothing to say about her anyway. I had recognized her from Justin's funeral, but didn't know she was Travis's sister. I looked back out the window and played the sudden events over in my head again, impressed at how quickly Clare had responded. I felt like an idiot just sitting here, too tired and bloated to aid someone in trouble.

She had a child in the car to think about. Her response was instant, while I just sat here with my gut pressed against the table. She was headed to Lorraine's now and would relive the events out loud to her loved ones. Clare would say something about how her life had flashed in front of her eyes. She reacted on impulse because all she could think about was her kid.

All I ever thought about was Justin. But my life was a slow flash, and I never reacted to it at all.

Lorraine

Like every morning, I was awake by dawn. I preferred the winter months when it would still be dark outside. The earth was quiet and asleep. I felt like I had it all to myself. The old habit of tip-toeing through the house, from back when I still had kids upstairs sleeping, had never gone away.

The coffee was on a timer, and if the smell of it brewing didn't wake me first then my internal clock never failed. I don't remember the last time I'd set the alarm clock on the nightstand. I didn't even keep a clock there anymore. It'd been in the dresser since Frank passed. When you are the last one left in a big empty house, with no kids to attend to or lunches to make, a clock-timed schedule is pretty useless. I got up with the sun, and sometimes went to bed "with the chickens" as my Granny had liked to say. And as long as my eyes opened on tomorrow, I'd get up and do it all over again.

I stretched my way out of bed and threw on my slippers and heavy housecoat. After the first cup of coffee, I picked the paper up from the front step. The obituaries were always read first. I had constantly skipped that section before I lost Frank. Now, it was as if I was waiting to find my name printed there, and I guess that would be the day I'd stop reading them again. After reading the paper, I load a pail with birdseed and go out into the backyard to fill up my three birdfeeders.

I kept a large plastic container just inside the back door filled with seed. Four bags from the dollar store filled it up. I attempted to keep it outside the back door once, but a raccoon discovered it one night and helped himself to it. I assumed it was a raccoon, and one with a sense of humor. He spilled the seeds all over the deck, ate most of it, pooped by the steps, and then carried the container off into the yard like a toy. A flock of sparrows had frightened me when I opened the back door the next morning. They had been devouring the leftovers.

Cardinals and finches anxiously watch me from the low limbs and the fence posts, accustomed to seeing me put food out for them but still keeping safely out of distance. The two larger feeders were pretty commercial looking, and could hold a whole bag of seed. I never filled them up that much because the squirrels would come around and chase the birds away.

The third feeder was one the boys had made for me from a craft kit for Easter or Mother's Day many years ago. It resembled a miniature barn the boys chose to paint red, white, and blue. It always made me laugh because, unbeknownst to them, three of the five children had been conceived in an old barn Frank and I use to stroll out to on the edge of the property. The barn had since been torn down when I sold several acres after Frank passed, but a coat of shellac each spring helped preserve my little barn birdfeeder.

A few weeks ago when I went to fill the barn-shaped feeder with seed, I found a small yellow oriole lying on the ground beneath it. It frightened me at first and I took a step back, expecting it to quickly fly away. When it didn't, I knelt by it to get a closer look. It had yet to snow so the bird was not wet. Its gold colored feathers were soft and dry. Its eyes were closed as if it was sleeping.

It broke my heart because the orioles only visit this area during the winter. I see mostly sparrows and robins during the warmer months. I wanted to blame the cat, Marcus, but he was so old he rarely chased birds these days. Back when he did, he'd leave them at the back door for me to find and they'd look all wet and matted from where he chewed on them.

I filled the last feeder with seed and then picked up the small fragile bird and put him in the empty pail. After I showered and dressed, I retrieved a garden shovel from the garage and dug a small grave next to the koi pond. Marcus sat on a rock next to the pond and lazily eyed me, proud as if he had killed the oriole or as if I should give it to him now. With it already being dead he'd have no interest in it at all, and besides, the little bird deserved a proper burial.

"Don't you go digging him up either," I said to the cat. I dipped my hand in the pond water and flicked it at him. He gave a hiss and ran under the porch. The fish flopped, wanting to be fed.

A few days passed, and I had just begun to get the thought of the unfortunate little bird out of my head. Then, another dead oriole startled me on my morning routine. This time it was right under one of the other feeders. It looked exactly the same as the other one had. I turned and looked over at the koi pond, expecting to find an empty grave as if the oriole had risen from the dead only to die again. The little brown patch of dirt where I buried the first bird was still intact, and so I planted his friend next to him.

"Could be the whole corn kernels in that cheap feed you're buying," the blatantly rude pet store attendant told me when I went in to inquire about the health conditions of orioles within the vicinity of town. "Some smaller birds can choke on the larger seeds and nuts."

"I had no idea," I said.

I was ashamed of myself. I felt like some exterminator putting out rat poison for unsuspecting rodents. I was Violet Newstead putting Skinny & Sweet in Mr. Hart's coffee! I never expected bluebirds to come up and tie ribbons in my hair, but no wonder the little critters kept their distance from me. I thought I was doing a service to nature by feeding the winter birds, but I might as well have been putting out arsenic for the raccoon.

"What can I do?" I asked the pubescent-faced boy as if he had a degree in ornithology.

"Stop buying that dollar stuff. Use this," he said, showing me a bag of something called Clydesdale Birdseed.

"Sounds like it's made from horses," I said.

"I didn't name it. I just sell it."

I bought three bags.

"I've got a new menu today," I announced out the back door the next morning.

I could clearly see hesitation in their black beady eyes that day, but they eventually came and they ate. I watched from the porch as flocks of bright red cardinals and green finches, and more orioles than ever emptied the feeders. The next morning I held my breath as I made my way out into the yard on my daily routine, but there was no body to be found.

It snowed that night and so I planned to fill the feeders in the morning and again in the afternoon. The koi pond had frozen over now, but we'd dug it deep enough for the fish to be able to hibernate in the bottom where the water was still thawed. Spikes of ice jutted out of the fountain like crystals on a chandelier. Marcus rarely came inside, not even during winter. He sat on top of the frozen water now licking a paw as if waiting for the fish to come up. I somehow envisioned a cartoon version of the ice cracking and the old black cat falling in. The air would be filled with squeaky laughter from the fish and the birds.

I stayed up most of last night and the early morning preparing food and cleaning the house to get ready for the arrival of the kids today. Christmas Eve. Travis was driving up from Memphis to stay for three days. It was still to be decided if anyone else would be staying the night, but if they did all the sheets were fresh and the beds were made. I put fresh towels out in the upstairs bathrooms, along with the girls' favorite soaps and lotions. I placed small bags of chocolates on the pillows in the bedrooms. These days, with everyone grown, there were no assigned sleeping quarters. The grandkids might end up in one of the boys' old rooms, but there'd at least be a surprise waiting there for everyone.

I spent an hour or so putting up more decorations. Small tabletop Christmas trees now adorned the vanities in the bathrooms and the nightstands between the beds in the kids' rooms. Back in the day when the house was full, I'd put a tree up in every room. The boys' bathroom had a tree decorated with American flags and green tractors. The girl's bathroom tree had lace, strings of plastic pearls, and small soaps wrapped in pink twill.

In the bedrooms, the trees had tiny stockings hung on them where the kids could find little treats and gifts all throughout the month of December. Even when it was just me and Clare here, I still bought stocking-stuffers for her. It'd been several years since she left. These days, it was not rare for several weeks to pass without me going into their old empty rooms. I kept the doors shut except to the spaces I lived in. It made the house feel smaller. With all of the kids here for Christmas this year, I just wanted the house to feel like old times again, for them and for me. So, I went through the house and opened every door this morning. It expanded and creaked, sighing with relief. Despite winter, the house was coming alive again.

After filling the feeders, I decided to take a walk down to the property line where the barn had been. The sun had just started to crack the gray sky. First, I went back inside to change into warmer clothes and to make sure the stove was turned off. When we bought this house in 1966 Martin, the eldest, was one year old. Frank and I married in 1963 and a small upstairs apartment in the city was our first home. When Martin was born in '65 we both decided we wanted more kids but would need a larger home.

The two-story colonial, built by the Dogwood family who also founded and named the community, was the first home we'd looked at. Back then, it was one of only four homes on the dirt-clad road that ran through Dogwood. There are over thirty homes on Main Street now. With the ten acres of trees surrounding us, we felt like we were the only house around for miles back then. Even in the winter when the apple trees had dropped their leaves and their thin limbs were practically transparent, we still couldn't see the neighboring house when looking out the window.

Many generations ago, the Dogwood family had planted a fruit orchard on the property to make a living. Mr. Dogwood kept a fruit stand out in front of the house and sold produce to downtown markets. Since the family business had long been retired and Mr. Dogwood had passed on many years ago, most of the property had been divided and sold for community development.

When Mrs. Dogwood died in early 1965, none of her few existing family members wanted to live in the house. The older generations were all resting in the cemetery nearby, and the younger generations had moved away and didn't care about where their roots had started. Frank and I purchased it for a steal from her money-hungry grandchildren. It'd practically tripled in value since then. With three bedrooms and two baths, this house was the perfect size to grow the family. Frank's mother passed in 1980. We used money she left us to add another bedroom and bathroom, and to make some other much-needed improvements to the house. I was pregnant with Sebastian before construction was done.

It'd been months since I walked the property line. The four acres I still owned were thick with old apple, plum, cherry, and pear trees that had stopped producing ample fruit back before Frank died. Like me, the trees had grown old and retired. It's odd how I remember things based on if they happened before or after I lost him. When the children were young, we spent many Sunday afternoons playing in the orchard and filling bushel baskets of fruit. I'd bake pies and bread, and Frank would give some of the harvest to friends and neighbors. In autumn when the leaves fell, we'd all rake them. The kids would play in the piles, while Frank and I bagged the leaves for the mulch bed.

The six acres I sold had yet to be developed. The land was still in much the same condition as when I divided the property except now it was overgrown with dead brush and a few trees had fallen, and the barn was gone. Its brick foundation had been left, but now looked as if it were slowly being claimed by the earth as the dead foliage collected around it. Even though I knew the old man who had bought the property, I still felt like a trespassing stranger. My heart raced a bit like a kid exploring wheat fields and making mazes by bending down the crop, hoping they didn't get caught.

I smiled, standing there in the middle of the foundation where the old barn had been. Frank walked the entire property once a week, an old farmer mending fences. When I started walking with him, it became our usual weekly stroll just to escape from the house and the burden of children.

The creak of the old barn door turning on its rusty hinges, and the long strands of sunlight leaking through the gaps in the walls took us back to a younger time. We were teenagers keeping warm in the back seat at a drive-in all over again.

Ellen, Travis, and Sebastian were the end result of three trips down to the barn over the years. Frank was a great lover, so adventurous. There wasn't a tree on the property that hadn't seen our aging bodies. We made love in the barn or on the ground beneath the spring blossoms many times.

After he was gone, the immediate decision was to sell off some of the property because I couldn't take care of it by myself. I hated to do it because I was selling off the playground of our memories. Not only was the land our funny love shrine, but it was also where the children grew up playing. Those memories would never escape my heart and my head, though. Frank was gone, the kids were all grown up and Martin and Ellen now had kids of their own, so letting go of the land where our lives had happened wasn't as hard as I thought it would be.

Clare

Obese fucker, I thought to myself. *Who just sits there and watches a car almost explode?*

His face looked familiar, but I was used to dirty old men gawking at me when I walked by. Eventually, they all started to look the same. Mr. Greer never looked at me that way. He might have been an old coot, but I felt comfortable around him. I didn't even need the milk for Jake. I just stopped there to sort of check in on Mr. Greer. I'd known him my whole life from my parents taking me into the grocery when I was small. He'd give me a sucker and tickle my arm. Later, I'd stop in to buy cigarettes from him on the way to high school.

Now living in an apartment downtown, I still stopped at the grocery when I came to visit mom. Then this whole mess with the gas happened. Mr. Greer would hate to see me ever drive up again. I remembered hearing on the news how a spark from static electricity can cause flames to ignite, but I never gave second thought to it. Something like that would never happen to me. It seemed that was my motto in life, but whenever I thought it, something usually did happen. Like two years ago when I had never planned to get pregnant.

My right hand stung. The hot metal handle of the gas nozzle had burned when I pulled it out. I was going to put the handle in the snow to extinguish the fire, but the blistering sting caused me to drop it. At a stop sign, I put my right mitten back on as if covering my hand would somehow make the pain go away. I couldn't find the left mitten. I'd search for it before I got out of the car at Mom's. It was probably in the back seat with Jake. Thankfully, the hum of the car and its rocking motion had soothed him back to sleep. I looked at him in the rearview mirror. The redness from crying so hard had faded from his fat little face. It had not faded from mine.

"Pull yourself together, Clare," I whispered to myself in the mirror.

I pulled strands of hair from my face and turned the radio back up a bit. Christmas music blared from every station. I left the dial on a station playing some guy I didn't know, but at least he wasn't singing about the holidays. Instead, he was singing about how everything can change in a New York minute.

"What about a Ruby Dregs minute?" I said out loud to the radio. "Nothing ever changes in this damn town."

I turned the heater down because I'd broken into a sweat. I wanted to crack the window for some cool winter air, but I was afraid the sound of the wind pouring in might wake Jake again. My stomach and chest felt tight. A hot ache pushed itself upward. I was only a few blocks from Mom's house, but I needed to stop the car right now.

I pulled the car off to the side of the road. I hesitated with the emergency lights for a second, but then there was no time to turn them on anyway. My throat burned. I opened my door wide enough to bend over and out. The cradle of the seat belt kept me from going much further. Resting my forehead on the door handle, I held my hair to one side and let the burning ache expel onto the pavement. Long spider-web strands of spit hung in the air, not wanting the poison to escape. I wiped them from my face with the mitten and turned my head to look down the street. There was a car in the distance. I leaned back up and shut the car door gently to avoid waking Jake. I didn't want anyone to drive by and see me getting sick, and I prayed it wasn't one of my siblings.

The oncoming car crept by. It was no one I knew, just some young cocky kid with a goofy grin trying to act like he was checking me out. He gave a nod with his chin as if he knew me, but every guy did that around here. I faked a smile but wanted to give him the finger. I turned on the left blinker and pulled back onto the road. Mom's house was just a few blocks away. The blinker was still flashing when I pulled into the driveway. I parked behind Travis's car. He and Mom were outside unloading his car. They paused to wave at me. Mom approached the car, waiting for me to cut off the ignition.

"Merry Christmas Baby Doll," she chimed before I had opened the door.

"Merry Christmas," I moaned getting out of the car.

Mom grabbed my neck and hugged me. I lightly patted her on the back.

"Want me to get Jake?" she asked.

"Sure," I sighed.

Travis just stood there looking at me with a bit of doubt. He could tell something was wrong. I cowered toward him like a scolded puppy wanting to apologize, trying to force a smile onto my face without bursting into tears over what had happened at Mr. Greer's. I actually was happy to see Travis, but didn't want Mom to think my tears were for him.

He leaned down to hug me as I hurried to him with open arms. I held him tight, trying to squeeze back my tears but it was no use. I closed my eyes and buried my face in the sleeve of his wool coat. I felt dizzy. Breaking loose from his grip, I wiped my snotty nose with my hand and ran inside the house, a sleeve covering my face to shield my expression from them. I ran upstairs and locked myself in the bathroom.

I splashed cold water onto my face in the old pink bathroom. Pink shower curtain, pink soaps, there was even a pink toilet seat. This was the girls' bathroom when Ellen and I lived here. I remembered playing with Barbies in the big pink bathtub. Mom even bought pink toilet paper for us. Back then, I liked to pretend I was a princess and often played dress up with Ellen. I'd sit on the vanity and pretend to do my make-up in the mirror. Now, I hated pink. I searched the drawers, unsure of what I was looking for. They were full of wash cloths and guest towels. Nothing comforting to be found.

I dug in my purse for my lipstick and eye shadow, both now darker, more adult shades unlike the pretty pink and red colors Mom bought us for dress-up back then. Up close in the mirror, I tried to reapply my eyes. Ellen had taught me how to put on eye liner in this very mirror. My hands were too shaky now to do anything.

"Pull yourself together, Clare," I whispered to the mirror.

It was no use. I had more crying to do. It wasn't my life that had flashed in front of my eyes back there at the grocery. My life had long ago lost its meaning and hope for any kind of momentous future. I was a mom now, and all I could think about was that baby. He was the importance of each and every day. I had to be there for him, to bend and break the day so that he would not grow up and be like me. And when something bizarre or accidental happened like today, it scared me to think that life was that fragile; and that sort of stuff was always happening to me. I cursed myself if Jake fell and scuffed his face when trying to walk. I stood over his crib at night, sleepless, just to make sure he was breathing.

Just a few years ago, I was not so responsible. At twenty, my upper arms and back were already filled with ugly tattoos. The tattoos covered the scars left by reckless boyfriends who beat me. I was thankful the bruises at least healed. Some of the scars I'd put there myself, but I no longer beat myself up—on the outside. I still didn't like the person looking back at me in the mirror now, but the girl from two years ago seemed even farther away.

My cell phone was full of friends. They were all wrong

numbers, the kinds of friends you never wanted your mom to meet because you knew she wouldn't approve anyway. They were from the "wrong side of town," I could hear mom say. I called them friends because I never knew anything—or anyone—better. Like me, they wore baggy clothes and skipped class. After high school, they snuck me into bars and bought me drinks. They shared their cocaine and their pot. They introduced me to strange alluring men who gave me chills when they touched my hand, who fingered me in dirty bathroom stalls. Instinct whispered in my ear that this feeling should have been fear. I should have been afraid, but I didn't listen. That's how I met Andre.

His real name wasn't Andre. Andre was the name of some cute jock in high school I had a crush on back then. He never looked my way, and graduated two years before me. He joined the marines and was killed in the line of duty in Iraq. His parents had taken out a memorial ad in my senior yearbook with Andre's senior picture and a photo of him in his uniform shown side by side. I drew a red heart around his photos, just like I did in the yearbook two years earlier when Andre was a senior. By giving Jake's father that nickname, it somehow made him less terrifying.

I didn't know his real name. Luckily, I'd never seen him again since that night. Me and a friend, Chelsea, were out at a bar on a typical Friday night. She lived in a trailer park on the edge of town, but liked to hang out at bars in the projects on Forrest Avenue.

Chelsea preferred to date colored men, and she wanted to go to some new bar called Project X. I had never been to those bars before, and was a little too trusting of her judgment. I had read about police raids and drug busts going down at Project X ever since it opened, but I let her talk me into going with her anyway. Surprisingly, we weren't the only white people there like I thought we would be. The bass of the music was so loud it hurt my ears and my teeth.

"You'll get used to it," Chelsea told me.

The thick sweet smoke of cigars was not like the smoke in the truck stop bars I normally frequented. It stung my eyes but had a pleasant aroma.

You'll get used to it.

We barely had time to finish a beer when Chelsea wanted to dance. Some tall thuggish guy immediately started to flirt with us. Chelsea went with him to the bathroom to score some weed. I didn't want to go, but I didn't want to stay on the dance floor by myself either. I must have washed my hands a thousand times while Chelsea let the man snort lines of coke off her breasts in one of the stalls.

From under the stall wall, I could see Chelsea down on her knees. Standing there holding her bag, I wanted to go home and knew the car keys were in her purse. I couldn't just leave her here though. Friends didn't do that to each other. I wouldn't do that to Chelsea, and I wished I could say she wouldn't have left me either.

I honestly didn't know.

When they finished in the stall, the man wanted to take Chelsea outside. He offered to drive both of us to another bar just down the street or back to his place. I didn't want to go, but was too frail to speak my own mind. I knew by now that she would go with or without me, and so I went too. But I knew that no matter what happened, I couldn't save Chelsea. I didn't even think I could manage to save myself. Outside in the parking lot, the man conveniently ran into a friend of his who decided to accompany us.

"Chelsea, we should go," I said to no avail.

She just laughed while the man whispered empty compliments into her ear.

"Chill out, Clare," Chelsea said.

"Yeah, Clare. Chill," the man said with a wink.

In the front seat, she squeezed the man's bald head now buried between her breasts. Soft moans bounced off the windows as she pushed his head downward. I didn't want to, but I let the man's friend play with my hair and nibble my ear.

I closed my eyes and envisioned a better place. I tried to envision a better man too, but I'd never met one.

A callused hand pinched my face, clasping my mouth shut and pinning me down in the seat. There was no breath to scream as he pushed my face into the seat and pinned my arms behind my back. From the corner of my eye, through tussled hair I saw fists flying in the front seat as the man wrestled with Chelsea. Panties ripped and private parts were exposed.

"Don't fight bitch. I ain't gonna kill ya," the man in the front seat yelled.

I didn't believe him, but I didn't fight back. The weight of the man on top of me was too suffocating. The invasion between my legs was excruciating.

You'll get used to it. Chelsea's words echoed in my head.

The man never hit me. It was the pavement that bruised my face and scuffed my elbows when I was thrown from the back seat. Chelsea was not as fortunate, with two black eyes and a missing tooth. Bite marks bled on my neck from some wicked vampire, but this was somehow much worse. We were just lucky to still be living. Funny, because I'd never had much luck at all.

I managed to help her to the car. I wanted to take both of us to the nearest hospital, but she refused. She just wanted to go home. With Chelsea soaking in a hot bath, I sat outside the bathroom with my back to the door and my knees pulled up to my chest. I cried the tears of a lonely insane person locked in a padded cell somewhere in a strait jacket, unaware of if or when daylight would come.

The only difference was that I could get up and walk away. I wanted to bust through the bathroom door and yell at her, "I told you so!" But no one had told me, so who was I to blame? Who's to say I would have even listened? Instead, I walked out the door and got in my car. I cried for a long time with my head on the steering wheel, and then I started the car and went home.

Two months passed and the phone rang in my apartment. I did not want to answer it when I saw Chelsea's name on the caller I.D. I still wasn't sleeping soundly and the sleeping pills weren't curing the nightmares that woke me. I let the phone ring several times and then go to voicemail. The recording told me I still had things in common with her. She was pregnant too, and wanted me to go with her to an abortion clinic across the state line.

There I was in the living room of some two-story house that had been transformed into a clinic. There was a warm fire burning in the fireplace. Magazines and crossword puzzles were spread out on the coffee table. Soap operas played on a black and white television hanging on the wall, and fresh coffee was brewing in the corner. One nervous man, pacing back and forth, took the blame from every woman in the room who just looked at him through squinted eyes. Two women chatted in the corner, obviously there just to support a friend because all of the other women in the room were quiet and looked apprehensive.

The sucking sounds coming from upstairs would haunt me for months to come. They reminded me of the vacuum the dentist used to extract excess spit from my mouth when I was a little girl, not a living human thing growing inside of me now. A nurse called me upstairs and told me to bring Chelsea's purse. She had to give them more money because she had lied about how far along she was.

"Your turn," she said lying on a sofa in the recovery room.

"I can't do it," I mumbled.

"What? You can't keep that baby."

"Yes, I can."

"Clare, it will be a constant reminder of what happened."

"My baby will remind me I can change all this. Life doesn't have to be this way."

I walked out and left her lying there. I never saw her again. Outside, a pro-life picketer tried to pull my hair.

"I didn't do it," I said.

"God bless you, child. Your baby will be blessed," they said letting me pass by.

Eight months later, Jake was born.

* * * *

There was a tapping at the bathroom door. I opened the door to find Mom standing there holding Jake.

"Is everything okay in here?" Mom asked.

"Everything's just fine," I said, taking Jake from her.

"Come downstairs and visit with us then."

"I need to get everyone's gifts out of my car."

"Want us to help?"

"No. No, I can do it," I said stuttering. I was still trying to clear the events of the morning from my head.

"Are you okay, sweetie?" Mom said putting a hand to my forehead as if checking for a fever.

"I'll be fine. Just need some coffee."

"I've got a pot brewing downstairs. I'll go make you a cup. Cream and sugar?"

"Yes, please."

I followed her down the stairs and watched as she disappeared into the kitchen. I hurried back outside and got in the car. I almost felt like I wanted to drive away and disappear. I had not wanted to arrive like this. I always panicked when life handed me the unexpected. Before, I would have shrugged it off as bad luck and thought I deserved whatever happened to me. But now, I took it personal. I still blamed myself, but now it was because I worried so much about Jake and whether or not I was a good mother. I had been a disappointment to my mother too much growing up; I didn't want to be that way with Jake.

I popped the trunk in case they were watching me from the window. I checked the ignition for my keys. They weren't there. I checked the floorboard and the seat. My purse was still upstairs in the bathroom, but I knew I had not put the keys in there. I opened the door and looked on the ground in case they'd fallen out.

"Looking for these?" Travis said, dangling the keys in front of me.

"Shit! You scared me," I said.

I didn't know how long he'd been standing there. I swiped the keys from his hand and got out of the car, and he followed me back to the trunk. I started loading his arms with gift-wrapped boxes. Travis remained quiet, just looking at me.

"What?" I asked him, like someone mistrustful of the person looking at them.

"I didn't say anything."

"You're thinking it," I snipped, rolling my eyes. It was a typical sibling reply. "I've been here five minutes and we are already arguing. Just like old times."

"I'm not arguing," Travis retorted.

"Then what do you want to say?"

"I'm just going to say I saw what's in the glove box."

I didn't look at him. I didn't say anything.

"You aren't going to find happiness in those little plastic bottles, Clare."

"I'm not looking for happiness. Just some nice substitutes."

With the trunk empty, I slammed it shut and hurried into the house. Travis stood there for a minute, lost and looking as if unaware I'd ended the conversation, and then he followed me into the house.

Lorraine

Frank was my first boyfriend, and the only man I'd ever been with. It was a bit odd to have taken interest in someone else now. Calvin was a retired farmer who'd lost his wife about three years ago. All the kids had met him, except Travis, so I was very excited about Travis being here for Christmas this year. There was some resentment among the kids concerning their mother seeing another man now, but I think they understood that even I deserved not to be alone the rest of my days.

"He makes me happy," I told Ellen.

"As long as he's good to you," Ellen said.

"He is," I said, feeling like she probably did when I questioned her about Mark back when they were dating.

"Have you guys had sex?" Clare asked with a giggle.

I blushed and laughed, and kindly told her it was none of her business. The truth was Calvin and I were both beyond the need for physical pleasure in life. These days an arm around the shoulder while watching a movie and sharing a bowl of microwave popcorn, or a kiss on the cheek at the end of the night was just as satisfying. The comfort of a man in the house or just someone to talk to instead of these walls was enough for me.

Frank and Calvin were totally different in demeanor and looks, so I have no idea why I was attracted to Calvin. As we get older, I guess our tastes change in lots of things. For instance, when I was young, scrambled eggs were a daily staple in my parents' house. My Mom raised chickens in a coop in the backyard, so eggs were plentiful. I hated them now probably because I ate them everyday for breakfast, and sometimes for dinner, when I was a little girl.

Frank was tall and lean. The man could eat two hamburgers in one setting, and I don't think he'd ever gained a pound since the day we married. His hair was thinning and he looked very studious. But he was a teacher and accustomed to wearing thin white shirts with bold neck ties, and heavy green or brown pants with freshly shined shoes. Over the years, the heavy wrinkles around his mouth and across his forehead became deeper and much more precise. When he smiled he almost resembled a comedy mask hanging above a high school drama stage.

Calvin was plump with thick bone-white hair that stood up on end with each hair looking like a perfect blade of grass. From years of spiking his hair with heavy pomade, it now stood permanently at attention. His skin was dark and spotted from years of working outside beneath the hot summer sun. He always wore blue jean overalls over a crisp tan or blue buttoned shirt. Bags beneath his eyes held stories of a farm boy who was up before dawn every morning to plow the fields. The wheat and the corn were his only friends until he came in at dusk when it was too dark to see to get any more work done. He has the same weighty wrinkles on his face as Frank did, even in the exact places. They reminded me of Frank, which is why I think I liked Calvin so much, except his age lines were there from different reasons.

He'd started coming to our church on Sunday nights because he'd grown tired of being a hermit after his wife died.

Sometimes when our heart empties out we want to be alone, but sooner or later it too yearns to be around other people. At first, he sat in the back next to Mr. Manny Black, who had also started back to church around the same time.

Calvin soon learned that good quality conversation with Mr. Black was almost nonexistent, or that Mr. Black was a bit crazy. Mr. Black always stopped me at the end of service to ask how Travis was doing. I remained cordial with him because I was sad about the loss of his own son, and I knew how much Justin had meant to Travis.

The sight of Mr. Black himself was pitiful. He'd gained so much weight. I don't know how he balanced himself sitting in the church pew, and seeing him stand up from it was quite a feat. His hair was usually greasy, and so was his skin. His old glasses looked spotted with paint and were held together with balls of Scotch tape. He smelled like he had not bathed in days.

Calvin was a fresh glimmer of hope when I saw him that first day sitting there next to Mr. Black. Mr. Black introduced me to him, and I thought maybe Calvin was a friend he had invited. I remember he'd winked at me, and I think it'd made me blush a bit. The usual church trustees had already pounced on him, inviting him to the morning senior service or to Sunday school, feeling him out to see if his soul was in need of being saved. Calvin politely shook their hands, but showed no interest in the activities they were eager to initiate him in.

A few Sundays later Calvin had moved from the back pew up to the middle where I sat. I had arrived early in the sanctuary and took the pew in front of him. I turned around to greet him and ask how he was doing. I'd made a sincere effort to remember his name. He remembered mine. He invited me to lunch after service, and with no hesitation, I went. Over chicken salad sandwiches at a darling little downtown cafe I'd never been to before, Calvin and I swapped life stories. The sandwiches became a usual Sunday afternoon routine for us, even after we caught ourselves repeating our stories.

He eventually asked to sit next to me at church. It sent the little blue-haired ladies gossiping, but after all, they needed something to pray for forgiveness about. Nothing was ever said out loud to me because they knew I wouldn't participate in the quarterly women's bake sale if they did, and my lemon ice box pie was always a best-seller.

Lunch with Calvin became dinner after the evening service, which soon became movie night at my house with a bowl of popcorn, a new weekly ritual of ours like the chicken salad sandwiches. That was four months ago, and my time with Calvin had been quite rejuvenating, some of the best moments I'd had since long before Frank died. I was happy that Calvin would be spending Christmas with us this year.

As I stepped out of the old barn's foundation to head back up to the house, I smiled over the whole birdseed episode from two days ago. It all seemed trite, but it was necessary sometimes to step back and take a look at ourselves as if we were a different person. We shake our heads in amazement at the things we do or obsess over. No matter how unimportant it was, the whole charade with the dead orioles choking on cheap birdseed would have to stick out in my mind as something much more important because there had been some discomforting news that day which was much worse.

After buying the birdseed, I had a doctor's appointment. It was to be a usual check-up for heart rate, blood pressure, and all the other things to be concerned with at my age; but I was also going there to get the results of some tests the doctor had run a few weeks prior.

It was official.

I had abdominal cancer, some rare cancer no one else ever had in my family that I knew of. It's a cancer that eats at your digestive system attacking the intestines and eventually the stomach. Radiation or chemotherapy was not an option, but I'm not sure they were options I'd contemplate anyway at this point in my life.

The doctor said I had eight months, maybe a bit longer. Eight months was plenty. I'd go right at the beginning of autumn like Frank did. That was always our favorite time of year because we enjoyed watching the leaves change. It's funny how fall foliage is the most obvious change each year we can always count on happening, but actually everything else is changing around us in life as well. Just sometimes we fail to take notice, or we don't want to.

At least this year would be a good Christmas. So, I chose not to tell them. I had not even told Calvin. I wanted the kids and grandkids to be able to look back and have fond memories of the last Christmas they spent with me. I had no plans for them all to be bedside this time next year watching me sleep, with hoses and monitors hooked up to me. Holidays should be special. I wouldn't have it any other way.

Back in the house, I reheated the oven and checked the foil covered pots under the burner. Homemade cookies and pies are the only thing that kept me up late last night. Thanks to the new mega supermarket with the huge deli section that just opened in town about a year ago, I bought everything else pre-made. Yams, green beans, corn, cornbread, baked beans, deviled eggs, potato salad, and even a fruit tray were all bought at the deli. And Mr. Greer was smoking the ham for me.

I just brought all the plastic tubs of food home and poured them into my own pots and pans to keep warm. It is more of a luxury to not have to cook for five children and four grandchildren. I still make the desserts they've been accustomed to for years, but if I could teach the bakery how to make my lemon ice box pie or chocolate almond cookies I certainly wouldn't hesitate to buy those either.

As I stepped into the den to plug up the Christmas tree and light some cinnamon-scented candles, I heard a car pull up in the driveway. Travis. I rushed to the door to greet him and to go help him unload his car. He was the first of the kids to arrive today; he always was punctual. I had not seen him in a few months, so hugging his neck now took all the pain of a distant child away.

I didn't blame him for moving away to the city. There never

would be anything in this small town for him except a factory job and his family, but a young maturing man like himself needed unridiculed love, whatever kind his own heart desired. Although Justin grew up here too, he and Travis might not have ever met, for a small Southern town like ours holds much prejudice. At least in a larger city filled with open minds, they were free to be who they wanted to be. But Travis had no qualms about coming back home to this town to visit us. Here in Dogwood, we were probably all that mattered to him. And for that and his arrival home, my holiday had officially started.

Ellen

"So long, see you tomorrow," Mark said standing at the kitchen door. He'd already put his suitcase in the car.

"Did you kiss Robbie and Rachel good-bye?" I asked.

"Yes."

"Did you wish them Merry Christmas?"

"Yes."

"Did you wish me Merry Christmas?"

He smiled. His eyes sparkled with a hint of the love I knew he still had for me somewhere inside him.

"Merry Christmas," he said with an exhale.

"Mark?" I said before he closed the door and left.

"Yeah?"

I wanted to tell him I loved him, but I was too afraid of his reply.

"Merry Christmas," I said instead, and went back to fumbling with a garden salad I was making to carry to Mom's.

He nodded and closed the door.

Mark was spending Christmas Eve with his parents this year. He'd return to the house early in the morning to put out the kid's gifts from Santa for when we come home tomorrow.

The kids and I were spending the night at Mom's tonight. For the most part, this would probably be my and Mark's last Christmas with each other, but we weren't really spending it together. I should say it will be the last Christmas Mark and I are married. The divorce would be settled in late January. I wanted it to be earlier, just to start the New Year off with a clean slate. Mark is the one who wanted to prolong it. He still loves me.

I love him too, but I don't know how much longer it's going to take for me to heal from all the pain of these past few years. It all started when Mark was laid off from his job at the plant four years ago. He drew unemployment or worked various construction jobs until he found steady work with a funeral home as a maintenance man. Until he got the funeral home job, the paychecks were barely enough to cover the mortgage.

With the kids in school, I decided to go back to work again to help Mark with the bills. I'd been a corporate secretary before Mark and I got married. My skills might have been a bit rusty now, but I landed a job as a court secretary for Judge Railen. At first, he didn't want to hire me since I'd been unemployed for seven years to raise a family. I turned on the waterworks for a bit of sympathy. I told Judge Railen about the hardships with Mark losing his job, and how I stayed awake at night worrying they'd foreclose on the house because I refused to beg Mother for money. I really needed this job to keep the lights on so my kids could see to do their homework, so my kids could have food to eat.

I dramatized things a bit, but everything I said was true. I feared the worst even though Mark had cashed in his 401K from the eleven years he'd worked in the factory. It was plenty of money to keep us and the kids clothed and fed for at least a year or so, but the crying worked. Judge Railen hired me that very day. Little did I know, my tearful plea opened the door for Judge Railen to be able to take advantage of my situation.

It all started in his office when he'd dictate notes to me. He had a habit of taking forever or making lots of changes. I later figured out he was just prolonging this time we spent together alone. He liked to lean over my shoulder to review my steno pad. Sometimes, he'd rest a hand on my shoulder or my back while reading my notes. I thought nothing of it in the beginning. When he lingered there for too long pretending to read, I realized it was because he liked to look down my blouse. Weeks passed and this routine continued. When he made me stay a few minutes late once so he could dictate a grocery list to me, things got worse.

With a hand on my shoulder while studying the list, he fingered my bra strap. I politely pushed his hands away, calling him a dirty old pervert but only in my head. Judge Railen was a bit offended, almost as if he'd heard my thoughts. He sat down behind his desk and asked if my paycheck was helping my family. It definitely was, although Mark had not been happy about me taking a job. Judge Railen reminded me of how I'd begged for the job that first day and how he didn't want to hire me.

"Things could be a lot worse for you right now," he said looking at me with lust in his eyes.

I ripped the list from my notebook and sat it down on his desk, then walked out. I was going to be late picking up the kids. I didn't want to go back to the courthouse the next day. At home, after fixing dinner, I took a long hot shower to try to wash away his touch. The water and my tears were not enough, but I went back to work the next day anyway. After court, Judge Railen had more notes to dictate. With his hand down the collar of my shirt to cup my breasts, he dictated a chocolate chip cookie recipe to me.

Judge Railen was a powerful man in the community, and he constantly reminded me of that when his hands were touching me. His brother was the District Attorney of the county, so his family had a stronghold on the legal aspects of Ruby Dregs. If I ever said anything to anybody, he threatened that neither Mark nor I would ever find work around here again. If we ever divorced, he'd make sure my kids were taken away from me.

For a whole year, I remained quiet and succumbed to his advances. He gave me a one-dollar raise. I cried in the car on the way home each day. I tried my best not to let Mark or the kids see me cry, but in the end no tears could cure my helplessness. No tears could wash away the pain I felt inside. No tears could explain why even Mark's touch at night in bed made me freeze with fear.

Eventually, I spoke up.

I wasn't the one who went to authorities first. Apparently, Judge Railen had his hands on several other female litigants and employees. Many of them were single mothers who had appeared before him during their divorces or for child support issues. The others were secretaries, like me, or clerks in need of the well-paying courthouse jobs because this economically depressed town had nothing else to offer us. Facing the community gossip, local and national headlines, and personal embarrassment, nine women gave an account of their humiliating experiences before a grand jury. I was one of them.

The judge was indicted on denying us of our constitutional right to be free of sexual assault in the workplace. Judge Railen was sentenced eight months later to twenty years in prison, but the emotional damage didn't end there. During the trial, a relative slipped him a cell phone while visiting him in prison. He called each of us and verbally harassed us over the phone to try to intimidate us the way he did in his chambers.

I'll never forget the day our phone rang. Mark had just been hired full time at the funeral home. I was home alone finishing the breakfast dishes. I had not been able to stay by myself for very long. Sleepless nights made the days weaker, but I still couldn't find rest when Mark and the kids were gone. I was too afraid to sleep in the house alone. During the day, I'd try to sleep at Mom's house or she'd come over and do housework for me while I rested. But even the security of someone else in the house didn't help much.

Eventually, I called Mom one morning and told her not to

come over. I had to fix this. For my and Mark's sanity, I had to get back to the closest thing I could to the life we had before I went to work in the courthouse. Our lives would definitely never be the same as they were, but I had to grasp for something new and familiar, a sliver of hope, anything we could at least mistaken for that old happiness. I was doing well for about two weeks, then the phone rang.

"Ellen," the rusty voice said.

I froze like a statue. A dish fell in slow motion from my hand and shattered on the floor into a million tingly pieces. My chest tightened. My heart stopped. My breath held. I was like an industrial but fragile engine that had come to a shuttering halt. I tried to drop the phone, but it was as if he were reaching through the receiver and forcing me to hold it to my ear to listen to what he had to say. The voice in my ear—the harsh grip of his hand—was all too familiar. A tear rolled down my face, stinging like a mosquito bite, but I could not swat it away. I let out a wince of air, acknowledging that I was listening.

"It's not too late to recant what you told them," Judge Railen whispered.

"Never," I managed to say after a hard swallow.

"You better hope they put me away for a long, long time."

"They will."

And they did.

Five more years were added to his sentence once a private investigator heard about the harassing phone calls. Twenty-five years behind bars would never seem long enough. After the immense settlements were passed out, based on the amount of time each of us suffered and the level of abuse, most of the women backed out of the way instead of pushing for a life sentence. Judge Railen had put his hand on one court clerk's leg under the bench right in court, and also forced her to perform oral sex on him in his private chambers. She received close to a million dollars, and was the first to sell her story to a national news channel and to a true crime author who conveniently popped up in town.

Having only worked under his authority for a year, I received the smallest settlement but was okay with that. I was more concerned with returning to being a housewife and taking care of my family now that Mark was working full time again. I was ready for the trial to be over so that I could start to forget about all of this.

All of the women, including myself, did insist that Judge Railen serve his time as far away as possible, as he had practiced law in six of the eight states that bordered Tennessee. Judge Railen had immediately pursued his appeal rights upon the basis that the indictment should be dismissed because the due process clause did not give protection against sexual assaults.

Highly educated and trained in law, he vigorously represented himself, so we did not want him to find loop-holes in the state courts that could eventually overturn his conviction. He ended up in a California penitentiary thanks to a motion that the grand jury made to the Supreme Court on behalf of the families of his victims. But even while in jail he continuously pursued a reversal by seeking a new trial, arguing that new evidence had surfaced.

The public embarrassment of having my family's name printed in the *Ruby Dregs County Gazette* every day soon faded. Being yesterday's news with a chunk of Judge Railen's dirty money in the bank was supposed to somehow make things better. Eventually, the women behind me in church or in the beauty shop stopped whispering. I still lay awake at night just knowing that evil man was still out there, still breathing. The pressure of all the small town scrutiny didn't help my marriage.

I demanded myself to bury all of this and move forward, but just when I'd made it through a day without once hearing the Judge's name, someone in line at the bank felt the need to give me their condolences over everything that had happened. This town wouldn't let me forget. Mark was growing tired of me jumping every time he casually put an arm around my waist or touched my shoulder. Sex was unbearable because I only saw the Judge's face hovering over me. Mark's kisses became distant and intermittent. I made them that way.

Two years passed. Answered prayers came one day when Mom called and asked if I'd seen the morning paper. Now, I'd never wished or prayed for anyone to die, and if I'd ever spoken it out loud it was out of sheer anger for what Judge Railen had done to me. And although no one would ever say it, reading the headlines that the Judge had died in prison was a lot like being baptized. The heavy burden of depression and victimization washed away, at least, for a little while.

He'd been dead for months but the black-robed potentate still haunted my dreams.

"Stop going to his grave," Mark told me.

I don't know why I went. Standing there, I'd break into tears over his gravestone like a mourning relative who cared about him. Instead, I grieved for the happier days when my marriage and family were stable and had meaning, all lost at the wandering hands of a perverted boss—king of the small town legal system, the very one that I felt turned its back on me.

A therapist told me standing over his grave was a huge step to facing my fears. There were no flowers there. There wasn't even grass growing back over the patch where they planted him. I expected to find graffiti sprayed across his marble-etched name some day, but it's as if this town just forgot about him forever. I wished I could be so lucky. I kept a safe distance, half expecting his menacing corpse hand to pop up out of the ground and chase me. I dreamt that once. The man haunted my dreams, when I was fortunate enough to get sleep, but still I went to his grave at least once a month.

I'd go after dropping the kids off at school in the morning. When there was a day with no bill to pay, no errand to run, and no groceries to buy, I'd find myself driving the winding narrow paths through Zion Cemetery to the Judge's grave in the far back corner. I memorized the names on the markers I drove past like they were old friends I'd see now and then. Some of them were friends once.

I don't know how long I stood there each time. A passing car would grab my attention and bring me back to the reality of the day. With a jerk of my wrist, I'd look at my watch thinking I'd lost several hours of time in a daydream, but usually only a few minutes had ticked away. Sometimes, the cell phone in my purse would ring. It was always Mark, as if he knew where to find me and knew I needed to hear his voice.

"Where are you?" he asked.

"I'm in line to pay the utility bill," I said.

He knew I was lying.

"Come have lunch with me today."

He never invited me to lunch until recently. Our time alone together was suddenly precious again. He'd hold my hand across the table and tell me whose body was at the funeral home that week. He told me how much their coffin cost, or about all the pretty flowers or lack thereof. How had death become such an important and inevitable part of our marriage, for both of us?

I pretended to pay attention, usually lost in the ripples of a bowl of potato soup. I wondered who would be sitting hear listening to him when he needed to tell someone about how this marriage had died. There would be no flowers at that funeral either, only a debate over what to do with the house or who got custody of Robbie and Rachel.

It's a lot easier to talk about someone else's passing when you aren't the one who needs to grieve. Grieving for when our marriage finally closes its eyes seemed almost impossible.

And so now it'd come to this, but there was always something delaying the divorce. In August the kids had to have school supplies and new clothes, and in September we celebrated their birthday. In October, there were pumpkins to carve and Halloween costumes to buy. Thanksgiving was my and Mark's favorite holiday. He'd help me in the kitchen in between quarters of football games on television. All four of us would put up the Christmas tree the next day.

In between helping the kids write letters to Santa and building a gingerbread house, we managed to schedule meetings with lawyers. So, in the dead of winter with all our warm memories buried deep in the snow, I'd find myself in a courtroom again making a decision that would change the one part of my life I thought I'd managed to keep consistent till now.

I finished making the salad to carry to Mom's. I chopped tomatoes and put them in a separate bowl because I hated them. I don't mind them cooked in a sauce or soup, but raw tomatoes on anything make me sick. I think Mom is the only one in the family who likes them. Dad didn't even like them. I remember Mom grew them in the backyard and put them on our dinner plates out of spite sometimes, knowing that we'd pick them off and push them to the side. She said a salad wasn't complete without them. So, before we eat tonight I'll toss them over the top of the salad when she isn't looking.

"Kids, grab your coats and shoes. We're leaving for Grandma's in a few minutes," I yelled into the living room where they were watching cartoons.

"Yay!" they squealed.

I washed my hands and then walked into the living room to survey the floor for toys to be picked up or snack wrappers to throw away. Rachel was already putting her dolls away.

"Good girl, Rachel," I said drying my hands on a dish towel. "Put your shoes on, Robbie."

The Christmas tree looked oddly bare as I reached behind it to unplug the lights. Mark had already packed the gifts into boxes for me and put them in the trunk of the car. The gifts from Santa, all wrapped and stowed away in the attic for now, would briefly make it look cheery again tomorrow morning. I packed our overnight bags last night and he'd put those in the car for us too.

"Mommy, I don't think Granny's tree is as pretty as ours this year," Rachel said.

"Don't tell Granny that. Let's at least let her think hers is," I said while helping Rachel with her coat.

"Okay."

I helped each of them to the car, fearful they'd either fall on a patch of ice on the driveway or they'd run into the snow to play. When I went back inside for the salad and the desserts, the phone was ringing.

"I was hoping I'd catch you," the voice on the other end said.

"Hello, Mom."

"Have you left yet?"

"You called the home phone, Mom."

"Oh! So I did."

"The kids are already waiting in the car so we will be there shortly. Did you need something?"

"I think I need one more can of cranberry sauce. I called Mr. Greer and he's holding a can at the counter for you. Would you be a doll and stop by there on your way over?"

"No problem. Is anyone there yet?" I asked.

"Travis got here a few hours ago. Clare and Jake are here too."

"Great. I can't wait to see them. See you in a few."

"Thanks, dear."

I hung up the phone. After putting the food in the car I went back inside for a quick run through the house to make sure I had not forgotten anything. Craving a treat, I peeled a gum drop from the roof of the kids' gingerbread house, which was sitting on the kitchen counter. The sweet replica of our family and home seemed oddly real, with only a mother and two gingerbread children standing in the snow-like frosting. The Daddy gingerbread man was gone because Mark had eaten him a few days ago.

My motherly instinct wandered through the house and checked for lights that might still be on in the kids' rooms. The peaceful quiet of the house was comforting, even with Mark gone. I wanted to just leave the kids in the car and sit down and enjoy it for a bit. I'd spent so much of the past few years unable to be alone thanks to Judge Railen, so taking notice of the serene house now seemed strange to me. It was just the peace of no television playing and no kids screaming that I was savoring right now. Otherwise, I don't think I liked the sound of being alone.

I knew Mom would warn the others that Mark would not be here this year, so no one would ask about him. We've all had struggles, but because it's Christmas we were exempt from talking about them. Mom, afraid talking about our problems with each other would ruin the holiday, wanted things to be perfect. Maybe Travis would want to toast Justin at the dinner table tonight. Maybe Clare felt like announcing that Andre had started paying child support. But Mom's desire for a picture-perfect postcard Christmas would keep all of us hushed.

The White family always managed to sweep their problems under the rug, especially when we spent time together. We never discussed our failures with one another. We each had too many. So, it was the diminutive bits of happy we have that we utilized at the holidays. My marriage was falling apart and about to end in divorce, but they already knew that. I didn't need to say it out loud. I didn't feel the need to talk about it with them.

Instead, I really wanted to tell someone how much I was still in love with Mark. That was the happiness I wanted to put on the table. I wanted to stand up in the middle of the living room tonight and scream it to everyone while they were opening gifts. Instead, I'd call Mark tonight. I'd tell him.

By the end of the day today, I'd call and tell him I still loved him.

Travis

"Wow, I wish she was always that happy to see me," Mom said after Clare came up and hugged me before running into the house.

"Do you need some help with Jake?" I asked.

"I've got him. I've got the baby boy," Mom sang.

Jake blinked his eyes awake with a wobbly head. He looked around to familiarize himself with where he was. Seeing Grandma's face made him light up with bliss. He grabbed at her neck with a baby hug. Mom hugged him back and gave him Grandma kisses.

"Hey there, lil guy," I said gently shaking Jake's arm.

Jake wrapped a tiny hand around my finger and looked intently at my face with intrigue. He had not seen me in weeks, but I could tell his tiny mind was trying to place me.

"I can't believe how much he's grown," I said. "How's he walking?"

"Honey, he doesn't walk anymore. He runs. Will you check the car and bring in her things?" Mom said, taking Jake into the house.

I wrinkled my nose at the sight of the inside of Clare's car.

The seats were damp in places from spilled drinks. The floorboards were filled with old bags from fast food restaurants. I collected Jake's bag and the gallon of milk that was sitting on the front seat. If Clare was staying the night or had brought gifts, the rest of her things must have been in the trunk. Curiosity told me to snoop in the glove box. It was locked. I looked over at the steering wheel and noticed she had left the keys in the ignition.

I took the keys and unlocked the glove compartment. The door fell forward, revealing a heap of clear brown prescription bottles. It reminded me of a box of spools Mom once kept from sewing. They made nice blocks for us kids to play with. I picked up a few of the bottles to examine the labels, but only found Clare's name on one or two of them. They were all prescriptions for Valium and various types of pain killers. I recognized some of the names from when Justin was sick and had to take all sorts of medication. I shut the glove box and went inside the house. I tucked Clare's keys into my pocket, waiting for an opportune moment to confront her about what I'd found.

I entertained Jake while Mom checked the pots on the stove and Clare was still upstairs in the bathroom. His heavy, sleepy eyes, fuzzy hair, and pouty lips reminded me of Justin rolling out of bed and waddling through the house in the early morning. He was always a light sleeper, often going to bed before nine if we were in for the night, and always waking up by five. He'd make coffee and check email while I was still in bed.

Sometimes, I would awake to find him sitting on our balcony. The sun had just come up and he'd be enjoying a cup of coffee in the cool morning air. I'd stand and watch him through the kitchen window over the sink, while pouring coffee for myself. Justin would be sitting at the small patio table and talking to himself, or to some ghost sitting across from him. I tried not to disturb him. I'd wander off into the house to watch television. On some days, out of the corner of his eye he'd see me standing there behind the window. He'd smile and wave to me, like a friend sitting in an airport or a café who spots a loved one they've been waiting for. His smile was like sunshine; I was happy to see it every morning.

I still woke up early now out of habit. I made my own coffee and checked email or read a few pages of a book. I enjoyed my time to myself in the morning before work or on the weekends. Not much had changed, except Justin wasn't a part of my morning now. Instead, it was me who sat at the table on chilly mornings and talked to his ghost.

"Do you think I should go upstairs and check on her?" Mom asked.

"I think she's okay. Give her a few more minutes."

"What if she's fainted?"

"I think we would have heard something."

"I'm not so sure. I'm going up there."

Mom leaned in front of me to pick up Jake. It was as if she didn't trust me with him. I didn't trust myself with him. Kids are fun, as long as a parent is close by when they start to cry or need a diaper changed. Mom hurried up the stairs with him to check on Clare. I went into the living room to admire the Christmas tree. It looked the same as it always had for years now, as if Mom just left all the lights and ornaments on and tucked it away in the attic like a piece of furniture.

She had never put lights on the tree when we were kids. There was a large spotlight that hung on the curtain rod to shine down on the tree. It had a motorized disk divided into four colors that turned in front of the spotlight, changing the color of the light from green to orange to red to blue. These spotlights were meant to shine onto aluminum Christmas trees. I still see them in vintage and antique stores sometimes. It was a firm brick in the foundation of my childhood holiday memories in this house.

When dad passed last year, Mom didn't want to put up the tree. I'd driven up to spend Thanksgiving with her. Ellen decided to cook and have everyone over to her house. After dinner, we came back to Mom's house and put the tree up for her. Since Ellen and I had planned on doing this, I'd gone to a store and bought strands of multi-colored lights to put on the tree instead of using the spotlight. I'd also bought a few dozen painted glass balls and a hodge-podge of Santa and toy-like ornaments. Ellen bought a new angel for the top.

Giving Mom's traditional tree a face-lift would hopefully keep it from reminding her of Dad. The spotlight was never used again; however, Mom insisted we put the tree up for her again this year because we'd done such a good job with it before.

I often thought Mom pulled out the photo albums to consult pictures from years past when it came to putting it up herself. Even the faded construction paper ornaments we'd all made as kids in school still adorned the tree branches with their pipe cleaner hooks. She always chose differently themed gift wrap each year and different colors of live poinsettias for the mantle, but the yard decorations always looked the same.

Mom made sure that one of us always took photos of the tree each year. All of the gifts were piled under it, often spilling out into the middle of the living room floor or onto an adjacent chair. With five kids, there were always so many gifts that they were leaned up against the wall in the back. If we were getting clothes, shirt boxes were stacked three and four deep against the wall like books on a shelf. Mom would insist we turn the camera sideways and take a long picture of the tree up and down, and then we had to take a picture of just all of the gifts, then the top half of the tree.

These three photos would receive a whole page in a photo album of hers labeled with that year on the cover. She'd take the two pictures of the top and bottom half of the tree and place them side by side overlapping to create one big image. Photos of each of us kids and each grandchild opening their gifts would follow. Although she usually made faces or conveniently ran out of film, we always took photos of her opening her gifts last. After dad died, the photos of her didn't find their way into her albums. The scrapbooks of our memories were all about us kids and the grandkids instead.

Making these photo albums was a year-long family tradition for as long as I could remember. There was an album for each of us, containing photos from every birthday and also every school yearbook picture in order from kindergarten through our senior year of high school. Mom always bought a package of our school photos in the spring and the fall. The white envelopes with the clear plastic windows and our school logo on the front, still containing extra wallet-sized photos we had never given away, were tucked between the pages of the albums.

Her Christmas albums alone filled up two shelves of the built-in bookcases in her sewing room. My photos of Justin and me were all digital and stored on CDs or on the computer. I wondered if my brothers and sisters kept albums or had other family photo traditions of their own.

Sitting on the floor by the tree, I was arranging the gifts I'd brought when Mother and Clare came down the stairs. Mother headed toward the kitchen with Jake still in her arms.

"Do you want some coffee? I'm going to make a cup for Clare," she said.

"Sure."

"Cream and sugar for you too?"

"Okay, just a little sugar," I said standing back up. I looked up to see Clare walking out the front door. "Where is she going? Is everything alright?"

"I think she's just tired. She's going out to her car to bring in her gifts. You should go help her," Mom said from the kitchen.

Since Mom was busy with Jake and making coffee, I decided to take this opportunity to ask Clare about the pill bottles I'd seen in her glove box. Besides, I still had her car keys in my pocket.

Giving her keys back after I accidentally startled her, she popped the trunk and loaded my arms with gifts. She was confrontational about the pill bottles when I brought them up, something about a substitution for happiness. I tried not to sound like Mom when talking to Clare, but with her being our little sister I'm sure she felt like she had a houseful of parents sometimes. She was closer to Sebastian than any of us, but only because they were closer in age. I remember they shared clothes and accessories when they were both into the punk scene and wore black make-up and shirts stitched with safety pins.

With nothing to say to me, she just walked away and went back into the house like she always did when she was tired of listening. Clare was unable to communicate with any of us very well except Sebastian, it seemed. It would be useless to ask him to talk to her because he had the same issues with drugs, and rather than try to console her or find out what's bothering her, he'd probably want to bum Valium from her if he found out she had any. Ever since Jake was born, I was pretty sure she'd given up pot and cigarettes. I don't even think she drank anymore, but the pills worried me.

Jake was the answer to our prayers that Mom would never get a phone call in the middle of the night telling her Clare was behind bars—or worse—dead. She was still young and a bit immature, and still rolled her eyes at her older siblings when they spoke to her, but Clare was a good mother. She had a steady well-paying job, a nice downtown apartment, and she could afford Jake's daycare on her own.

Back inside the house, Clare was sitting on the sofa with Jake and attempting to keep his hands off her coffee mug. The boxes she'd brought in lay beside her. Mom was sitting opposite her holding a mug for me. I had the odd feeling I'd interrupted a hushed conversation between them. Mom stood up and took a few boxes from me, placing them on the floor. I sat the rest under the tree and took the hot coffee from her.

"Thanks, Mom," I said, wrapping my bare hands around the coffee mug to warm them.

"Why don't you sit down and visit with your sister? I'm

68

going to attend to some things in the kitchen," Mom said.

I got up to arrange Clare's gifts under the tree. From the corner of my eye, I caught her rolling her eyes at me. She bounced Jake on her knee, content with pretending I wasn't in the room. This awkward silence between us was typical. We didn't dislike each other. She was the youngest, and she and Sebastian had been equally rebellious compared to us other kids. I don't think there was any resentment she housed particularly against me.

With Jake, she'd had to grow up fast and I think the transition from her teenage years into her twenties was still taking place. Although, before the age of sixteen she'd probably illegally done most of the things you are not supposed to do until you are twenty-one. Clare was still poorly clinging to the days of being daddy's little girl. The look on her face now was just a facade she could almost keep in a jewelry box with her belongings. We were quite accustomed to seeing it.

"She'll grow out of it. Sebastian did," Mom would say when we'd speak about Clare's anger.

Sebastian was never really angry. He was too strung out to hold defenses against anyone. Although he was a loser in high school, he was quite popular as the class clown. He flunked almost everything or was kicked out of class, but Mom made him finish. He begged her to let him quit and get his GED, but she just knew he'd end up in a fast food joint flipping burgers. After five years of high school, he ended up there anyway for a while. Now, he was a bartender in some college pub. Completely emerged in the party lifestyle of never-ending music, drugs, beer, and girls, Sebastian wasn't much different from Clare. He just knew how to make better with the cards life had dealt him.

It's not fair to say his life was supposed to turn out this way. Sebastian could have straightened up and studied harder. He could have gone to college and became a doctor or lawyer, but Mom and Dad never pushed us to do anything we didn't want to do. They just wanted each of us to be happy, so I didn't feel sorry for Sebastian. He certainly didn't feel sorry for himself, and never asked for our sympathy. The cards he'd been dealt were the ones he was content with playing.

"So you have a really nice apartment in Memphis," Clare said from behind me.

"Why are you asking?"

"I'm not asking. Sebastian told me."

"He did?"

"Yeah. He said he had a really good time staying with you."

"He told you about staying with me?"

"Yeah. Why wouldn't he?"

"He told me not to let anyone know he was there."

"He went there to dry out."

I didn't know why Clare was bringing all of this up. Sebastian had either already told her everything, or she was fishing for information. Sebastian got pretty messed up after losing a girlfriend back in the summer. He called me in the early morning one night and wanted to drive down right then to stay with me for a few days. He needed to get away. By the time the cops were looking for him, I had convinced him to at least call the police department and let them know where he was. He had nothing to hide, but coming to Memphis definitely looked like he was trying to run away from what had happened.

"Clare, if you ever need a place to stay—"

"I don't."

"I'm just offering."

"Thanks, but no thanks."

"Clare, just listen to me. I know you've never really had a chance to get away from this place, this town, and I know what that can be like. If you ever need a break, just call me. Jake can come too, if you want."

"It's easy for you to run off to your skyscrapers at the end of the day."

"It'd have been harder to stay in this small town. I don't know how you do it."

70

"This is home," she said.

"And it will always be home to me too, but sooner or later the birds leave the nest. You can't sit there and tell me honestly that you are happy still living here in Ruby Dregs, can you?"

"Is everything okay in here? Travis, why are you yelling?" Mom asked, standing in the doorway to the kitchen.

"Sorry, I didn't realize I was."

I walked to the front door as if someone was knocking, or as if I was going to walk outside into the snow, anything to escape the tension I'd created. Lucky for me, I noticed a small red car pulling up into the driveway.

"Whose red car?" I asked out loud.

"Sebastian," Mom and Clare said practically in unison.

Sebastian

Going to Mom's for Christmas was a lot like detox. I usually didn't drink or smoke anything for two days before. I also would wash whatever I planned to wear at least twice or have it dry cleaned if I had the money. I brushed my teeth for an hour the night before and that morning, and chewed half a pack of gum while driving there.

It was rare for me not to smell like booze or smoke, especially since I worked in a bar. My siblings were well aware of my addictions and weaknesses. If one of them wasn't standing by at the hospital while my stomach was getting pumped, then they were visiting me in an actual detox facility. I spent at least a week or two there during each year of high school. I was pulled over for drunk driving before I was eighteen. Mom and Dad left me in jail for the night, hoping it'd "scare some sense" into me. I stayed sober for only about a week, but I did stay out from behind the wheel long after that.

Getting a job in a bar didn't help. Mom frowned at the idea and said I was putting the nails in my coffin, but at least I was earning a paycheck. She no longer had to pay my rent or buy my groceries. Kids always seem to gravitate toward whatever their parents fear the most, at least for a little while. Once Clare got pregnant, their interventions toward me stopped.

I was the kid who was just trying to get by. I had no plans for the future. I lived for today and that was about it. I would have dropped out of high school if Mom would have let me. The words "when are you going to do something with your life" stopped after Dad died. We all learned that our time together was precious, but for me it was just another excuse to drink. The excuses came to a halt when I met Lind.

Although I had no children of my own, I knew what it must be like for a parent to lose a child to the poisons under the sink or the unlocked gun cabinet. They are the news stories we take for granted when they happen to someone else, but also the blame that beats us up when the mistake does happen to us. We shake our head in sorrow at the disturbing front-page news, but have forgotten all about it by the time we are reading the funnies. It feels a lot different when we become the headlines.

I'm not talking about my Dad. He woke up and died in the middle of the night from a stroke. Losing him was a different kind of pain. I still felt empty inside, but it was more like losing a best friend. With my sister's arms wrapped around my waist, or my own arms wrapped around my mother's neck, I knew I wasn't feeling this way alone. In time, that pain healed even though it might have left a scar on the inside. The sickness I'm talking about has never gone away.

I wonder sometimes if it's the way Mom felt that night. Dad probably shook her from her peaceful sleep to get her to call for an ambulance. She probably burst into tears, unaware of what she could possibly do to help him. There was nothing to do. She sat in the floor next to the bed and held his hand, and he went. A piece of her, deep inside somewhere where those feelings are kept, died with him. That's the ache I'm talking about. I just can't kick it.

I first met Lind at work. I was doing five nights a week, Tuesday through Saturday, at a bar called Zero's over on the end of The Row. That's what we called the line of buildings across the street from the fraternity houses. It's an old shopping mall, now home to mostly frat bars. There was a gas station at one end and an all-night diner on the other. A coffee shop, a textbook outlet, and a Laundromat broke up the neon bar signs.

Lind was short for Lindsey. She was dancing with the wall on a slow Wednesday night. She played horrible '80's music on the jukebox most of the evening. I would have threatened to unplug it on her but she fed my tip jar three or four bucks for every beer she drank, and two hours into my shift she'd emptied about six bottles. Soon, we were the only two in the bar. After wasting a few quarters between the video games and the pool table, she settled down on a bar stool to flirt with me.

"You got a girlfriend?" she asked.

"Nope," I said, wiping down the bar, stocking the cooler, and going through the typical routine of a bartender trying to look busy to pass the time. "What about you?"

"I don't date girls," she snickered. It was a loud animal-like laugh through the nose.

"Got a boyfriend?" I asked. Drunken bubbly sorority girl humor never fazed me.

"Nope. Not anymore. Tonight, I'm celebrating being single again."

I refrained from asking any more questions. It was the number one rule of bartending on a slow night. Never open the door to confessional. It could be hours before any one else walked in if at all, and I didn't want to make the night go by any slower by having to listen to her cry and bitch about why her boyfriend left her. Smashed girls and sob stories don't mix, and I found it highly unusual that she was out celebrating alone. Usually there's a flock of girls in here when a relationship has called it quits.

Some regulars wandered in for a game of pool. More guys came in to celebrate a basketball game victory, and some more from a study break. Lind lost herself in the crowd of jocks and frat guys, flirting with them all. As my shift picked up, she fell out of sight and out of mind. I assumed she'd left until one of the guys came up and told me some girl was passed out on the bathroom floor.

I got him to help me pick her up and put her in a booth. Some guys, who had crowded around to watch, joked about taking advantage of her. I was afraid that someone already had. Her pants were unzipped. She might have just fallen off the toilet, but I still feared the worst. I called a chick bartender from the joint next door for advice. She had coverage so she offered to come over and help. She checked Lind's pockets for an ID. The address on her license was local. We contemplated calling her a cab. Lind woke up just as we were looking through the numbers on her cell.

"Can we call you a cab?" I asked.

She shook her head no. "Call Shelly. She's my roommate. She'll come and get me."

A few weeks later, Lind was in the bar again on my shift. I was relieved to see Shelly with her. Lind seemed much more reserved and together this time. She sipped one beer for about an hour while sitting in the corner talking to Shelly. I caught myself looking at her several times, unsure if it was the same reckless girl who'd been in here that night. I spoke up when Shelly came to the bar to buy another round.

"How's she doing?"

"Hey, thanks for calling me that night. Lind doesn't even remember. That was a tough week for her. Her boyfriend was killed in Iraq."

"I'm sorry to hear that. I hope she's okay."

Lind certainly wasn't the first inebriated girl I'd picked up off the floor at Zero's or at any of the other bars I'd worked at, and a couple of them I'd put into cabs more than once. They'd drowned their sorrows in cheap beer for flunking a test, celebrated a twenty-first birthday, or finally graduated from college. The difference between them and Lind was that most of the time, there was a friend here for them.

My only intervention was usually calling a cab, handing out bottled water, or making an ice pack. The fact that Lind had been here alone that night still intrigued me. Shelly was obviously a friend, but where was she that night when Lind needed her most? Suddenly, Lind seemed more appealing.

I hate to sound like I wanted to take advantage of her situation. A sad lonely girl losing a military boyfriend and passing out alone in a bar can seem awfully vulnerable. Lind was pretty. She had full sandy-blonde hair right from a shampoo commercial. Her green eyes were probably contacts and her glossy pink lips were painted on. With a nice rack, an hourglass figure, and a heart-shaped ass, she'd have another boyfriend in no time.

I admired the fact that she appeared sensitive right now at the table with Shelly. No one would have ever believed how sloppy drunk she was that night. Her slow buzz tonight must have cured her grief because she winked at me when she came up to the bar to buy the next round. She giggled and tossed her hair to flirt. It was much more innocent than the loud pig snort laugh I remembered from before.

"This one's on me," I said pushing her money back across the bar.

I was a bit surprised when they left shortly after, but I knew she'd be back. And it was sooner than expected. She was waiting for me outside that night when the bar closed. Before I had a chance to speak, she'd pinned me against the wall and kissed me. Since it was a week night, the only place still open was the diner just a few doors down. She suggested we go back to my place. I liked her idea better.

The love we made that night was exciting and familiar. I'd had plenty of one-night stands before, but usually only after a night on the other side of the bar when I'd had a chance to drink and socialize. Exploring a girl's body for the first time was always a thrill. I remember studying her appendix scar while kissing her stomach, something I'd never taken time to notice on a girl before.

I don't remember ever having had sex sober before that night. It'd never been this easy. I think it was the only time

Lind and I would ever make such clean love. Smoking pot was a bit simple for her and pretty much a staple for me. She preferred cocaine, and ecstasy on the weekends if we went out dancing. Her purse was an illegal medicine cabinet and reminded me of my younger sister.

The Lind I'd seen that very first night soon reappeared, and stayed around quite often. There was never a night we went out that she didn't drink too much. We'd end up having to call it an early night because she'd pass out. I'd get pissed and try to dump her off at her apartment, but she always conveniently woke up in my car and wanted to go back to my place. She'd beg me to make love to her and then pass out again in the middle of it. This practice was also a little too familiar, but it was usually me who fell asleep.

If we had not had sex that first night, if she had not been such an easy piece, I think I could have fallen in love with her. She was a trophy on my arm in the eyes of my buddies, but it wasn't even fair to call her a "catch." There had never been a hunt or chase. I knew that sooner or later I'd call it off before she got too serious. I'd break her heart before she wanted to leave a toothbrush and some clothes at my apartment. When I found out the spiel about the boyfriend in Iraq had just been a lie to reel me in, I didn't feel so bad about letting her go.

It all started when I decided not to call her for a few days. I ignored her voice messages and went out alone. I think I even took a different girl home one night. Dating girls I met at work doesn't make the break-up so easy though. A few nights later, Lind was there waiting for me when my shift started. She yelled. I ignored her. She dumped a bowl of popcorn across the bar.

I'm glad there were only two other guys in the bar to see this, and I knew both of them. It was still embarrassing, but I'm sure they understood such trouble with girls. I walked around the bar and grabbed Lind by the shoulders. She tried to pull away, arms flailing. When she'd stopped and calmed down long enough for me to say something, I told her to go home.

She left in tears. I look back on that moment now and wish I had broken up with her. Things might have been a lot different now.

Instead, I picked up the phone and called her the next day. When you aren't getting laid, apologies come much easier. She came over that night for what was to be a quiet evening at home with just the two of us. I was bored. We were drinking. Soon, Lind was scraping lines of cocaine across a mirror on my coffee table.

Lying on the floor naked, I woke up when it was still dark outside. The sun had just barely touched the sky but I squinted my eyes as if it were rising right there in my apartment. My crotch ached from sex I didn't remember having. Lind was lying in bed. I crawled into bed and threw my arm around her. When I woke up again, it was noon. I crawled out of bed and took a hot shower. My head throbbed. I didn't have any aspirin, so I was going to make a trip to the drug-store.

After getting dressed, I sat down on the edge of the bed to put my shoes on. I reached over to wake Lind. She wouldn't wake up. I put my hand on her chest and put my head up close to her nose and mouth. Her heart wasn't beating, and she wasn't breathing. I called emergency services. They let me ride in the ambulance. Again, I knew what it must have felt like to be my mother, leaning over an emergency technician in the back of an ambulance as they tried to revive someone right there in front of you, but couldn't.

The only difference was that I didn't love Lind the way my mother loved my father. Before, I didn't think I loved Lind at all. Now that she was gone, some feeling from deep inside kept interfering with the pain, overwhelming me with confusion. I was still coming down from the alcohol and the drugs from the night before. I passed out before the ambulance had reached the hospital.

* * * *

"Is Sebastian there?" I could hear my Mom asking Travis on the phone.

"Yeah, Mom. He's here."

"What has he done?"

They were four little words I'd heard her say quite a bit over the years. What had I done? Doctors had revived me in the hospital. Knowing that Lind was gone, I panicked. I was hysterical, and on the verge of a breakdown. I managed to keep myself together long enough to sneak out of the hospital. I caught a cab back to my apartment. I threw some clothes in a bag, and without even thinking about what to do or where to go, I drove to Memphis. When I got to the city, I called Travis and told him where I was. He gave me directions to his apartment. I had already told Travis what happened before Mom called. The police had come to her house looking for me. They'd told her about Lind. She had never met Lind and didn't even know who she was.

"They just want to ask you some questions," Mom said on the phone.

"I'm a suspect now."

"You should have thought about that before you ran away," Mom told me.

A detective and two cops were knocking on Travis's door an hour after we hung up with Mom. They didn't arrest me. The detective told me Lind had died of a lethal concoction of alcohol, cocaine, and Valium. An overdose. Doctors had tested my blood when I passed out and found the same levels of alcohol and cocaine, but no Valium. Passing out in the ambulance was the only thing that saved me from going to jail for murder.

The detective asked about the Valium. I told him about Lind's pill addiction. Her purse was in my apartment and its contents would prove it. I agreed to take him there. It wasn't the first time I'd ever been in the back of a cop car, but it was the longest ride I'd ever taken in one. The eighty miles from Memphis back to Ruby Dregs only took about twenty minutes at the speed the cop was driving. Travis agreed to go with me.

"Why is my door open? Did you send someone here already?" I asked the detective.

"Stay here," he ordered.

With guns pulled, they ran up the stairs and flanked the doorway. They glided around the wall and into my apartment. I heard them yell, "Police!" Travis looked at me wide-eyed when we heard scuffling inside.

"Do you have a roommate?" he asked.

"No."

"Did someone break in?"

Neither of us dared to go up the stairs to find out. Soon, the cop emerged, escorting a woman with her hands cuffed behind her back.

"Who is that?" Travis asked.

"It's Shelly. Lind's best friend," I said.

"Why is she here?"

"I don't know."

"Murderer!" she yelled at me as the cop put her in the back seat of his car.

Shelly had broken into my apartment to steal Lind's purse. It still contained around a dozen bottles of Valium. I don't know if she wanted it for personal reasons or to make me look guilty of being responsible for Lind's death. Probably both. We had arrived just in time to stop her. The detective told me that if she had gotten away, the story I'd told him would have looked false and I would have been arrested. Lind's purse would have most likely disappeared, and I'd have been sent to jail.

Lind had no family, or at least no relatives who cared to press charges against me. A bag of cocaine found in Lind's purse cleared me of the responsibility of possession for the drugs that killed her. A receipt in her purse from a gas station near her apartment confirmed she'd bought the beer we drank that night. The marijuana they found in my apartment was mine, but luckily we had not used it.

With nothing firm to charge me with, the judge gave me a break. The amount of drug paraphernalia found in Shelly and Lind's apartment was proof to the judge that Lind was gambling with her own life and it was only a matter of time before something like this would have happened. My older brother Martin agreed to drive me back to Memphis to pick up my car a few days later. Travis took off from work to stay in town and offer his support if I needed it.

"Hey, wasn't this your girlfriend?" A guy asked me one night at the bar. He was holding up a newspaper with Lind's death as the front-page cover story.

After the cops let me go, I picked up a few shifts at Zero's. They didn't want me to leave town for a few days, not even to go get my car.

"No, she wasn't my girlfriend." I said. I was hoping to stay out of the public eye.

"Sure, she was. You woke up next to her dead body, right?" the guy continued to harass me.

"Hey, man, I don't want to talk about it," I said trying to keep things low.

"This guy sleeps with dead chicks," he said, laughing with his buddies.

I refrained from jumping across the bar and hitting him. Ignoring another guy's taunts two nights later got a beer thrown in my face. The manager of the bar suggested I take a few weeks off until things calmed down. I was too afraid to drink or smoke anything, just knowing the cops would call me back in and bust me for something. I was walking on egg-shells, and not having a job to occupy my mind was going to drive me insane.

Lind might have been dead, but her soul was not resting peacefully. She haunted my dreams. I'd wake up in the middle of the night in a cold sweat on the floor. I just couldn't sleep in that bed where she had died. After several sober and sleepless nights, I got a phone call from the detective. I was all clear of any charges and anything to do with Lind. The case was closed as a wrongful death. Finally, I could go to Memphis and pick up my car. I could have a drink, or two, or three and smoke a joint.

Instead of a bottle of vodka clearing my head, it made it worse. I tried to go out to a bar, but everywhere I looked I saw Lind. Every girl on the dance floor had her face. The more I drank the more dead she looked, skin peeling and bugs crawling out of her mouth and eyes as she called me a murderer. I bought a dime bag of coke from someone, hoping it would numb my brain.

A buddy of mine gave me two pills that I chased with a few shots of tequila. He said it would help me chill. Instead, it sent the room spinning. Now, Lind's face was every face in the room, men and women. I crashed to the floor as several Linds hovered over me. They were asking if I was alright, but all I heard was "Murderer! Murderer! Murderer!" over and over again.

I woke up in the back of Martin's car. He and Travis were in the front seat. I felt like I'd been asleep for days, but they told me only a few hours had passed. Martin was taking us back to Memphis. Travis was going to let me stay with him for a few days to "straighten my life out."

I didn't know how I was going to do that. I didn't have much of a life to figure out. I was twenty-two years old and had probably killed enough brain cells from so much intoxication that I should probably be legally deemed a teenager all over again. The only job I'd ever held was in a bar. I'd worked as a bar back right out of high school, and as a waiter for a year, finally moving my way up to tending bar. I wasn't like Martin or Travis. They'd taken the right path and gone to college. They'd settled down and got good-paying jobs. The pieces of my puzzle didn't fit together like that. Although I'd run away to his place just two weeks ago, unsure where to go, actually, I didn't want to spend days with my fag brother so he could remind me all the time about getting my shit together. I'd heard enough of that from Mom over the past few years.

I should have gone to stay with Clare, but I agreed to Travis and Martin's plan instead. Besides, they had the keys to my car, and I'd need their help moving out of my apartment when I came back home. As soon as I got back to Ruby Dregs, I was definitely going to find a new place to live. There was no way I could stay in my old place after what had happened there with Lind.

It'd been six weeks since then. No twelve-step programs. No Alcoholics Anonymous. At Travis's place, he didn't preach to me one bit. He even took me out to a night club after a few nights in Memphis. He bought me a couple of drinks and drove us home afterwards. After a week, he gave me my keys and told me to be safe driving home; he was letting me go all on my own. He drove up a week later and he and Martin helped me move into an apartment across town.

I don't know why none of them, not even Mom, said anything scolding to me since the phone call with Mom the day I ran away. It's as if they were finally treating me like an adult. It almost worried me. I expected the finger-pointing and ranting from them, at least from Mom.

"Why is everyone pretending nothing happened?" I asked out loud at the dinner table that night. Mom had offered to fix a meal for us after a long day of moving my stuff.

"We're not pretending," Martin said.

"No one has said anything about all of this," I said.

"What do you want us to say?" Mom asked.

"I don't know. I've been building myself up for a long counseling session from all three of you, an hour of 'I told you so,' especially from you Mom."

"We're tired of all that," Mom said.

"What?"

"Sebastian, we've wasted our breath trying to talk to you. Telling you to stop drinking and stop running around with the wrong crowd has been a waste of time. It's time you took responsibility for your own actions," Mom said.

"I didn't kill that girl."

"I didn't say you did. But that girl was a drug addict you'd been dating for some time. Both of you were drunk and sniffing cocaine. I'm not saying it doesn't matter that she died that night, but you were passed out on the floor. You were practically knocking on death's door yourself."

"I'm okay—."

"You're okay now, and I'm thankful for it. But what about the next time? You're not a cat, Sebastian. You don't have nine lives, so I don't know why you constantly toy with the one you do have. As soon as the cops dismissed you from the charges, what did you do? You went to a bar and right back to your old habits."

"Okay, fine. Whatever."

The slap across my cheek came from nowhere, a motherly reflex as if she were killing a fly in the kitchen in mid-air. It stung my face and brought uncontrollable tears to my face.

"Whatever? Is that how you feel about your life? Whatever! If that's how you feel, then why in the hell do you sit here at my table and ask why we haven't said anything? You don't listen to us, so we're all tired of talking!"

That was the first time I can remember ever hearing my mother swear.

"I'm outta here," I said slamming my chair back and getting up from the table.

For effect, I threw my tea glass on the floor. Walking toward the front door, I heard the shattered glass settling behind me. I felt a hard grip on the back of my shirt and knew it was one of my brothers. Martin spun me around to face him and then slammed me against the door. As if in slow motion, I tried to raise my arms to block him. His fist moved in the realness of time and landed across my face where Mom had slapped me. I fell to the corner of the threshold and buried my face in my knees.

"Martin!" Mother cried, still standing next to the table.

"Don't ever disrespect this house or disrespect her like that. She's your mother!" he screamed down at me.

It was anger I'd never seen before, not even in Dad. Martin left out the back door. Travis came over to help me up, but I jerked away from him. With my burning face buried beneath my arms, I sat there in embarrassment and shame. I could hear Mom sweeping up the broken glass. I don't know how long I sat there like that.

I don't know why I still didn't listen to any of them. After that, I kept drinking. I kept smoking. I occasionally snorted a line at a party if it was offered to me. But every sip of alcohol, every joint I rolled, every grain of white powder sucked up into my nostril after that day was infected with guilt. My Mom's words echoed in my ears when there was a beer bottle in my hand. Her face formed in the smoke I exhaled, but she wasn't saying, "I told you so." She was just looking at me and weeping.

No matter how much I drank or smoked, this time the guilt wasn't going away.

Travis

I held the door open for Sebastian, watching him walk up the drive. He was holding a stack of red envelopes, probably Christmas cards for each of us. He was never one to shop for personalized gifts.

"Hey, little brother," I said to him as he walked in.

I expected him to ignore me. I had not seen him since that day Martin hit him a few months ago right here in the doorway.

"Hey there. Merry Christmas," Sebastian said handing me an envelope with my name scribbled on it in his scratchy penmanship.

"Thanks," I said taking it from him as he stepped inside. "Yours is under the tree."

"Hey, sweetie," Mom chimed.

There was a much different vibe in the air today than when I'd last been in the same room with Sebastian and Mom. Maybe it was just because of the holiday. I sometimes felt like I was kept in the dark with my family, mainly because I was the only one who had moved away from this town. Although I came back and visited regularly and spoke to Mom on the phone on the weekends, if anything happened in between no one made it a habit to let me know. Being gay probably aided in making me the black sheep. Today, Sebastian's demeanor told me I'd missed out on something. My Mom's next words confirmed it.

"How is school going?" she asked him.

"School?" I said.

"Sebastian enrolled in night classes," she said.

"When did this happen?" I asked, looking back and forth from Mom to Sebastian.

"A few weeks ago," Sebastian said with a shy grin.

"What are you going to school for?" I asked.

"Massage therapy."

"Are you still working at Zero's?"

"No, the manager wouldn't let me come back after what happened. I'm waiting tables again."

"In a bar?"

"In a restaurant down on the court square."

"Wow, that's great! I'm proud of you," I said.

"Hey, Sebastian, if you need someone to practice massages on, keep me in mind," Clare spoke up from the sofa.

"Will do, Sis," he said walking over to her and giving her a light squeeze on the shoulder. He took Jake from her and held him up in the air to say hello.

"How's my little nephew doing?" Sebastian said playfully.

Although I'd just found out his good news, I was happy for Sebastian being enrolled in classes. We've all had our hardships the past few years, but Clare and Sebastian had provided quite a few gray hairs for Mom and Dad since high school. Now that Clare was a mother and Sebastian was in school, I think their course in life was finally leading them in a mature direction.

Sometimes I wondered if they thought we were boring. Martin, Ellen, and I had all gone to college and established lives for ourselves after that. For the most part, we stayed out of trouble and all landed steady jobs.

Although Clare and Sebastian probably thought of me as a

stiff, I certainly wasn't without sin. It'd been years since I'd gone home drunk with a stranger after a night of partying. I could count on one hand the number of times that actually happened and have fingers left over.

Clare still played with dolls and Sebastian collected model cars back when I was living the life they are now. I think it was easier back when I was growing up, although that hasn't been but a decade (or two) ago.

No matter how reckless their lives had seemed, I can't help but be a little jealous of what they have experienced so far. I never drank a drop of alcohol before I was legally old enough, and I've still never smoked anything, not even a cigarette to this day. Both of them had done much more than that before they were eighteen. To them, I *was* probably boring.

With work hours to clock and bills to pay, the rest of life quickly slips away from you. No reason it was a never-ending party for Sebastian. Clare was too young to have a baby when she did, but she chose to catch up with the rest of us who'd entered that fuzzy part of being where we think we finally have everything figured out. Maybe she always looked depressed because she was still clinging to those good old days, debating on whether or not to admit she was growing old like the rest of us.

We all couldn't wait to get out from under our parents' wings back then. We wanted a car and a credit card, and our own place. When I received my first credit card bill in the mail, or maybe it was the bill for the car loan, or when I wrote that first check to pay the rent, I knew there was no going back. After twelve years of school and four years of college, was this what I'd been waiting for? Justin was my answer to that question.

In all the ten years we'd spent together, I never knew loneliness the way I do now. It's the kind of feeling that makes your throat sore from swallowing or coughing too hard during the night, that constant nagging at your insides during the day when you know you are about to come down with something.

It's always there, in the back of your mind, and all you can do is get through your day and wait for the worst to come. I doubt they'd ever been in love, but I wondered what kind of loneliness Sebastian and Clare felt.

Just then, the door bell rang. Mom rushed to answer it.

"Trick or Treat!" Robbie and Rachel yelled when Mom opened the door.

"Trick or treat? Where are your costumes? There's no Halloween candy here," Mom said, teasing them.

"Mama, we fooled Granny," Robbie said, turning to Ellen who was walking up behind them.

"Granny, I have a gift for you," Rachel said

"You do?"

Rachel pulled a can of cranberry sauce out from under her coat and presented it to her with a flourish.

"Thank you, sweetie. It's what I always wanted," Mom said, playing along by taking it from her and clutching it to her heart.

She knelt to hug both of them. They kissed her on the cheek.

"Merry Christmas, Granny," Robbie and Rachel both chimed as they pulled away from her and peeked around her to see who was inside.

"Merry Christmas to you too. Go inside and say hello to Uncle Travis, Uncle Sebastian, and Aunt Clare."

"Hi, Mom," Ellen said.

"How are you?" Mom asked, hugging her neck.

"I'm good," Ellen said with a smile.

After hugging Robbie and Rachel, I stood behind Mom to greet Ellen. It was good to see her smile. I'm sure it came easier to her these days. Mom, Sebastian, and I all accompanied Ellen to her car to help her bring in their things.

"Where's Mark?" Sebastian asked outside.

I hit him on the shoulder to get him to shut up.

"What did I do?" he asked.

"I thought you would have told everyone by now," Ellen

said to Mom.

"Tell me what?" Sebastian asked.

"Mark isn't coming this year," Ellen said.

"Shit, who am I supposed to watch football with?" Sebastian said.

"Don't look at me," I replied.

"You can watch football with Martin. Are you and the kids staying the night?" Mom asked Ellen, changing the subject.

"Yeah, our bags are in the trunk. I hope that's okay."

"Of course, everyone can stay as long as they like," Mom said.

Who could blame Sebastian for asking about Mark? He had not been here long enough for Mom to tell him. I had never been really close to Mark since I didn't live here, but I knew that both Sebastian and Martin considered him to be a close friend. I had always found him to be a bumbling heterosexual idiot. I imagined he blamed himself for what happened to Ellen. If he had not lost his job at the factory, she would have never gone back to work and been subjected to the horrible things that judge did to her.

Mark was a narrow-minded guy who'd never known a day outside of this town. He'd been born and raised here, gone to work here, raised his own family here, and he'd die here. When his glory days of being the quarterback and prom king were over, he was lost. An assembly-line factory job was the only option for someone who didn't want to go to college or join the armed forces. His arrogant haughtiness kept Ellen at home to raise the two kids, but broke his pride when he lost his job and was no longer the bread winner.

Landing a job at the funeral home should have been a metaphor for the end of the road for him. I figured any job that required him to do more than punch a button or turn a key was going to be a challenge. Steady work would not keep his family from falling apart, though. While Mark thought he was picking up the pieces, and Ellen thought she could help him out by going back to work, the mirror they'd been looking into shattered all over again.

I think Mark pretty much gave up after that. By the time the Judge's soap opera was revealed and their names were in the morning paper, Mark had forgotten how to reach out and touch his wife. I doubt Ellen wanted to be touched. It wasn't her fault. The touch of any man was the feeling of the Judge's hands crawling on her. She froze up even when I hugged her. She didn't want it to be that way, but it was like the terror of looking upon a gruesome auto accident. Those images and feelings were burned into her memory and could not be washed away.

I think he tried to be there for her in the very beginning. He sat beside her and held her hand in court. He cheered when the Judge's sentence was announced, and when Ellen's reparation check came. He mistakenly felt their story now had a happy ending, and Ellen could somehow magically go back to being a happy house-wife since he was working full time again. Mark was impatient, though, when it came to her healing process. He fell out of love with her.

Sebastian had wanted to treat Martin and me to lunch the weekend that we helped him move. After a long morning of transporting his belongings across town, he took us to a bistro called Poteet's where he once worked. It was a sports bar steakhouse-type place, with outbursts of yelling at the television and rounds of high-fives, adjacent to the shopping mall and the movie theater. The three of us sat at a pub table in the far corner of the restaurant, away from the busy activity surrounding the bar where everyone was watching a baseball game.

I was tired, but leisurely enjoying just sitting there and people-watching while Martin and Sebastian talked. That's when I noticed Mark sitting at the bar nursing a pitcher of beer. I immediately noticed there were two mugs sitting in front of him, and he wasn't acting like a tired guy grabbing a cold one after a long day at work. After all, it was the middle of the afternoon! He was smiling and seemed joyful, with his eyes glued to the overhead television like everyone else around him. He didn't notice us. Rather than point him out to Martin and Sebastian, I waited to see who would join him.

It was not Ellen who returned from the restroom and sat down beside him. It was a young buxom blonde who reminded me of a stereotypical cheerleader in a pink fuzzy sweater from some B-movie. She giggled and fell into him when she sat down, a bit intoxicated. He wrapped his arm around her and pulled her close, whispering into her ear as she smiled and fluttered her eyes. He filled their beer mugs. I could tell she was rubbing his leg beneath the bar.

If Sebastian and Martin were not with me, I would have approached him. I still refrained from telling them because I knew they'd run over and knock him off his bar stool. He deserved that, but I kept quiet. My mind refused to believe what I was seeing. This town was so small and although I didn't know anyone in the bar besides us, chances are half the waitresses had gone to my high school, and half the patrons either worked together, lived next door to one another, or went to school with each other. Everyone in this town knew everyone else, either by face or by name or both.

Certainly more than half the restaurant knew Mark's wife, if they didn't know him personally. Her name and picture had graced the pages of the local newspaper for months, pictures of her coming out of the courthouse or getting out of her car at home. So, I couldn't believe Mark was publicly cheating on Ellen right here in one of the busiest restaurants in town. Maybe no one cared. Maybe everyone minded their own business, or maybe the testosterone-filled air made everyone relate to him in some sick way.

I was frozen in anger as I stared across the bar at him. I imagined Ellen sitting at home with the kids. I wondered what lie he had told her about where he was tonight. How long had this been going on? Staring across the bar at him, I failed to notice right away that Mark caught me looking. The icy and empty look of his eyes snapped me out of my daze. I squinted my eyes at him, evilly disappointed. He looked away from me, asking the cheerleader if she was ready to go. He threw some bills on the bar and they left. At the door, he turned and looked back at me one more time. I hoped the expression on my face was enough to let him know he was making a mistake. He was aware. It just took something like this to bring it into focus for him. I wanted him to lie awake at night, worrying over the day I'd tell Ellen what I saw.

But I've never told anyone to this day.

Martin

The doctor had diagnosed me with high cholesterol and high blood pressure, and he said I should lose about twenty pounds. That wasn't exactly the news I was hoping for at my age when I went to have a physical. Marline had done a good job of trying to correct my eating habits. She bought less junk food, fried fewer foods, and made me eat more vegetables. Why did I never listen to my mother back home and finish my spinach or carrots?

After lying on the examination table with a doctor's finger in my rear, hearing that everything else about me was fine was a relief, I guess. The doctor reminded me that Dad had died of a stroke. If I kept up my eating habits and current lifestyle, I'd be seeing Dad again sooner than I wanted to. So I took the doctor's advice and started walking. That was last summer, shortly after Travis's boyfriend died. I'd lost twenty-five pounds since then, but I still kept up the walking.

We live next door to Mom, and the distance between our property and hers is equivalent to almost an acre. I'm pretty sure the four acres our house sits on was once part of the Dogwood family orchard many years ago. A few old spindly apple trees lapsed over onto our land back when we bought the house. I had them removed since they no longer produced fruit and we replaced them with a row of dogwoods all the way down the property line, paying homage to the neighborhood.

Marline liked looking out the windows on that side of the house in the springtime and seeing all the pink and white blossoms. I liked seeing the kids running and playing beneath the trees as the petals rained down. It reminded me of my own childhood back when I played hide and seek with Ellen in the orchard while Mom and Dad picked apples.

I preferred to walk early in the morning before the sun was up. A year ago I was doing it because I didn't want anyone to see me out walking. I didn't want anyone I knew to drive by and frown at me the way people do when you are struggling to get into shape. They pity you for being out of shape, rather than applaud you for trying to do something about it. I'd always been an early riser so getting up and walking at that hour was not hard to do. Even back when I was the only kid in the house, I remember being a light sleeper and crawling out of bed as soon as I heard Mom stirring downstairs. She always tried to make me go back to bed, but I wouldn't go. She'd fix me a glass of milk or a link of sausage, and then turn on cartoons for me in the living room while Dad finished sleeping.

Standing at the sink now, I filled the pot with cold water so the coffee would be ready by the time I got back. Looking out the window, the dogwoods resembled boney hands sticking out of the ground. Their branches were covered in the fluffy white snow that fell in the night. We lived up a hill, so from the kitchen window I could just see the roof of Mom's house over the branches. A billow of smoke rose from her chimney and disappeared into the cobalt morning sky. I was admiring the fading stars when I saw a light come on in one of her upstairs windows. Like always, she was awakening to start her day too.

The crunching of the snow beneath my boots was the only sound as I wandered around the yard for a bit before starting my two-mile walk. Although we only have four acres, walking the property was an old habit I'd picked up from Mom and Dad. Mom hated the thought of selling off part of the property back when Dad died. With Dad gone, it was as if enough of the house was gone already. Why should she downsize anymore? When the old barn crumbled, I asked the new land-owner if he wouldn't mind cleaning it up and hauling it away. I offered to help him if he needed me to. We'd told Mom the guy had just torn it down. It'd break her heart to know that barn caved in right after Dad went. It had been their get away from the world on Sunday afternoons when they went out walking.

After a slow amble around the property to stretch my legs, I walked to the end of the gravel driveway and turned in the opposite direction of Mom's house. Back when I first started walking, I would go in her direction because it felt good to pick up the pace by having to walk down the hill. Once, Mom had just stepped out to pick up her newspaper and saw me. Of course, I stopped to say hi and see if she slept okay. The day after that she was sitting on the porch waiting for me to come by. She waited by the road for me a few days after that and decided to join me for the walk. It was nice because I had not spent much time alone with her in quite a few years.

We talked about my work a lot of the time. Like my father, I became a Biology teacher. I shared my stories of the week with her, having already recited them to Marline at the end of the day before. I think Mom found them consoling because Dad had done the same thing at the end of his day. Protozoa, bug collections, plant phylum, animal kingdoms, and frog dissection were parts of regular conversation at our dinner table then and now. Mom was always eager to listen to Dad, and to me. I knew that she found my classroom stories comforting because they reminded her of him.

Teaching school was much different now than when Dad did it. My stories often involved confiscating knives from students, breaking up fights caused by racial tension, or going in early to monitor the metal detectors as students entered the building. Sure, dad had to break up fights, but those were over girls. He searched lockers monthly and picked up porn magazines and cigarettes. Students could come and go through the doors as they please without having to have their bags x-rayed, unlike now.

Walking each morning was not only working on the gut, but it also helped to clear my head. I felt much better about facing the day after accomplishing a brisk stroll. In the early spring, I watched the grass turn green and the flower stems stretch for the sky. Rabbits and quail greeted me along the roadside, awake from the long winter. In summer the flowers bloomed and baby rabbits chased each other in the tall grasses. I watched the leaves change in the fall from lush green to crispy brown and orange. I always looked forward to that first morning dew of the season and knew it'd be time to pull my windbreaker out from the top of the closet.

This walk was practically meditative on the days Mom didn't go with me. The quick wave of my arms, the cadent steps of my feet, and the rising heartbeat inside my chest was the percussion of nature's sympathy around me. Birds chirped in the trees and the crickets settled down from their night song. Wind whistled in the limbs overhead that hung over the narrow road.

My route was to walk to the end of the road. Once I reached the highway, I turned around and came back one block, turning opposite the side we lived on. One street over, I walked the length of the main road until I reached another crossroad that came out just a few feet up from our house. The long rectangular path was exactly two miles. I'd walked it everyday for six months straight. Mom still joined me about twice a week.

"How are things going this week?" she always asked.

"Great," I would answer, and then usually rattle into how I stayed up late the night before grading tests, or how I'm debating on whether or not to make the kids do a leaf collection this year.

There had never been a day of bad news on my behalf to

break my mother's heart. I was my father's son, but I could not be a father to the broken lives of my four siblings. We babysat Jake for Clare when she had to pick up a shift at work. I drove Sebastian to Memphis to pick up his car, and helped him move to a new apartment back when that girl overdosed in his bed. We picked up Robbie and Rachel from school and let them stay with us for a couple of days while Ellen was testifying in court against Judge Railen.

Travis was the only one who had never asked or expected something from us, not even when he lost Justin. I don't know why. I remember the shock on his face when Marline and I came to the funeral home. He humbly told us we didn't have to come as I hugged his neck, as if his loss didn't affect us. It was as if paying our respects was somehow bothersome. Travis had always been like that. He'd step back and let Clare and Sebastian go in front of him when in line for anything, always giving up part of his dinner or dessert when there wasn't enough.

As the oldest, the only standards I was expected to set were the ones in the eyes of my proud parents. Ellen followed almost immediately in my footsteps, going to college and finding a good job. We were the only two in the family married with children. Of course, then Clare had Jake. Children out of wedlock were kept hushed back when I was her age, but there had been at least one pregnant girl in school each year for the past six years where I taught.

Seeing a white boy dating a white girl had become uncommon these days. The guys who dated guys even flaunted their homosexuality with rainbow stickers on their notebooks and pink triangle buttons on their jackets, symbols far more advanced than the white dove and the peace sign of my day. Love was still free, but just not as safe.

Love was also not always permissible, but the human heart possessed no knowledge of the laws our society bestowed upon us. Our brain may know right from wrong, but the heart doesn't always listen. The rules of love may certainly be unwritten. It's whom we fall in love with that can find us breaking the rules that are penned in a law book somewhere. I don't know why we act upon such urges. The temptation is there, and we know it can send our world spinning out of control. It's a hunger, a sin to some that demands to be satisfied.

I was no different.

Her name was Danyele Child. Her friends called her Danny. She had crisp brown eyes and stringy brown hair when she was in my sixth-grade homeroom period. She would not become an actual pupil of mine until eighth grade. Like all the other girls going through puberty around that time, Danyele attracted the attention of her share of young men. I'd had other students who pretended to have crushes on me, but Danyele was different. Her notebook for my class had MR. WHITE'S BIOLOGY painted on it with white-out encircled with a large heart and several small hearts around that. I dismissed it as the doodling of an eighth-grader. All the kids decorated their notebooks with hearts, crosses, initials, peace signs, and the renowned I WUZ HERE that made the English teachers cringe.

She had a habit of dropping her pencil if I walked by her desk, and meeting me face to face beside her desk when I knelt to pick it up for her. She always seemed to be wearing a skirt in my class, which she pulled up a bit to cross her legs in the aisle. She was an honor student and passed every test with flying colors. I was relieved that she never had to stay after class to ask questions or complete a lab experiment. She never made reason to have time alone with me, so when she graduated I dismissed her actions as being my own perverted thoughts. I had always kept student-teacher relationships extremely professional, and had only known one teacher to cross that line during all my years of teaching.

Two years later, I'd forgotten all about Danny when I took a teaching position with the high school science department. All the students had passed through my junior high classroom at one time or another and were excited to have me as their teacher again. I'll never forget the day that Danny walked through the door and took a front-row desk. She was taller with make-up and full-bodied hair now. She wore tight blouses that brought attention to her perky breasts. Her jeans were also tight, except for the days she wore a skirt, which was a bit shorter than the skirts that had met the junior high dress code.

High school Biology was just a bit more complicated for Danny. She stayed afterward to complete tests and was always finishing late on lab day. Her A-average was slowly dropping to a B, which truly brought fear to her eyes because it endangered her fully paid scholarship to the college she'd chosen.

"Is there anything I can do to keep this from happening?" she asked one day after class in an ill-attempted slow and sultry voice with her back arched so her chest stuck out.

"Study harder, maybe get a tutor," I said, walking out of the classroom and leaving her standing there.

Weeks later I was touching her chest in the supply closet in the back of the lab. I don't know what language temptation speaks, only that it had taken control of my body. My brain had shut down. Common-sense left me. Danyele loosened my tie and kissed my neck. Chills rocketed through every nerve ending down my back, both from the soft touch of her lips against my skin and from the thought of getting caught.

There, among the microscopes and beakers, I jeopardized everything in life that I had. My wife, my kids, my job, and my freedom were all at stake as I reached under the skirt of a seventeen-year-old girl. I wouldn't call it blackmail, but Danyele passed the class with an A. Without my "assistance," she would have received a high B. Although it seemed inane, I wondered if Danyele would look back on our small affair some day while in college and think about how she prostituted herself for just three average grade points. It probably didn't matter to her. In her eyes, those three points were worth about ten thousand dollars each towards her college tuition.

Danyele had two other male teachers that semester. She

received A's for both of their classes. One teacher was Coach Powers for Health. Sitting next to him at lunch, I envisioned Danyele practicing her CPR on him instead of the dummy. The other teacher was Mr. Kindle for Business and Typing. Role playing adventures of secretary and boss polluted my head while sitting across from him at a staff meeting.

I only snuck to the supply closet twice with Danyele. She disappeared six weeks before the end of the school year, like a ghost. Her chair sat empty in my class, a haunting effigy for me. Her classmates gossiped in the hallways about what happened. I listened with intent to make sure their rumors didn't involve me. They didn't. Her picture graced the cover of the local newspaper for several days. POLICE HAVE NO LEADS IN MISSING TEEN CASE, the headline read.

"Did you know this girl?" Marline asked reading the story.

"Yeah, she was in my junior class," I said with as much grief as I could muster.

"A good student?"

"Straight A's. No signs of any problems. Never slept in class. No boyfriend trouble that I know of. Nothing."

That's what all of her teachers told the police. They called us for a meeting one day after class. I was thankful they didn't want to meet with each of us individually. I looked hard in the faces of Mr. Kindle and Coach Powers, but saw no signs of worry or fault. Like me, they looked very concerned. I *was* concerned for Danyele's safety and I hoped that she was okay. In the lounge, the other teachers had picked up the stories that were circulating among the students. A nameless boyfriend had kidnapped her or killed her, but Danyele's closest friends had all confirmed that she wasn't dating anyone that they knew of.

Guilt was the name of the monkey on my back. I had not had time to feel any sorrow about the affair between Danyele and me. The possible repercussions had blinked in my head a time or two, but were shadowed by the lust in my eyes when I was in that dark closet pushed up against her. Then, she was gone. It was as if some phantom lurked in the dark beside us and was on my side. Before we were exposed, before I lost my job and went to jail, before my family was torn apart, it stopped all of this by taking Danyele out of the picture.

Danyele's picture, taunting me, soon disappeared from front-page news. For weeks afterwards, groups of volunteers could still be seen searching the sides of the roads, or holding bake sales in front of the grocery stores to raise money to help fund further investigation. Posters with the word MISSING across them in bold letters above Danyele's face hung in windows of businesses across town for months. On my walks, I caught myself searching the ditches along the road for clues: a scrap of cloth from her skirt, a biology book, her body.

I woke up at night having dreamt that I did find her body beside the road while out walking. I knelt beside her and brushed the hair from her face. Her eyes were closed. Her skin was cold to the touch. In the distance, in the trees, I could hear laughing. It was that deep boogeyman laughter from cartoons that sounded like a slowed-down tape recorder. Someone wanted me to find her.

I didn't know if it was Danyele showing me these thoughts at night or if my mind made them up out of fear of being exposed. There was no evidence that I had kidnapped or killed her, because I had not done it. But what if? What if someone devised a plan to frame me, and they planted clues to point toward me? Every morning, with the family still asleep, I persistently walked the property to search for anything out of place. I checked the house for a window that might have been left open allowing someone to plant something inside the house while we slept. I searched my car every time it was left alone for any period of time. I even ran to the mailbox everyday expecting to find a blackmail letter or some incriminating photographs.

Nothing ever came.

The MISSING posters faded and were replaced with yard sale announcements and day camp advertisements. The yearbook staff dedicated the yearbook to Danyele. The bake sale volunteers soon went home to their own families to enjoy summer vacation. As the temperature rose, Danyele's case went cold. We started the new school year having forgotten all about her, but I didn't forget. It had now been almost one year since what happened between us. I stopped checking my car and stopped dreaming about finding her body. I stopped waiting for the day the police would knock on the door wanting to ask questions, but in the back of my mind a part of me still couldn't help but think someone thought they were doing me a favor.

"Hello darling," I whispered into the phone.

It was a little joke Mom and I shared. When I called her, I always said that when she picked up the phone. It was from an old Conway Twitty country western song she listened to back when we were young.

"Hello there. Did you just come in from your walk?"

"Yeah, I did."

"Sorry I wasn't out there to walk with you this morning. I was up late last night cooking and cleaning."

"That's okay. I know you have things to do to get ready for today."

We all knew that Mom didn't cook much these days. Most of her Christmas spread came from the deli. We didn't mind, though, and never said anything about it. When taking the trash out a few years ago after dinner, I found a bag already in the trash can filled with empty plastic containers for green bean casserole, creamed corn, and mashed potatoes. I'd known ever since then most of the holiday dinner was store-bought, but Mom had slaved over that stove year after year when Dad was alive. She deserved a break now.

Instead, I knew she'd spent last night wrapping gifts while watching old black and white holiday movies. She'd also put out all those little trees in every room like she did when we were kids, wanting us to believe they had been there all month long. Before going to bed last night, I looked out the window and saw her lights still on across the grove of trees. I could barely see the yellow light of her bed lamp glowing in the window as the heavy snow fell. It was a comforting feeling to talk to her on the phone now and look out the window and know that she was there at her house in the distance, even though I could not see her.

"Mom, are you in the kitchen?" I asked.

"Yeah. I just came in from feeding the birds."

"Come to the window."

"What? Why?"

"Just come to the window, the one above the sink."

"Okay, I'm at the window."

I saw her shadow appear there. It was still too dark outside to see her clearly.

"Can you see me?" I asked.

"Martin, you know my eyes are bad. What am I supposed to see?"

"I'm waving to you."

"Hello dear. What am I doing?"

"I think you are giving me the finger," I laughed.

"Martin White! I am not!"

"I'm just kidding," I laughed.

"You silly boy."

"Merry Christmas, Mom."

"Merry Christmas, Son."

Justin

A monitor beeps in my left ear. A ventilator rises and falls over my right shoulder. Long thin plastic tubes lay against my skin, but they've been resting there for so long my skin is numb to their touch. Although my eyes are closed, I imagine that I must resemble Frankenstein's monster or some kid's eight-grade science project. A band of black stitches encircles half my bald scalp on the right side, starting behind my ear and ending at my temple.

I am naked beneath the cotton sheets, having made the nurse and Travis pull off my gown last night before I slept. I doze in a slightly reclined position because I have been watching the television mounted high above me on the wall. The television has now been turned off because Travis thinks I want to sleep. The room is quiet, except for the machines and the almost meditative rhythm of his breathing beside me.

I've been in and out of hospitals so much recently, but I always look forward to the bed. I wish Travis and I had one like it back in our apartment. Like a kid, I raise it up as far as it will go and then feel like a kid cradled in its mother's arms as I push the button to lower it completely flat again. Travis laughs at me for playing, but I tell him I'm just testing to make sure the bed works properly. To convince him, I push the button to call the nurse. There's a knock at the door and a tall thin male nurse lets himself in. He's cute, blond, and shiny. His ceil blue scrubs are crisp and clean. Travis and I whisper like school girls behind him when he leaves.

"Forget the bed. We need one of those buttons at home," Travis says with a laugh.

I sometimes see those movable beds advertised on television late at night. Some elderly woman is inclined in bed and channel-surfing, or eating, or reading the paper. Stuffing pillows between my back and the headboard of our flat mattress just doesn't feel the same. Once, I thought about calling the number flashing at the bottom of the screen and having one of those beds installed for us. I'd wait and do it for an anniversary or something just to have an excuse.

"Your insurance will pay for a hospital bed if you want one," Travis told me.

I shake my head no. He thinks I'm just being stubborn. I am. I don't want to look like an invalid at home for as long as I can prevent it, but I also don't want to sleep alone. The only thing that makes our bed comfortable now is him sleeping in it next to me.

It is protocol for the doctors and nurses to put on a pair of rubber gloves when entering the room to examine me. There is always an IV to change or blood to be taken. Some of the regular nurses don't put on gloves to just take my temperature or blood pressure. They know nothing I have is contagious. The regulars are also accustomed to seeing Travis next to my bedside. They greet him and call him Mr. White, and share my progress with him. They know who he is to me.

A new nurse covering a shift will see Travis and then nervously check my chart while reaching for the gloves from the box on the wall. Because their first impression is that we are a gay couple, they assume they will find the letters HIV on my chart. A second glance at the clipboard assures them I'm clean. A young female nurse blushed at her assumption. Travis and I eyed her quietly, adding discomfort to her mistake.

"Diseases hold no prejudice. Only humans," I groggily whispered to one nurse who'd done the same.

Travis hushed me.

The nurse looked at me with a bit of shock over my reading her mind. We didn't see her again.

It's been four days since I was admitted this time. Travis shaved my head for me the night before the surgery. I refused to allow any nurse to do it, even a cute one. I'd shaved Travis's face for him before out of some loving favor I thought would be romantic. He was hesitant about letting me do it because I never had to shave. The absence of body and facial hair had made me look like some prepubescent grade-school kid all my life. It only grows in the private places, not even under my arms. I looked worse after the chemo. Travis joked about buying a toupee for me, but he knew I'd settle for a ball cap. I still felt like a pale psychic alien being from some movie.

I say psychic because that's exactly how I feel sometimes. It's not a strange side-effect listed in all the small print Travis and I had to read, but the possibility should be explored. With the ball cap on, and sunglasses to cover the absence of eye brows, people still look intently at me. I try to ignore their expressions of sorrow, but I know what they are thinking. Back home, their kids will tell the other family members about the strange bald man in the grocery store. The parent will hush them and feel the need to explain how pitiful I looked. Cancer may not have a cure, but it all looks the same.

That's why no matter how much Travis begged, I refused to go out. Forget the grocery store. Forget a quick trip to the bank or post office, and restaurants are definitely not an option. I'm content with my time spent behind walls at the hospital or in our apartment, like Quasimodo lurking in the shadows. It seems a waste to number my days, biding my time, between these two places. When we learned the cancer was malignant, the daily chore of being anywhere else except for in the hospital seemed overwhelming. Spending the rest of my time at home was much more comfortable, and between the two places, as long as Travis was with me, I never got bored being there.

The chemo failed. It seems the vomiting, diarrhea, nausea, loss of appetite, and hair loss were not the only side effects of the treatment. The tumor originally in the right hemisphere of my brain barely broke down, but metastatic offshoots from it became secondary neoplasms on the opposite side. I'd just begun to fully recover from the treatments. I almost had a full head of hair back. Then, the headaches came back.

Gamma knife radiosurgery would have been the next option had the neoplasms chosen a different organ to take refuge. A craniotomy would remove the remainder of the original tumor, which is the reason for being in the hospital now. Then, it's a waiting game to see if a tumor develops at all on the opposite side. The doctors keep saying there's a 50 percent chance it will be benign if it does develop, but isn't there a 50 percent chance at everything? It will either rain or it won't. One team always wins, one always loses. Unless it's a tie, but there are no ties in cancer. I will either die of this or I won't, but somehow I think those percentages are much different.

My parents came to town to offer their awkward and daunting support. Mom cries and holds my hand too tight. Dad just stands there with his hands in his pockets, eyeing his watch as if he has somewhere more important to be. I pretended to be asleep for most of the time they were here, leaving Travis to deal with them. He's always had more patience with them than I ever did. He coaxed them into a hotel for the night because he knew I'd rest better without them being here. It's Travis I prefer to stay with me anyway; and he has been here, never leaving my side through all of this.

"Are you tired?" I asked him.

"No, I'm fine, Justin. I napped a little while you were asleep."

"That's not what I mean."

"What do you mean then, sweetie?"

"Are you tired of dealing with all of this? With me?"

He was silent for a bit, thinking about what I had asked him and how he was going to answer. I looked at him for a long time, wondering if he was going to answer at all. Maybe he was pretending I was just a little child asking an embarrassing question when the grown-ups in the room all act like nothing happened. Then he spoke.

"I think both of us are tired of it. If there's any place I'd rather be right now, I'd want you to be right there with me. I'd want you to be healthy."

"With hair?" I asked, trying to laugh but it hurt too much.

"I don't know. I kind of like the bandages," he said studying my head. I knew he was joking.

* * * *

Back home, Travis removed the bandages for me every other day to change them and let the stitches get some air. The stitches resembled a large puffy closed eyelid across the side of my head, like some strange giant conjoined twin that my body had absorbed at birth. My hair eventually started to grow back. The black peppery fuzz reminded me of a GI Joe doll I played with as a child, except now he was recovering from a massive head wound inflicted by some backyard war.

Somehow I found it easier to face the world with a hairless fish bone-like scar on the side of my head than with no hair at all. I was no longer the sad pale cancer patient for strangers to feel sorry for. I kept my hair buzzed short, mainly to prevent infection near the wound while it healed, but the military look gave people a different impression. Suddenly, they were happy for me instead of apologetic.

"God bless you, Son," an old lady said grabbing my arm, assuming I was a troop. I just smiled and didn't say anything. It felt better to be appreciated than spurned with the plague.

I let Travis talk me into going to a restaurant, but I would only go for lunch and take the chance that it would be less crowded than dinner service anywhere in this city. Avoiding public places now just felt like an old habit I needed to break.

The scar was permanent; the hair would not grow back to cover it entirely, but I found myself forgetting about it. Patches of pigmentless hair or no hair at all are like mysterious pieces missing from a human puzzle. I was really the only one who took notice. Others ignored it because it wasn't such a rarity these days to see someone with a harsh visible blemish, and their behavior or lack thereof helped me to disregard it too.

The restaurant was a quiet sky-lit place on the roof of some downtown hotel skyscraper. It was enclosed in glass and you could eat inside, where they often opened all the windows, or outside on the terrace if it wasn't too windy. It was a place Travis and I had eaten at in the past for birthdays or celebrations, or just for an excuse to go downtown. The menu is filled with anomalous dishes like Seafood Ragout and Wild Mushroom Pizza. Travis laughed at me for sticking to the simple dishes I knew like Pimento Cheese on Rye or Chicken Strips with Hot Mustard. He always ordered one of the more irregular items and let me sample some from his plate.

The sudden epileptic seizure was an awkward tingle I had never felt before. I jolted back in my chair like an astronaut at lift-off. A strong force felt like it was pushing against my face and all I could do was shake to escape its push. It was out of control and violent, forcing me onto the floor. I was not conscious enough to know what Travis did, but I do know his patience greatly outweighs his fear. He probably rolled me over onto my back and turned my head to the side so the vomit could drip from my mouth and I wouldn't choke. A waitress might have screamed. Some of the other patrons stood up from their tables and watched. Travis begged someone to call for an ambulance as I lay there convulsing.

"These seizures are transient symptoms due to abnormal, excessive activity in the brain," the doctor told us.

The word *transient* made me think of those particles from the original tumor taking root on the opposite side of my brain. They'd set up camp and another tumor was forming.

"What are his choices?" Travis asked the doctor.

"In a few months, we could attempt chemo again," the doctor answered.

"He may not have a few months!" Travis yelled. It was the first time I ever heard him raise his voice. I liked it.

"I'm not doing chemo a second time," I mumbled. No one was listening to me.

"The gamma surgery is also a possibility if this new tumor becomes malignant. We still need to give the right side of his brain some recovery time. Right now, it's still too early to weigh the options."

"No more surgeries," I whispered.

"What do you want to do?" Travis asked in a much calmer voice, turning to me, unaware of the things I'd already said.

"I just want to go home."

And so we did.

That was the last time I ever saw a hospital in this world.

* * * *

"Can he come here and be with us?" My mom asked Travis on the phone.

I knew she would ask. I was mouthing the word no to Travis and cutting the air with my hands like a referee.

"Sure, I can drive him up. We'll leave whenever he feels like it."

"Why did you lie to her?" I asked Travis when he hung up the phone.

"If I didn't tell her that, they might come here and try to make you go back with them," he said.

"I don't want to go there."

"You don't have to go there. You never have to go."

Speaking words of hope felt good. Hearing them felt even

better. But neither of us could ignore the inevitable. At some point, I was going to go.

I imagined my mother and father at home in Ruby Dregs preparing a place for me, but it would be a place I wasn't acquainted with. Mom would pick up the newspapers and magazines that always cluttered the floor. She'd move the dust around with her hands and spit shine the pictures on the wall. She would open the door to my room and let it air out. She might change the sheets on the bed. Dad would just sit and wait, with his hands folded neatly across his belly, in silence.

Mom would stand at the window periodically throughout the day, pulling back the drapes and peeking through the yellowed blinds, waiting to see Travis's car pull up in the drive. She'd envision the passenger door opening and me stepping out and running to the door to greet them with a smile on my face. I'd come home.

From the moment I left it and moved in with Travis, that wasn't my home anymore. I felt like a foster child every time I had gone home to see them. A summer weekend, Thanksgiving, Christmas, or whenever all seemed like I was on guard and walking across a frozen pond. At any moment, the surface could crack and I would fall in to a chilling drown.

Several days passed, maybe weeks or months. I stopped counting. Travis had second thoughts, and he said I should go home and see them. The phone had not rang once. They never showed up at our door unexpectedly. Mom had most likely pulled the curtains to and closed the door to my room again. Dad had gone back to doing whatever it was that he did each day. They were just waiting for their phone to ring to bring the news they knew would inevitably come.

It was my time to go; to leave Ruby Dregs and never have to think about going back, to leave my parents although it felt like I'd left them long ago. And sadly, to leave Travis though I could never imagine life without him. I didn't have to imagine that. My life was almost over.

"It's not about them anymore," I told Travis when he

carefully chose his words to try to get me to go.

"It never was about them. I know that. Don't you want to see them?"

"No. It's too late, Travis. I've got to go now," I said crawling under the bed sheets.

"Justin, not now!"

"Please…just hold me close and be strong for me now," I told him.

"I can't be strong when you are my only weakness," he said as tears fell from his cheeks.

"You've done so much for me, Travis, more than anyone else ever has. Let me go."

"Okay," he whispered, squeezing my hand and crawling into bed beside me.

"Let me go," I repeated.

I closed my eyes, resting my face against his side. He wrapped his arm around my shoulder.

For just a moment, I was allowed to step back and look at us from across the room or maybe above it. My scar was hidden against Travis's shirt. To anyone else we would have looked like a normal couple resting on the bed. All the pain was hidden or gone. I held my transparent hands in front of my face with ease, as if holding a camera, and I pretended to snap a photo to remember this. I didn't need a photo to remember, because I knew I would never forget him.

I left the room alone or maybe with someone from my past I didn't remember or had never met before. I tried to turn back and take another look at us, but had somehow quickly forgotten I was ever there.

I felt light on my feet. Every burden, and even the cancer, had been lifted. It had all washed away. Passing through the door, I went away too.

Mrs. Black

I woke up to find all the lights on the tree had gone out. I leaned behind it to see if it had come unplugged. It had not. The last of the working lights had just burned out during the night. A few days ago the tree looked like some odd planetarium map of the constellations with some parts still twinkling and others in the dark. I had left the tree up all year, since last Christmas, and left it plugged in. About mid-January this year, I intended to take it down. Then, February came and it was still there. I cut pink and red hearts out of crepe paper and tucked them onto the limbs for amusement, shamrocks for March, and Easter eggs for April. Thanksgiving was here before we knew it, when others had just begun to look forward to putting a tree up again. Ours was already up, adorned in the traditional symbols from every holiday that had passed since last Christmas.

I stood at the tree, unraveling the strings of lights from the branches and letting them fall to the floor. After a few feet of lights and knocking a few ornaments off in the process, I decided this was too time-consuming. I was just going to throw the dead lights away anyway. I went to the sewing machine table and retrieved my fabric scissors from the drawer. I returned to the tree and unplugged the lights from the wall just to be sure there was no electricity or a shortage in the wires. I used my scissors to cut the strings of lights so they could be removed from the tree more easily in smaller pieces.

Trimming them like hair, I threw the twines of lights behind me and let them fall to the floor with a crackle-like snap. I avoided breaking any more ornaments in the process. Having to touch almost every limb stirred up the layer of fuzzy dust that had settled over the branches during the year. I would have Manny buy new lights to store away for next year. Christmas had almost come and gone again now. It amazed me that some of those strands of lights had lasted all year.

The tree looked sad in the dark, sadder than it looked when it was only half-lit. Maybe the lack of its glow would inspire me to take it completely down this year. I went to the kitchen to get the broom to sweep up the tangles of wire and bulbs. From the darkened doorway, the tree looked like a stranger waiting in the shadows. It would bother me, or startle me, each time I came down the stairs. So, it would have to come down now.

I ignored the crunching of some of the tiny bulbs beneath my shoes on the hardwood floor as I walked back by the tree to go upstairs. The ornament boxes were kept on the floor in Justin's old room. Manny had never placed them back in the attic last year after I put the tree up. I'd made an effort to carry all of the boxes back up the stairs and sit them in the hallway. And there they sat half way through December. I pushed them into Justin's room and closed the door upon the unexpected arrival of a guest or some boring relative. I don't remember who.

I had not actually been inside that room at least since last year, although Manny had left the door open from time to time. I had walked past the open doorway and looked in, wondering why the door was left open. I assumed that Manny might have gone into the room for one thing or another since it had become a somewhat temporary storage place and an excuse for not having to crawl into the attic. Maybe some old house ghost liked to leave the door open.

The cat had died in Justin's bedroom this year. Apparently, it was a mute cat. I'd never heard it cry or scratch at the door. Not once. Or maybe I just wasn't paying attention, and neither was Manny. We left the door closed for too long. It pissed on the bed and eventually lay down to sleep forever. Manny discovered it and removed its body in a trash bag. The outline of its stiff body against the black plastic made me nauseous. I had Manny gather the bedspread and sheets and dispose of them too. Since the room was on the second floor and faces the back of the house, we left the windows open for a week to air it out. The mild breezes of spring didn't help much. It still stank of cat piss.

I pushed the door open now, letting go of the knob as the door creaked open, like some snooping parent spying on their kid's doings. The room was cold and musty. The smell of cat urine still lingered just a bit, only adding to the stale scent of mildew. The bare white mattress on the bed reminded me of white sheets draped over the furniture in a house that had been boarded up for the season. I knew it was a bed but it still looked like the shape of something else, perhaps a coffin. I folded my arms to somehow shield me from the cold bitter air now escaping the room. These days, everything reminded me of death.

Justin's room was a tiny square space filled now with boxes and crates, all waiting for something useful, or meaningful, to be put in them. The ornament boxes had been moved further into the room, stacked neatly on the floor against the bed. Stacks of magazines we never read lined the walls and hid the top of Justin's old desk.

There were some empty shoe boxes I kept to recycle next to two or three thin plastic grocery bags, each stuffed with more grocery bags I always kept. Manny had added some empty milk crates he collected from work, and some packages of model trains.

He and Justin had built a model train replica of the town when Justin was a kid. It encompassed over half the basement. Manny left it alone for several months after Justin moved away, but he spent more time in the basement now than he did when Justin was here to help him with it.

The room and its contents were all alike. Even this house was like that, waiting for something meaningful that would never come. I knew what it felt like to be an empty box sitting in a cold room.

The ornament boxes had perforated handles cut into the sides of them. I lifted two at a time and moved them into the hallway. Under the bright light outside the room, I could make out a thin layer of white dust across the boxes. I pressed a finger down on top of the first box, leaving a perfect fingerprint in the ashy film. I examined my finger, holding it up close to my face, rubbing it against my thumb until the dust I'd collected was gone.

After moving six boxes into the hall, I carried two of them down the stairs and sat them by the tree. Piece by piece, I began removing glass balls from the limbs first, leaving the hook on each of them as I tucked them between the dividers in the box. After filling the two boxes, I put the lids on and pushed them aside. Most of the other ornaments were heavy ceramic figurines, characters blown from mercury glass, and craft projects Justin had made as a kid. With their gold macaroni pieces, crayon-colored popsicle sticks, and red pipe cleaners, they were as faded as the rest of the memories I clung to.

I climbed the stairs to pick up another box. Removing its lid, I discovered crumpled pieces of yellowed newspaper I had used to wrap the ornaments before storing them away. When I unwrapped them and hung them on the tree last year, I stuffed the wrapping back into the box with intentions of using it again. There were plenty of fresh papers and magazines in this house now. I could throw out all the old paper and wrap the ornaments in yesterday's news. I emptied the box on the floor next to the pile of Christmas lights. Tinkles of red and silver glitter littered the floor, remnants that had rubbed off some of the ornaments from the last time they were in the box. The flat, folded corner of one of the papers caught my eye.

Bending to pick it up, I smoothed out some of the creases with my hands. The paper was so old some of the ink transferred to my hands, blackening them. I immediately noticed the date. The paper was from two days after Justin had died. I laid the paper on the coffee table and picked up more pieces of it from the floor. Unraveling the wadded paper and smoothing the pages out on the glass top of the table, I felt like some television detective slowly recovering some sort of evidence, or an archeologist digging up clues to our past.

Some of the pages were missing, probably in another box or thrown away because I had not used them. The headlines were words I don't remember reading. When a mother loses her only son, the rest of the news in the world is easily forgotten, if heard at all. The rectangular pieces of the newspaper were still quite wrinkled but intact, and I stacked them neatly on the table giving the gazette back its shape. I found one page that had a neat long rectangular piece missing from where someone had cut out an article. It was a full-page ad for a car lot. I immediately turned it over to find the obituary page. I didn't remember cutting out the article on Justin, but I must have. I did remember where it was though, tucked between the pages of the Bible in my nightstand drawer. I walked upstairs to my bedroom to get it.

I don't know how much time had passed between trying to take down the tree and sitting on the bed to read Justin's obituary again. Hearing Manny come in the front door brought me back. I looked at the tissue in my hand, soaked in tears and stained black from the newspaper ink on my hands.

"Helen?" he called from downstairs.

"I'm up here."

"Why are you taking down the tree?"

I wanted to tell him that sooner or later we all had to move on with our lives, but I'd already grown tired of him telling me that.

"All the lights burned out," I yelled down the stairs.

I heard him grumbling about the mess on the floor. I could hear him picking up the strands of lights and stuffing them into a trash bag. Like the cat and the bedspread, he cleaned up the problems and took them to the curb. I checked my face in the mirror to find a smudge of black ink on my cheek from touching my face. A clean line ran through it from where a tear had fallen.

"Guess who I ran into at Greer's?" he said as I was coming down the stairs.

He was always running into someone there, or at the bank, in line at the post office, or in the parking lot at work. It was always someone from church, back when I went, or an old neighbor I'd done a favor for once. It was never anyone I'd thought of since. I never remembered them. Manny often had to go through neighbor genealogy to get me to remember.

"Sheila. You remember Sheila. She's Mr. Barnhill's granddaughter. Her parent's lived in the old Parker house before she was born. Mr. Barnhill passed away about a year ago. The Barnhill's moved to town, but they would bring her out here to go to church sometimes with her grandparents. She went to high school with Justin."

Half the time, I still never remembered. Later, I'd fade into a daydream with their name on my mind. Bake sales, pageant plays, piano recitals, trips to the grocery store all flooded my mind like I was thumbing through a directory in my brain. Faces flashed from church pews, department store aisles, or community barbecues. Eventually, I sometimes found the one Manny had run into that day just as they were back then. I never knew how long ago it had been since I saw them last. Every event was placed in time either before Justin's death or after, and I had not seen too many people outside this house after it.

"Who?" I asked him, as I stood there and watched him picking up the mess I had made.

He always waited for me to respond, a sign that he knew he had my attention. He stood up from kneeling on the floor. His sweater had risen up a bit to reveal a roll of pink flesh. With the movement of my eyes, he saw that I had noticed so he pulled the sweater down. He huffed out a large breath before speaking again. Getting up from the floor took a lot out of him.

"Who did you see?" I asked again to speed things along. He was accustomed to my impatience.

"Travis White," he said through another exhale.

Now, that was a name in need of no explanation. He popped into my head immediately. I knew exactly who he was, although I had often wished I didn't. It was hard to think of my son without thinking of Travis, but I eventually learned to dream of a Justin prior to him meeting Travis. It kept Travis from creeping in to the memories. He wasn't there back then. He didn't know the Justin I knew. Yet.

I wanted to walk away and leave Manny standing there. I clinched my fists closed and then opened them again. The imprint of my nails in the flesh of my palms stung. Manny looked at me like a happy puppy that had just pissed on the newspaper. He was waiting to see a smile grow on my face, but it just would not sprout. Instead of waiting for my reply, he continued.

"He's in town to see his family for Christmas. All of his brothers and sisters are staying at his mom's house for the holiday. You remember Lorraine, don't you? Nice lady. She hasn't aged a bit. I see her at church all the time. She always says hello and asks about you."

I didn't believe him, the part about Lorraine asking about me anyway. I doubt anyone ever asked about me as much as he said they did. It was a lot like when a couple gets a divorce late into their marriage, if Manny and I were to divorce now after forty-two years. The neighborly thing to do is to ask how one of us is doing, but no one wants to ask because they fear they will embarrass you. They think it might be rude to ask. No one wants to know your business when you might need a shoulder to cry on.

Since we weren't divorced, maybe Manny wasn't lying. I'm sure at one time or another, right after Justin's death, everyone did ask about me. Manny had rehearsed his answer and recited it by heart many times by now.

"She's fine. Thanks for asking," is probably about all he knew how to say.

Fine is a routine word that really means, "I don't want to talk about it." It's used to politely dismiss the subject. So, eventually, they just stop asking.

I never cared much for Travis. Even before Justin's death, I blamed Travis for what my son said he was. I blamed him for taking Justin away from me and off to that stinking city to live in sin. The thought of two men together still sent my stomach on edge, but it's a different sickening when your son comes home and tells you that's what he likes. I forbid him to tell anyone else. I wanted to put soap in his mouth and erase it like a cuss word slipping out of him when he was eight years old. I wanted to bend him over my knee and wear his ass out with a belt. I cursed the heavens every night.

Why me, Lord?

After he told us, it was as if I didn't know who he was. Everything we thought we were doing to raise our child right was a lie. Were we not praying hard enough in church? We were there every time the doors were open. I wanted to blame Manny. He was a eunuch when it came to being a father. He wasn't here enough. He didn't spend enough time with Justin. He didn't pass along the manly traits and actions a son should inherit instinctively from his father, if Manny had them to pass down at all.

Or was this my sin, my punishment, for having married Manny? Justin was my only child, a blessing I was humble to receive. But maybe I smothered him. Maybe I babied him too much. I forced him to take piano lessons. I made him sing in the choir. I never encouraged him to play with other boys when he was small. Maybe they picked on him or picked him last for games, if they picked him at all. Maybe Justin preferred to play with the girls. He did like stuffed animals when he was a young child, instead of trucks and dirt. Did that make him gay?

I wasn't there to watch my little boy grow up every second, or was I there too much? Maybe Manny and I are both to blame for what our son became. Was it our fault he didn't ask a girl to prom? He didn't even go to prom. Did he search his health class textbook for answers about sex because he had no one else to turn to? Did they even write about that sort of thing in textbooks? I don't know, and I obviously didn't know enough about my son, or about what he was, to answer his questions or even my own.

"It's not what I am, Mother, it's *who* I am," he kept telling me.

And I wouldn't listen.

I didn't know who I was anymore, or who I was when Justin was living. I was a stranger on the sidewalk who I avoid eye contact with every time I look at them, every time I look at myself in the mirror. When I turned away, the face was forgotten. I might turn back for a second look, thinking I knew that person from somewhere. But it's too late. They're already gone.

That's probably why I resented Travis so much. He too was a stranger to me, until he came into Justin's life. I'd known Justin much longer than Travis, but already it was as if he knew my son better than me. At last, someone just like him had reached out to my Justin. The missing piece in his puzzle of life was complete. He knew love, and the touch of someone I only dreamt about when I was a school-girl.

Maybe I resented Justin too, or was jealous, because he had someone to love and who loved him back. And it's not out of convenience or because we can't imagine doing anything different with ourselves. Too much time had passed for Manny or me to know a different life. How dare I think I could drag

Justin down with us? There was no time to learn anything outside my indifference; no matter how many times Justin tried to get us to be more open to such things. In a flash, the cancer took him. I don't know who was to blame for that either. But when your only child is gone it's then that you realize the time you wasted. I knew I couldn't change that, but I couldn't stop beating myself up over it either.

"Do you want me to take those boxes upstairs?" Manny asked.

He'd finished sweeping up the lights and picking up the paper. He thumbed through the sheets of news on the coffee table with a look as if he thought they were today's paper.

"If you don't mind, and bring down a few more of the empty boxes from the hall," I said.

When he was done, he sat down on the sofa and turned on the television. I wandered aimlessly between the stairs and the poor Christmas tree, as if waiting for someone to knock on the door. Manny had mentioned that Travis might stop by, so maybe it was him I was waiting for. I doubted he'd come, but a part of me secretly wished he would. Something inside felt that if Travis came over, our house would be alive with Justin again. I knew it wouldn't bring Justin back, but being the last person to have seen Justin alive, I felt Travis was somehow magical.

I wandered into the basement and pulled the chain to turn on the overhead light. The concrete room was cold, but not damp. I approached Manny's train miniature of the entire town of Ruby Dregs, which was built atop four large Ping-Pong tables pushed together. It was an elaborate replica of every building and house in Dogwood; even the cemetery where Justin was buried looked almost identical to the real thing. With all the lights and trains turned off, the town was eerily still and seemed deserted except for the miniature people frozen and faceless.

The miniature of our own house seemed much cleaner. The aluminum siding was not dirty; the yard was neatly cut. The tree in the front yard, the one lightning had hit this year, was alive and vibrant instead of half-dead and clinging to its last living branches. Lorraine White's house was the same, except that is how her real house looked in real life. It was lively and bright, nestled in its grove of countryside and between rows of fruit trees. I had never been inside, but I had driven by it many times.

I leaned down to look into the windows like some giant. With my thumb and forefinger, I grasped the sides of the roof and pulled. With a quick snap, the gum paste holding the house onto the Styrofoam land gave way. Holding the small house in the palm of my hand, I admired it for a few seconds before dropping it onto the floor to step on it. It shattered beneath my shoe like a crunchy cockroach. Satisfied with its demise, I lifted my shoe and pushed the remains under the table with my toe.

Travis

I put on my coat and slipped out the back door. I had been here less than two hours with my mother, three of my siblings, and my niece and two of my nephews, and already I needed a break. They're much easier to handle in smaller doses. During previous visits, I've had Mom all to myself or visited with only one or two of them. I doubt if any of them felt the same way I do. They all still live here within minutes of each other. They're accustomed to seeing each other once or twice a week.

Mom has always done a good job of keeping me caught up on things via the telephone when I couldn't be here. A conversation with Ellen or Sebastian on the phone rarely lasts longer than five minutes. Martin and Clare never call. But hearing about the lives of your loved ones from a voice on the other end of the receiver just isn't the same. Email is a little more personable to me. Someone has to actually sit down and type it, but no one has time for that either. Instead, I usually have a mailbox full of jokes and forwards from Mom. Ellen sends the same ones to me because she doesn't notice that Mom already copied me on them too. Of all things, family should feel the closest, but when we are actually close we don't have much to say to each other.

Mom's cat, Marcus, circled my feet. He meowed a few times and purred loudly, the most anyone had said to me since being here. I knelt to scratch him under the chin before walking out into the yard. Looking beyond the snow-covered trees, memories of all of us picking apples in the fall or having snowball fights in the winter played out before me. I found Martin and Marline's initials carved in a heart on one of the trees from back when they first started dating. Sebastian's old tire swing hung motionless. The orchard looked like some wintry canvas where a painter had captured the foundation of all of our lives here. Only we had changed. I envied Mom for getting to wake up to it everyday.

Her contributions to the yard had stayed much the same as well, as if she tried hard to preserve it just the way it was back then. Her birdfeeders were the same and in the exact same places. The little koi pond lay motionless, frozen beneath a sheet of ice. I brushed the snow from the ice to somehow look through it, wondering if those were the same fish she'd had for years. Marcus had stayed on the back porch until I knelt next to the pond. He bounded through the snow and stood on the ice watching my hands carefully as if I was going to be his accomplice in getting to the fish down below.

"There's only four or five koi left down there. I'll probably have lost another one by the time the ice thaws."

I looked up to find Mom standing there over me with a gentle smile on her face. The snow had silenced her footsteps, or she had snuck out the backdoor deliberately so I wouldn't hear her approaching. Marcus leapt over to her to rub against her boots.

"Are they frozen in the ice? I can't see them," I asked.

"No, there's a dip in the middle at the bottom where they go because it doesn't freeze completely. They are probably hibernating in some way, if fish do that."

The thought of the fish in their icy grave saddened me, but I guess it wasn't a grave at all. Like the flowers, they rebound

126

in the spring. The daffodils, the leaves on the trees, the fountain in the koi pond, even the birds all spring back to life. It seemed childish for me to wish humans didn't have to die. What if we could just hibernate in a hole in the ground until the ice over our life melted?

"Is something bothering you, Travis?" Mom asked.

"I just stepped out to get away from all the noise. It's so peaceful out here so I thought it would be nice to enjoy the backyard for a few minutes. I was remembering all the fun times we had out here."

"It's the only reason I won't let Martin cut down more of the trees. Half of them are dying. You can't tell now because all of them are leafless, but some of them look pretty spotty come spring time."

"Everything dies," I said with a sigh.

"I'm afraid so, dear."

"If you could go back and live any part of your life over again, Mom, would you?"

"Nah, I don't think so."

"Why not?"

"Travis, there were so many bad days. I couldn't wait for them to be over."

"What about the good ones? What about Dad? You wouldn't want to see him again."

"Of course, I'd love to see him again, but in a way he never left. Your dad is still here, the house, the trees; he's still here with us. He's in here," she said placing a hand over her heart.

She placed her other hand over mine.

"I'd give anything for one more day with Justin," I said grasping her hand in mine.

"Just one more day?"

"Well, maybe two or three…months," I said with a smile.

"Are you going to go see him?"

"I think I might wait till tomorrow. I'm debating on going to see his parents. I ran into Mr. Black when I stopped to pick up the ham."

"He's such a sad, pitiful-looking man. He's really let himself go. I see him at church, but I haven't seen Helen in a year or so."

"Do you ever go to the cemetery? For Dad?"

"At first, I went all the time. Then, I was going at least once a week. I make an effort to go about every two weeks or once a month now."

"Do you talk to him?" I asked.

"Travis, I talk to him here. I don't have to go to the cemetery and see his name on a marker to speak to him. The body we buried beneath the soil was your father's, but it's not who he was. His soul is a lot more than that. It's never left me."

"Mom, you have such a calm way of dealing with things."

"Calm? I'm a mother, dear. All I know is calm, at least now that all you kids have moved out of the house," she said with a laugh.

"I don't know how you do it."

"Travis, it's okay to grieve and there's no reason to feel guilty for not going to visit him everyday in the cemetery. I think you are doing fine. If you weren't, you would have gone to the cemetery as soon as you got into town, instead of coming here."

"Yeah, I guess you are right."

"Of course I am. I'm a mother. Now let's go back inside before the others come out here looking for us and try to start a snowball fight."

She picked up some snow and packed it into her hands and threw it at me. I jerked my shoulder to dodge it but it hit me on the back anyway. I pretended to lean down to pick up some snow. With a laugh and an apologetic plea, she hurried over to dust the snow from my back. I put my arm around her waist and wrapped hers around mine. We walked across the yard to go back inside.

* * * *

Clare and Sebastian were entertaining the kids with a board game on the floor in front of the Christmas tree. The warm glow of the lights on their faces would have made a great picture. Thinking the same thing, Ellen grabbed her camera from her purse to snap a photo. Mom, Ellen, and I stood there for a few minutes watching them letting the kids win. It was good to see Clare and Sebastian smile.

Mom disappeared into the kitchen to position the foil-wrapped plates and bowls of food Ellen had brought in, adding them to the buffet line of food on the counter, dividing them according to how she thought everyone should eat them. The ham and my turkey would go first, followed by rolls, salad, deviled eggs, yams, and other vegetables. Desserts were on a small card table across the room.

I crept away and walked upstairs like a sneaky kid with the house all to himself. I walked room to room opening the doors and turning on the lights to look inside for a few seconds, expecting Mom to have put up new wallpaper or painted a bathroom. Maybe she bought new furniture or bed linens for herself. But everything was just as it had always been, like the backyard, and I found that soothing. I noticed the small tabletop tree on the nightstand between the twin beds in what had been my and Sebastian's room. The tree was decorated with matchbox cars and tiny gift bags intended for jewelry size items. I walked over and peeked into one of the bags. There was a chocolate truffle inside wrapped in shiny gold paper. I turned around to see if anyone was watching from the doorway, like a kid about to take a peek at his gifts under the tree. With no one there, I dug my fingers into the bag to pick up the candy.

This routine was well-known to me and reassuring, a longtime tradition from our childhood. I remember us emptying all of the bags by the end of each week, but they were magically filled again when we came home from school. I sat down on one of the beds now to enjoy the rich sweet candy.

I peeked into another bag to find a piece of peppermint. I hated peppermint now. Mom kept pieces in her purse when we were kids to appease us during a car ride or while sitting in church. The teller at the bank or the secretary at the doctor's office always had a jar of mints for us to pick from, too. I don't think I ever really liked it as a child. I just accepted the treat and its sweet flavor as a free piece of candy.

A small green army man was in another bag. I lifted him out and stood him up in the palm of my hand. He was down on one knee and aiming a grenade launcher to the sky. There were probably two or three more in other bags hanging on the little tree, more pieces of my past that had never changed. I always swore that when Mom ran out of things to fill the bags, she just dug the army men out of our toy closet to make us think we were getting new ones.

Back then, Sebastian enjoyed the army men more than I did. We had hundreds of them, and they were always popping up between the cushions of the sofa, clogging up Mom's vacuum cleaner, or becoming mangled out in the yard after being run over by Dad's lawnmower. Blowing them up with fireworks in the backyard on the 4th of July was practically a rite of passage for all three of us boys. Eventually, I preferred the GI Joe and *Star Wars* figurines with jointed and movable arms and legs. Their costumes and rugged faces were much more appealing to my imagination.

"Aren't you too old to be playing with those?" Ellen asked, standing in the doorway.

I blushed a little, having been caught in the act.

"Have you checked the tree in your old room?" I asked.

"Stickers, paper dolls, and—"

"Peppermints!" We both said at the same time.

"You hate them too?"

"I'll give them to the kids," she said.

"You are just like Mom."

"Scary, isn't it?" Ellen walked over to the tree and began to look in a few of the bags on the tree. "No fair, you got chocolate."

"There's more?" I asked with excitement.

"You've already had one?"

"Yep. A truffle."

"I think I'll have a truffle too, if you don't mind," she said digging it out of one of the other bags and sitting down on the bed opposite me.

"Go ahead. We should raid the other trees before anyone else comes upstairs."

"Good idea."

We were quiet as Ellen enjoyed her chocolate. Then, she spoke up again as the silence became awkward. We both knew what the other was thinking.

"You aren't going to ask me about Mark?"

"I thought I wasn't supposed to."

"Did Mom tell you that?"

"Not really."

"Well, she just doesn't want any of us to put a damper on the holiday by discussing our problems. It's the one day of the year we are supposed to pretend nothing has ever happened in our lives."

"I'll still be in town the day after," I offered.

"The 26th? I'll see if I can pencil you in. I think Kwanzaa begins that day, though."

"Kwanzaa? Don't give Mom another excuse to try to get all of us together!"

"True. So, how are you doing?"

"I'm good," I said with a shrug.

"How are you really doing?" Ellen asked reaching over and putting a hand on my knee.

Before I knew it, I'd spilled a rant of words that must have been bottled up inside of me, and only because I knew Ellen didn't mind listening. I had always been closest to her out of the four of them. I told her about how much I missed Justin, and how lost I felt without him. He had been my first true love, the only person I'd spent any length of time with that mattered.

I didn't know how to start over. Right now, I didn't know if I even wanted to start again.

"There are few second chances in life, Travis, and the ones we do get are only at things that don't really matter. We only get one really meaningful true love in our life. Sure, we'll find love again, but we'll compare all the others to the one that meant the most."

"You said we?"

I felt a bit selfish, taking into account her own looming setbacks, but I went ahead and asked her though Mom had already filled me in on Mark.

"Mark wants a divorce."

"Why?"

"He says I'm still distant, which I am. I know he's my husband but I just don't know if I'll ever be able to trust the touch of a man again. Mark can't even come up behind me and kiss me unexpectedly on the neck without me flipping out. When I do let him hold me, he says I still feel tense."

"Doesn't he know these things take time?"

"It's been two years. I guess he's tired of waiting. I can't blame him. I'm tired of waiting too."

"What are you waiting for?" I asked.

In my mind, I expected her to answer with something prosaic like waiting for her dignity or self-respect to come back, maybe she was waiting for the day she'd wake up and find that it was all just a bad dream. None of us are that fortunate. Instead, she looked down to her lap and just shook her head. Like me, she didn't know what she was waiting for.

"I have no idea," she answered with a soft exhale.

"I know it sounds horrible to say this, but I thought things might have improved for you when the Judge died."

She thought so too, and said things were actually looking up as soon as the trial was over. A bit of the burden had definitely been lifted from her back, and the stress it had on their marriage had finally begun to cease. She kept the entire newspaper from the day a story about the Judge, the trial, her, or any of the other women involved *didn't* grace the front page.

When she was told about the Judge's death, a sigh of relief did escape her. However, her days of knowing he was safe behind bars were over. The questions racking her brain began again. What if the Judge faked his death to escape prison? What if he came back to Ruby Dregs to seek revenge? They were far-fetched ideas, but they easily planted a seed of worry in her head. Ellen had to go to his grave to prove to herself there was no reason to worry. Then, the dreams started.

Every night, if she was lucky to get to sleep at all, she relived those horrific sessions in his office. She felt his hands crawling on her and she'd wake up screaming and kicking the covers off the bed. He had to be dead, haunting her from the afterlife, but still she had to go to his grave for reassurance. Mark thought she was sick. He refused to go to counseling. And so, he too waited, taking two years to decide that the best solution was to distance himself from the problem.

"I'd have preferred if he'd just left me. He could have just skipped town and changed his name without telling any of us. At least then I would have felt I wasn't the only one going mad because of all of this. I could have blamed Judge Railen for one more thing instead of blaming myself."

Ellen broke into tears.

"Don't say that," I said taking her hand. "Mark didn't do that, because he loves you."

"Mark blames himself. If he had not lost that factory job, I would have never gone to work at the courthouse."

"And the Judge might still be on the bench and taking advantage of other women if you hadn't."

"It drove one of the other girls to suicide, having to sit there in a courtroom next to another judge and verbally say all the things Judge Railen did to her, while Railen sat there across the room looking at her. She hung herself that night after giving her testimony. I'd be lying if I said I never thought about doing it too, Travis. The kids, and Mark at the time, were the only things keeping me going."

Seeing Mark in the restaurant with that other girl immediately popped into my head. My conscience was telling me Ellen needed to know. I imagined a small devil on one shoulder and a tiny angel on the other. But weighing the consequences, I wasn't really sure if telling her would be a good or a bad thing. Besides, it was Christmas, and now was definitely not the time.

Instead, I got up and moved over to the bed beside her. I cradled her gently in my arms. She took to my shoulder, pushing her face into my collarbone, and let go. They were the tears she'd needed to cry for a long time while someone held her.

Clare

Recently, Ellen had let me baby-sit Robbie and Rachel for her. I liked being called Aunt Clare. I would always be older than them, someone they could look up to; and at last it felt like my own siblings had stopped looking down on me. I would always be their baby sister, but I hated being called the baby. I rolled my eyes when Mom called me "baby girl." Her baby girl had a baby of her own now.

Keeping my niece and nephew helped me to realize I wanted to have at least one more child. I wanted Jake to have a little brother or sister. I'd do it right this time. I'd get married and have a loving man by my side during the pregnancy. We'd raise our kids together in a stable home, like Mom and Dad raised me. Maybe he'd have a good job that could afford me to be a stay-at-home mom.

I liked my independence for now. But at the end of the day when it was just me and Jake going home to our tiny one bedroom apartment above the old downtown drugstore, it still felt like something was missing. Even now, sitting here in the floor beneath the tree, entertaining Robbie, Rachel, and Jake with Sebastian just felt comforting.

"Do you ever want to have kids?" I asked Sebastian.

"Who? Me? I haven't given it much thought. I mean sure, I'd love to be a dad, but I don't think I'm ready," he said.

"I don't think anyone is ever ready to be a parent. There's no way to be 100 percent prepared. Look at me."

"Yeah, but Jake was an accident—Sorry! I didn't mean that."

"It's okay. It's not like I haven't heard it before."

"You're a good mother, Sis. I'm proud of you."

"Thanks."

Although Sebastian was not completely aware of how I got pregnant, he knew there was no Andre. We were only two years apart, closer in age than any of the kids, which meant Sebastian had graduated high school with the real Andre who I had a crush on. Sebastian had never said anything, but I saw it in his eyes. He may not have known the truth—no one did except me—but I knew he worried about me.

I also knew something about Sebastian that he may or may not have known. Shelly, Lind's roommate, had got a job at the diner where I worked as a waitress part time. She started shortly after Lind died in Sebastian's apartment. After noticing my last name on the schedule, she asked me if I was related to Sebastian. I lied and said no, but that I had read about him in the paper. If she chose to talk bad about him, I'd set her up to get fired. I thought any information she shared might be useful if Sebastian ended up in trouble.

It was all that she talked about for several shifts when we worked together. I was the quiet type, so I let her spill her guts like the stupid ditsy blonde ones love to do. A lot of the regular patrons who she spoke to about it said nothing and just glared at her like she was an idiot. They knew Sebastian was my brother. I pretended not to hear her, but I was always listening.

The diner was open 24 hours, but I never worked past eight because of Jake's sitter. It was a slow night and my shift was about to end. The tables were clean and prepped, and there wasn't really anything to do, so Shelly and I were just standing there until it was time to change shifts. She asked me if I'd seen the paper that day. I said no, knowing it was just her way of bringing up something about Lind or my brother. Lind's memorial service had been the day before.

"Did you get to see her and say good-bye?" I asked.

"What do you mean?"

She looked at me like I was bleeding out of my eyes.

"Was the memorial at the funeral home or at her parent's house?" I asked, trying to explain myself.

"Oh! No, it was just a get-together at a friend's house. It's what Lind would have wanted," she said.

I somehow doubted a beer bash pool party at a friend's house in honor of Lind counted as a memorial.

"That's nice," I said out of a lack of words, and my typical response to her pageant queen tone.

"Did you know they burned her?" she asked.

"What?"

"Her parents had her cremated."

"That's nice."

"You think so?"

"Sure, I want to be cremated too."

"Really?"

"Yeah."

"I wonder if they knew about the baby."

"The baby?" I asked, puzzled.

Shelly revealed to me that Lind was about eight weeks pregnant when she died. She was with Lind when she bought a home pregnancy test. Lind was not completely sure if the baby was Sebastian's, but intended to tell him it was. I had little sympathy for a girl, now dead, who had been pregnant and still using illegal drugs. Apparently, the words *drug use* and *pregnancy* had not registered as a bad combination with Shelly, or Lind for that matter.

Having immediately given up drugs, drinking, and smoking when I feared I was pregnant, I had certainly not been an angel but I did care enough about the well-being of my baby. Finding myself sitting in an abortion clinic contemplating the fate of a child—my child—sent me over the edge. I needed no further convincing that cleaning up my life was the best choice.

Somehow, I convinced myself that the baby was not Sebastian's, and I wanted to dismiss Shelly's story as pure gossip given the turn of events. For the most part, I chose not to tell Sebastian because the whole situation had been life-changing enough for him. I had never met Lind, but was pretty sure she was a negative person. I don't know why members of the White family have a tendency to attract such people, and why the result is always horrific and unbelievable. The outcome always tends to be the secretive dirty laundry that curses a family and parades itself in the newspaper for the entire town to see. Any therapist would be rich off our family alone.

"You still have the nightmares, don't you?" I asked Sebastian.

"How did you know?"

He was surprised.

Everyone seemed to forget that I was a user too. By some means, me having a baby wiped that from everyone's memory. I wished I could forget.

"I still have them too."

"Lind is in every single one of mine," he said.

"It's because no matter how sad and terrible, she's responsible for turning you around. It's like the last thing someone remembers in an accident before they lose consciousness. It's what haunts you the most."

"How do you know all of this?"

"I've gone to a couple of meetings. Nothing serious. I just sit there and listen to other people tell their stories."

I had stood up and told my own story once, but I didn't tell Sebastian that.

"What do they say?" he asked.

"It's anonymous so I'm not really supposed to say, but believe me. Everyone else feels the same. It tears them up inside."

My own nightmares started out with me and my girlfriend drinking and using. Sometimes, we were in her trailer or my apartment, or at a party I don't ever remember going to in real life. We were playing music and singing out loud while snorting lines of coke off a mirrored coffee table. Then, I'm putting on make-up in the mirror, only now it's floating in the air so that I don't have to hold my head down to look into it. My girlfriend is floating in the air too.

While suspended in midair, the mirror shatters into a million tiny pieces for no reason at all. All the tiny pieces pull away in slow motion. I look through the pieces and can see my friend screaming her head off, but I can't hear her. I stand up and push the tiny mirrors out of my way so that I can step through them to help her. As soon as I sweep the pieces out of the air with my hand, it's like someone pushes play on a recorder and everything catches up with real time.

I pull my hand away because it feels like I've cut it on the mirror. I look at my hand and there's no blood or pain. I still can't hear my friend screaming, but when I look back up at her we are no longer in the trailer. Now, we are in the club, Project X, and we are on the dance floor. She's having a good time and looking at me all wide-eyed and wondering why I'm just standing there looking at my hand. All of a sudden, the noise of the club registers in my ears like someone pulled out a plug. The music is loud and covers the garbled chatter of the people around us.

Flash to the club's bathroom where I'm standing in front of one of the mirrors while she's in a stall with the guy we met. She screams and this time I can hear her. All the mirrors on the wall explode just like the one before, but this time they aren't moving in slow motion. I can vividly hear all the tiny pieces of glass falling across the floor. I shut my eyes tight to protect them. Shock registers in my hand again and I jerk it up close to me to examine it. It feels like someone has a hold on my wrist.

When I open my eyes, I'm pinned beneath a man in a car in

the parking lot. His hands are wrapped around both of my wrists and he's forcing them down so I can't struggle. I'm naked. I can't see his face, only a yellow smile in the dark and the whites of his eyes. I don't know where my friend is. This time, I scream. It's a long continuous scream but it's like only I can hear it. He laughs and puts a hand over my mouth, cutting off the noise. As soon as his large hand claps over my mouth I shatter into a thousand pieces just like the mirrors, then I immediately wake up. I sit up in bed, usually in a cold sweat, and look at my hand because it's actually hurting from the dream. I don't know why.

It's always the same exact dream, every time.

I just knew Sebastian was going to ask if he could come to one of the meetings with me, but he didn't say anything. I think he knew it would be easier to discuss your problems without having a relative in the room. Besides, there were plenty of outlets and meetings around town he could go to; he knew that from working as a bartender. The groups hung up flyers on the bulletin boards in bars. I could see his head filling up with questions he wanted to ask, but he kept them to himself. Being a typical guy, he probably thought he was too macho to go to a meeting. Maybe hearing that his own sister went had changed his mind. Recovery is difficult, but we don't have to do it alone. That's one thing the meetings had taught me.

"Are you guys having fun?" Mom asked, walking in from the kitchen.

"Yes, Aunt Clare and I beat the boys twice," Rachel said.

"You did?" Mom sang.

"Uncle Sebastian cheats," Robbie teased.

"I do not."

Sitting in my lap, Jake cooed and laughed at the excitement of his little cousins.

"Where did Ellen and Travis go?" Mom asked.

"Upstairs," I said pointing.

I watched her playfully tip-toe up the stairs to eavesdrop on them. She looked back at me and winked, with a finger to her mouth to be quiet. I was too rebellious and still clutching to my youth to admit it to anyone, but I admired my mother so much. I knew she wasn't that old, but I always imagined that she was a teen during the time of gentleman callers, like in that Tennessee Williams play. I smiled at the thought of my mom sitting on the front porch serving cold lemonade to a dozen or so men who came with hopes of escorting her to a summer picnic.

Frank White was the lucky man, standing among them, who later asked for her hand in marriage. She became a house wife while he went to work to support them. This was their first house. The bank probably loaned them the money in good faith, or maybe it was a wedding gift from their parents. Then, they started having kids and it all went downhill from there. Their cookie-cutter lives were filled with disappointments all brought about by their own children.

I'm sure they thought they only got it right the first time with Martin. His life had turned out just like theirs was back then. But then Ellen got felt up by her boss and her marriage was on the rocks. Travis was a gay. Sebastian and I were both insubordinate teen drunks who couldn't get a decent job if our lives depended upon it. I had a mixed baby. I'm sure that topped her list of frustrations brought about by her kids.

"All I'm going to say is that I'm highly disappointed," I could hear her say.

It was her final answer to all of our confessions. And like she stated, she never really said much at all. She didn't have to. The look in her eyes and on her face was enough to make you regret what you'd done. She never said anything like, "I regret ever having you."

Those were the cruel words I'm sure lots of kids heard these days, but we never heard it from our mom. Tears blocked her smile, but they eventually dried and her gleaming smile would come back. She always hugged us when we walked in the door, so tight as if she had not seen us in ages, even if she'd just seen us two days prior.

Being the last child, there was a brief amount of time when I had Mom and the house all to myself after Dad passed. I'd moved back in with her briefly because I thought she might like having someone in the house with her; the others thought it was a good idea, too.

As a younger kid, I snooped through their dresser drawers and closets poking around for birthday and Christmas gifts. Mom's closet was a palace full of dresses when I liked to play dress-up and pretend I was someone else. A few weeks after Dad died, Mom was napping on the sofa, and I was up in my room. For some reason, I felt the need to go through Dad's stuff. I needed to take something of his—a tie tack, a watch, a photo, anything—and hold it in my hand. I wanted something to keep to remember him by, as I felt him slipping away in my mind. The joint I'd just smoked at my open bedroom window didn't help, but I still felt it was too soon to be forgetting him.

Instead of going to their bedroom to rummage through his closest or bureau, I went to his office. Dad had an old roll top desk. I remember pretending it was an oven when I was a kid. Mom would send me up the stairs with a sandwich for him when he would be in his office grading papers. I wouldn't let him eat it until we had sat it on the desk and rolled down the lid, then turned a few imaginary knobs to bake the bread. Dad had bought the desk at a yard sale with intentions of refinishing it. It also had a broken lock he never bothered to fix either.

It had been years since I had used it for bread-baking, and I honestly couldn't remember the last time I saw my Dad sitting at the desk. In the age of computers and less children in the house, he usually sat in front of a laptop at the dining table downstairs. The top of the desk disappeared with its soothing sliding noise as I opened it. In my head, I could still hear the heavy metal slam of an industrial kitchen stove that I dreamed up as a child.

The inside of the desk was filled with pockets and cubbies of all shapes and sizes. Some were open like an old post office from the past, and some had doors with little grooves in the wood, instead of knobs, for your fingers to open them. As a child, I envisioned a grand hotel for my dolls or a henhouse for chickens that laid magic eggs, but Dad never allowed me to play inside the desk. I was only allowed to bake in it with him in the room.

I could feel him standing over me now, scolding me, as I pried the doors open to look inside the little spaces. Most were empty. One was filled with blank envelopes, another with pens and pencils. Canceled checks, old receipts, and bills marked paid all had their own pockets. They were the thousands of pieces of paper that blandly ruled our lives but also held it together. I remembered seeing Dad almost pull his hair out when he couldn't find a statement or specific paper he was looking for, although now it looked like he had always kept things in specific order.

At the bottom, there was a long slender drawer with no notch to open it. It could have been a secret drawer I would have ignored had it not been open just a bit now. I found a ruler in with the pencils and wedged it into the crack to open the drawer all the way. Inside, there was a single brown legal-size file with a name written on it in large black block-style letters: HANNAH. Something, or someone, told me not to pick up that file, but when had I ever listened?

I picked up the file and opened it. A small Polaroid photo fell out and landed on the desktop. It was of an infant child and almost looked like a photo taken in a hospital when the newborn was just a few days old. I did not remember this picture being taken, but I knew the baby in the photo was me.

The other contents of the file were a thin stack of papers held together by a paper clip. Removing it revealed a clean white imprint of the clip underneath, indicating just how much the papers had yellowed over time. I sifted through small print lines of legalities and agreement terms, anxious for any key words jumping out at me that would immediately tell me what this document was. And there was just such a word. One word.

Adoption.

I learned that Hannah's parents were both deceased. It seemed they were victims of a brutal murder. When no relatives came forward to claim the baby, Hannah was turned over to a Catholic orphanage in Savannah, Georgia. Frank and Lorraine White adopted her three days later. Baby Hannah's last name was missing from any of the documentation, but there was a photocopy of a birth certificate showing her name was now Clare Marie White. The lines for the mother and father were filled in with Frank's and Lorraine's names.

My birth parents had been completely erased, and in some way I felt my identity had been too. I wanted to feel thankful to have a home and to be with this family, and be glad that I was not raised by nuns among other bratty orphans. I should have felt that way. Yet, a part of me kept wondering about my real parents and who I might have turned out to be had I known them. Many believe that God has a predetermined plan for our lives, and before I was even born, I was destined to be right where I am. But rather than accept that, my free will thinking wanted to know how things might have been different if my birth parents had lived.

Looking back on my life, I couldn't have asked for better parents than the Whites. I always had a playmate in the house with my four older siblings, and they were always watching out for me. I went to a good school and made friends. But I still thought about where Hannah might have been raised, where she would have gone to school, and what type of family she might have had. I still felt cheated when the reality of it set in, although there was no way to know how my life might have been. I returned the papers to the drawer, walked out of dad's office, and returned to my life as a White, never saying a word to anyone about my discovery and also wishing I'd never found it. Sometimes we yearn for the truth that we think is hidden from us. It's only when we find the truth we've been looking for that we often wish we didn't know after all, and then we see why it was kept from us in the first place.

Today, as I sat here in the floor across from Sebastian with our niece and nephew and my child around us, I looked into Sebastian's eyes and contemplated if he knew who I really was. The others would have to have known since I was the youngest of them and Mom would not have been pregnant again after Sebastian. Why was this the one secret of the family everyone managed to keep so well?

I've been tempted to take Jake and leave. We could disappear in my car and head West cross-country, but what's out there for me? I couldn't imagine starting over again as someone new. There was no birth family to search for, and who's to say they would have known who I was anyway. If I did find them, maybe their answers to my questions were not ones I needed to hear. And so I stayed here, pretending I never discovered those adoption papers last year. I may not have been kin to this family by blood, but at least I had a family to call my own.

I would definitely have felt alone in this world without them.

Mr. Black

After picking up the newspaper and cut up Christmas lights from Helen's cleaning frenzy, I collapsed on the sofa to channel surf. Wholesome black and white holiday movies were repeated on every channel. I left the television on some version of Dickens *A Christmas Carol* that I may or may not have seen before. I thought I heard the basement door open and Helen going down the stairs, but Helen never went in the basement. The only thing down there was my train menagerie, something to tinker with when I was at home. I was too tired from work to care where she had gone. Although school was out, I'd been responsible for cleaning the furnace and checking the heating units in each room.

I became the janitor at the high school about a year after Justin graduated. The position had been open when Justin was a sophomore, but he begged me not to apply for it because my working there would embarrass him. I had been in accounting during much of my marriage, and landed another desk job with a local furniture company till Justin graduated. When the janitor position came open again, I immediately jumped in line for it. I was tired of crunching numbers, and the pay was the same.

Only one or two of the kids knew me from church. They nodded at me like they would to anyone on the street, but never spoke. To the others, I was just a strange man mopping the hallways. I was always in their way and they were always in mine. Some would smile and whisper, "Excuse me," when stepping over my dust mop. Others rolled their eyes, blaming me when they walked into my dust pile because they weren't paying attention to where they were going.

I got to work late nights when there was a dance or a ball game. It was a good and legitimate excuse to be away from the house and away from Helen. I made a habit of taking my time so that I didn't get home until around midnight. Helen had long since gone to bed by then, so I always fell asleep on the sofa watching television.

I was amazed at the number of used condoms I'd find under the bleachers. When sitting on the bleachers, if you try hard enough you can look down between the foot boards and see the floor underneath. It's dark, lit only by the light that comes through those small gaps, and littered with candy wrappers, gum, popcorn kernels, and spilled drinks. The bleachers were nestled between two flights of stairs. The gym was open and sunken into the main floor. You could climb down the bleachers or look down over the gym from the cafeteria up above, or you could walk down the stairs to access the basketball court and the bottom of the bleachers. There were locker rooms at either end and, despite their putrid lingering smell of sour body odor, they tended to be popular places for kids to sneak off to as well.

Although the bleachers were retractable and folded up into the wall for you to be able to clean underneath them easier, there was a door at either end that led below them next to the stairwell. It was a safety precaution to retrieve keys or cell phones so that the unfortunate owner didn't have to wait till the end of the night for the bleachers to be retracted. The doors should remain locked to prevent kids from playing underneath, or doing other things, but I intentionally left them unlocked on "active" nights. Finding the refuse of sloppy teen lovemaking excited me. I wish I could have had this job much earlier in my life, and before prophylactics were treated with spermicidal lubricants. Helen could have had another child.

I think another reason the kids all ignored me was because I had caught several of them during their trysts on game night or during the prom. If I kept the bleacher doors locked that night, like a spy, I hung out in the crowd leaning against the rails up above to watch the game. Young hand-holding couples loitered in the stairwell and waited for when no one was watching. Discovering the door was locked, the guy cursed the heavens. The girl told him to forget about it, but he was determined to get laid. He would tell her to c'mon and then pull her up the stairs. They'd disappear into the hallway leading to the classrooms. I gave them five or ten minutes to find a comfortable spot. The library was quite popular because it had sofas and overstuffed chairs, another door I purposely left unlocked sometimes.

Now, the principal was totally unaware of any of this happening because I never reported anyone. I'd sneak off behind the teens and almost make a game of trying to find them. Groans of ecstasy echoing down the hallway usually made them easy to find. I'd sneak up on them, hoping to get a peak of a butt or a flash of a boob. Then, I cleared my throat and put on my deep booming scolding voice.

"What's going on here?"

They always frantically jumped to their feet to put their clothes back on, if any garments had been taken off at all. The boy would turn red in the face while zipping up his fly. The girl turned angry, buttoning her blouse. I'd offer to give them a break this time and not report them because they were such "good kids," although I had no idea if they were well-mannered or not. A couple of the guys even bribed me with money before walking back to the game. I could always tell the bribers from the rest just by the nice expensive shoes they wore, and so, I let them speak first and take out their fine leather wallets. Who knew that pretending to be a hall monitor could pay so well?

I'm taken aback when I come across two boys who have hooked up and crept down the halls. They never went together. One would wander off, pretending to go to the restrooms although there were toilets right by the gym, and the other followed five or ten minutes later. They've obviously prearranged a place to meet up. I've never found two boys in the library. Being comfortable isn't as important for two guys, I guess. Most of the time, I came across them in one of the boys' bathroom stalls or in the lighting balcony in the theater. I took my time breaking them up. If I have a good view, sometimes I ignored them all together.

I memorized their faces so that I could be sure to avoid them if I ever saw them in the park. Letting one of them get in my car could put my job in jeopardy if I ever pissed one of them off at school. Backseat etiquette, if there was such a thing, was to never say anything if you run into one another outside the park. I've never had that problem so far, but now I cruise a park closer to the outskirts of town. It's closer to the neighboring county's school, so few of these kids will travel there just to get off.

Occasionally, I do see some frail pimple-faced kid who probably borrowed his parent's car and lied about some study night at a friend's house. He thinks he's the only questioning kid in town, and he heard about this nameless park in a chat room online. His heart is racing because he's driven all the way out here and he has no idea why. Rather than sit in his car, he's out walking the trails and sitting on top of the picnic tables. The other men in cars see him but they won't approach him for fear of spooking him. It's tempting, but they know he's new and will eventually learn the ropes.

Maybe nothing happens, and the kid jumps back in his town car and leaves, or maybe he disappears in the woods with someone taking advantage of his vulnerability. I'll pass the kid in the hallway on Monday. Before, he stood to the right side of the hall with a clutch of books in his hand and his eyes on the ground. He was one of the few kids still carrying a backpack. He's a math or chemistry nerd with an expensive calculator. After his trip to the park over the weekend, sometimes he looks the same. But sometimes, his chin is up and he makes eye contact now. He's tucked his thick black glasses into his pocket and put some gel in his hair. It's on those occasions I can pretty much guess what happened to him in the park that night.

Someone made him a man.

I never saw the same two guys together twice and rarely caught the same guy and girl together. The girls are usually the repeat offenders. Sluts. The most popular one was a girl named Danyele Child. With as many times as I had busted her having sex in the library or in a classroom, I had caught glimpses of almost every part of her naked body. Danyele's boobs were big, with some boy's face often buried between them. She was thin, like all of these voyeur girls, and the sight of her ribs when she arched back on a sofa or desk made me sick. Her full bodied long hair reminded me of some rock star girl on the hood of a car in a music video. Her confident demeanor made you believe she could snap the head off her lover's neck once he fell between her thighs.

Danyele used that appeal to her advantage in the classroom as well. It was not uncommon to find her sitting in the front of the class and wearing a low-cut blouse if the teacher was tough. I wasn't supposed to see how she charmed Professor White that day in the biology lab last semester.

Professor White had requested extra trash cans every day that week because the labs would be dissecting frogs. They would need them for disposal of the waste. After each class, Professor White would collect the smaller trash bags and put them into one large can in the supply closet at the back of the class. The supply closet was a walk-through space shared by the Biology lab on one side and the Chemistry lab on the other. When the Chemistry lab was not in use, Professor White would push the larger trash can to the outside of the door so I could come by and collect it. On this day, he'd left the door on the Chemistry lab side cracked open. When I stopped by after the first class to collect the trash, I saw Danyele with Professor White inside the supply closet.

Martin White was a well-respected member of both the staff and the community. I knew he was Travis's brother, and I'd seen him with his wife and kids around town shopping or dining. Despite all of the very public hardships Lorraine White's family had been through over the past few years, such severity seemed to have skipped over Martin White. His rendezvous with a temptress like Danyele Child was on the threshold of changing all of that.

Being a large man, there was no place for me to hide and spy on them. Any communication between them outside the classroom was kept to a bare minimum and practically nonexistent. That didn't stop her from still getting caught with two football players in the girls' restroom one night at a basketball game. There was no way Martin White could be thinking clearly. He'd been seduced by her only to secure a passing grade, and so I felt the need to save him. Their actions angered me, and I knew he was in need of an intervention.

I took a chance they would eventually make plans to meet earlier in the day, so I made it a habit to sweep the hallways on the Science hall just after Professor White arrived each morning. One morning, Danyele arrived at the lab before Professor White did. I ducked into an empty classroom so she wouldn't see me. She was eyeing her watch and soon stepped into the dark supply closet out of sight. On an impulse, I approached the closet through the Chemistry lab. Grabbing a heavy microscope off one of the tables, I swung the door open and caught Danyele by surprise. Her blouse was unbuttoned. She looked at me, quite startled, as I stepped into the closet. The look on her face told me she was trying to think up some sort of excuse for her being there.

Before she had a chance to scream, I smacked her across

the face with the scope. She fell to the floor in a heap, knocked out cold. I crushed her skull with the microscope again to be sure she would not wake up, and then I buttoned her blouse back up. I had no interest in what was underneath. Without hesitation, I picked her up and dumped her into the large trash can and covered her with smaller bags of waste.

I flipped on the light in the closet to clean up any trace of what I'd done. The floor was surprisingly clean except for a small pool of blood and some spattered on a cabinet door. The scope had a bit of blood on it too and was dented. I buried it in the trash with her and wheeled the can to the boiler room. I came back to the lab right away for a second look just to make sure nothing looked out of place.

Professor White had still not arrived. Upon returning to the boiler room, only then did I come to realize what I had just done. I had no choice but to dispose of her body, but could not risk doing it now at the beginning of the school day. I would wait until the end of the day when classes were out and the building was empty. I locked the trash can in one of my broom closets and then returned to the hallways to go on with my daily chores.

"Good morning, Manny," Professor White said passing me in the hallway.

He seemed as if he was in a rush to get to the lab, although classes didn't start for another hour.

"Do you need extra trash cans today, Professor White?" I asked.

"Not today. We'll be dissecting fish in a few more weeks and will need some then. I'll give you plenty of advance notice." He turned the corner to the Science hall and disappeared before I could reply.

Without him seeing me, I cut through a few of the classrooms to a view through the windows to his lab. I watched as he knocked on the closet door. When no one answered, he opened the door slowly and peeked in. I could see his mouth moving. I imagined he was calling out to Danyele lovingly, or whispering words of affection to her, although I could not hear him. Through the window in the closet door, I saw the light come on. Professor White came back out with a puzzled look on his face. He sat down at his desk and crossed his arms, waiting.

First hour came and went. Danyele was in the second-hour lab. He seemed uninterested by her empty desk, probably assuming that she was just absent for the day. I knew I'd have to act fast by the end of the day. When Danyele didn't return home after school, her parents would call all of her friends first. Upon discovering her friends didn't see her at school all day, they would contact the police.

After school, I kept to my usual schedule as well to avoid looking suspicious to anyone. I stopped in at Greer's Grocery to pick up supper for Helen and me, and then went home. After eating, I told Helen I had to go back to work which is something I did at least two or three nights a week anyway. There was always something to do to pass the night away. The parking lot was empty and the front doors locked. I was in the clear for what I needed to do.

It was six weeks before summer vacation. The school was heated by an old radiator system that wouldn't need to be turned on until late November. Heat was generated by a huge gas boiler that looked like a giant furnace or stove you'd expect to see in some old steel mill. It was massive and black with soot and grease. In the dark, the red and yellow of the fire inside made it glow like a monster. With a wrench, I turned on the gas. A match lit the gut of the thing with an intense whooshing sound, and the smell of heat filled the air for a minute or two like on the first day of winter. The dial on the outside, measuring the degree of heat, quickly rose to 870 degrees.

I found a pair of work gloves and opened the two iron doors on the side, which was already as hot as an oven. Flames licked at the edges of the open space. I adjusted the gas to pull the fire back inside while I retrieved the trash can from the utility closet. My stomach churned to find it empty if Danyele had escaped, but the bags of trash on top under the weight of the microscope were undisturbed. I pulled them out to look down inside. Danyele was still there, pale, with eyes open. She looked frozen. Blood had painted most of her face and matted her hair. The slut didn't look so likable now.

I tossed the smaller bags of trash into the belly of the heat. A singe of the plastic expelled air from one of the bags like a popped balloon. The rubbish spilled out across the broad grill and ignited, eventually dripping into the bottom as black liquid matter and ash. The vapors from the extreme warmth inside clouded my eyes. I tipped the trash can off its wheels and over onto its side. Pulling at the plastic still wrapped over the sides, I was able to maneuver her out of the can without having to touch her. The strength of the bag amazed me as I pulled at it to wrap it tight around her. It never broke once, not even when I pulled up to lift her body off the ground.

With my arms now underneath her, the feel of collected blood in the bottom of the bag felt like a full bladder of water or an IV drip. It squelched in my grasp and I was afraid it would break. If blood spilled on my clothes, I would have to burn them too. Luckily, there was a mechanic's jump suit in my utility closet that I could wear home if it came to that. Pinched between her lifeless body and my arms, luckily the bag never broke.

I supported the weight of her upper body in the palm of my hand, pushing her head-first into the boiler. Once her shoulders touched the retort, it was easier to grab her by the legs and push her completely in. I folded her legs under so I could close the doors. The trash bag had already started to cling to her like shrink wrap on a gift basket. A sporadic hissing sound came from her blood dripping on the grill like water on a camp fire.

Had it been winter yet, the boiler room would have been nice and toasty in only a matter of a few minutes after I turned up the gas. The smell of cauterized flesh and burning hair did not invade my nostrils because I stepped out to clean the restrooms to pass some time. Three hours later, I touched one of the radiator units in the hallway. It was just turning luke warm. I returned to the boiler room and stood next to the furnace listening to its crackle. It did not sound like the rapid burning of anything inside, only the steady flicker of flame slowly providing heat to the building. I turned down the gas and opened the doors to look inside.

The retort glowed and the grill was empty. Danyele Child was now a pile of cremains, bone fragments, and one badly charred shoe in the bottom of the boiler. I dimmed the flames to only a glint and doused the base with a bit of gasoline I kept in a squirt bottle, soaking the pile of ash and the shoe. I shut the door again before turning the flame back up. An explosive flash lit the inside of the boiler as the gas ignited. I let it burn for another two hours before shutting the boiler down.

The police did come the next day. They took the contents of Danyele's locker and held a meeting with the teachers, then had a meeting with just the teachers who had Danyele in class. Professor White looked nervous, but he didn't look guilty. With no breaks in the case, and the headlines in the paper moving on to some dead girl who had overdosed in Martin's brother's apartment, Danyele faded and became a yearbook dedication. A rumor surfaced that her locker was haunted.

Before the end of summer break, the boiler always had to be cleaned and checked. I removed the few remains from the bottom and put them in a bag with the microscope, which until now I had kept hidden. I wrapped the bag in duct tape and thought about burying it. Instead, I threw it off the Nicks Bridge late one night. The scope made a perfect anchor to sink the bag to the bottom of the muddy Forked Deer River.

If he'd known, I think Professor White would have thanked me. I had saved his job, his marriage, and his family. He didn't owe me anything for it, though. I'd do it again and again for any relative of Travis White. For some reason, taking a life to spare one didn't bother me. A need for my service did not present itself again all summer long. School was back in session this fall and Danyele Child was like a forgotten graduate. The urge to kill again had been growing inside me. I thought about practicing on a boy from the park, appeasing my need to play God. But I waited.

Helen had nothing else to live for. She'd said so herself many times since Justin left. So, I pondered what to do about that. It would be too risky to try to get all of her into the boiler room, at the same time at least. But if I took a bag or two of trash to burn each week or once a month, what's the harm in that? There is a crawl space beneath the trains in the basement, but I couldn't keep her there for too long. I don't want her in this house with her ghostly spirit nagging me like she does in this world. In death, she'd probably still make me pick up after her.

Death was too easy of an answer, but we all reach a point in life where it's the only answer, the final one. I didn't see any problem with it coming a little quicker for Helen. School was out again for Christmas, and the boiler would still be on for at least two more months. So, I had some time to think about it. I still needed to come up with a diversion, a story to tell the police and the last of her living relatives. I'd be the first suspect; the husband always is. Maybe I could turn myself in and just go to prison. Three meals a day, no bills to worry about, and no job to go to doesn't sound too bad. At my age and with the life I have lived, what else is worth being on the outside for? Or I could stage a suicide. Everyone knew she was depressed. The array of medication she ate everyday could be an easy accidental death by overdose.

On the television, Scrooge was stumbling through a grave yard to escape the Reaper. He falls over a grave and the Reaper stands over him. The name on the tombstone of the grave presents itself with a flash of light. It is Scrooge's grave, but I seen Helen's name there in my mind. I see my face beneath the black cloak standing over her like Death at her side.

I smile. A burp escapes me and rattles my stomach. The taste of Greer's chicken gizzards lingers on my tongue, mingled with the savory thought of freedom from the burdens that could be lifted from this life.

Travis

The sky looked cold and pale that day. Frost covered the grass outside, twinkling like confetti after a party. The sun was rising lazily in the sky, painting it with beams of orange that no one seemed to care about. Pumpkins had grown faces and ghouls had collected candy at neighbors' doors a few nights ago. The cool breeze of autumn and the rain of crisp leaves had lasted only for about two weeks. Winter was falling upon us fast.

Potted plants still adorned my neighbors' balconies like pets forgotten in the cold. Some drooped and sagged from the weight of the frost that had crept up on them in the night. Justin and I would have had coffee on the balcony on a morning like this. It was a tradition I had continued now without him, but the icy chill in the air chased me back inside only after a minute or two.

It had been a long hot summer that seemed like time was standing still for me. Justin had only been gone for a few months. Sitting in my car that morning, waiting for it to warm up and defrost the windows, was a frigid slap in the face that time would keep moving forward no matter how badly I wished it could go in reverse.

I cursed myself for trekking back home for the weekend without a coat. I thought this would be a week of chilly mornings cured by hot coffee or an extra blanket on the bed the night before. I wasn't ready to give up my short-sleeved shirt closet space to sweaters, jackets, and long-sleeved sweatshirts still packed away from last year. I couldn't believe I was running my car heater in November. Yellow and red leaves danced behind the car as I pulled out of our apartment's drive and headed toward the highway to home. I still say *our* when referring to the things that Justin and I shared. It didn't sound so lonely.

I was going home because Stuart's Monuments was supposed to set Justin's headstone later that day. Hopefully, this was the last burdening reminder that still lingered and felt undone. I never considered Justin's death a burden, but all the tasks that followed it were just that. Justin had no will, but it's amazing what legalities and bills we are tied to that try to keep a hold on us in this world, even after we are gone. He only had two credit cards, which were easy to contact. One of our cards had both of our names on it. I left his on it just so it would appear on the bill each month. I would eventually have it removed, but I liked seeing it there for now.

Our lease and utilities were in my name, but I had to call the finance company concerning his car. Manny and Helen didn't want it and could not afford it. A part of me wanted to keep it, but I didn't need two cars. Two months passed before it was finally repossessed. There had been notices of late payments in the mail. I called each time and had to tell them Justin had passed on and they could pick up the car. I had to call Helen to get her to fax a copy of his death certificate to some office, but I doubt she ever did. I wasn't home when they took the car, but our apartment's leasing office stuffed a notice in my mailbox that had been left when they picked it up. DECEASED was the reason across the bottom of the card.

Manny had called just days after Justin's funeral to tell me

Helen refused to go with him to Stuart's Monuments to pick out a marker for her son. She thought they couldn't afford it and should just wait a year. Manny did not want to tell her about the money I'd given him, so he called me instead. I'm glad he did. I almost expected him to waste the money on something else.

"I can't do it, Travis. I'm no good at these things," he said on the phone.

"Thanks for asking me to help."

"You knew him better than Helen or me. You should pick it out. He'd want you to."

"I'll come this weekend."

"I can give you back the money," he said.

"No, just keep it. Why don't you come with me?"

"You really want me there?"

"Sure. Go by Stuart's and see if we need an appointment. If we do, meet me there around noon on Saturday."

Manny didn't show, but he'd written a check to me and left it with the clerk for when I arrived. I walked around the nameless graveyard, an outdoor showroom of markers and headstones to choose from. I was content now that this task had been left entirely up to me without Manny and Helen lingering in the background and waiting to override my choice.

I chose a black marble flat marker with a granite inlay where his name and the date would be engraved. Although Helen would have insisted there be a piano pictured on the marker, I chose a simple staff of music notes across the bottom rather than an instrument. Justin's parents made him take piano lessons, and although he loved the piano, he rarely played after moving to Memphis to be with me. I was afraid he'd given up who he was just to be with me, but I don't think he liked who he was before. He assured me I had no effect on his piano playing, or lack thereof. His passion for it, or his parents' fervency for him to play, got left behind in Ruby Dregs.

"Instead of the music notes, we can add a cross or a rose for free," the clerk told me when I'd gone inside to confirm the order.

"Is that some kind of a sale or special?" I asked.

I wasn't interested, just curious.

"No. They are just easier to engrave," the clerk said.

I appreciated her honesty.

"I'll stay with the music notes," I said.

"Suite yourself, but this check Mr. Black left isn't enough to cover the black marble," she said, waving the check in front of me daintily between two fingers as if it were dirty.

"Mr. Black isn't paying for it, and besides, that check is made out to me."

I snatched the check from her fingers and tucked it into my wallet.

"Do you need to set up a payment plan then?"

"Do you take cash?" I asked with a stern tone, becoming annoyed with the clerk's preconceived notions that I couldn't pay for the marker.

"We do."

I paid for it in full and got a courtesy call weeks later telling me the stone was ready and when it would be delivered to the cemetery. I had not told any of my family I was driving up that weekend. Although I did pack an overnight bag, I had not made up my mind if I would stay or not. I wanted to go to the cemetery alone and see the marker for the first time by myself. I prayed they'd spelled his name correctly and got the dates right.

And, it had never happened before, but I liked the idea of driving home to take care of business and not feel obligated to pay a visit to Mom, or to one of my brothers or sisters. The best way to avoid it was to not tell them I was coming, despite having talked to Mom the evening before I left. It was like I was having an illicit affair, but instead of driving to a neighboring strange city to see someone privately, I was going back home where everyone knew who I was. I was a spy; fearful I might pass Sebastian on the highway or even worse, run into someone. But I took the chance anyway and told no one I would be there.

This would be the first time I visited Justin's grave since the day after his funeral. I did not know how I would feel seeing his grave with his name now in its permanent place. I wanted to see it by myself, but afterwards, I might want to jump back in my car and just drive the two hours back to the apartment, not needing condolences from anyone. I was still grieving, but I did not want anyone standing there beside me while I sobbed, if I cried at all. I didn't want it to be like his funeral all over again. This time needed to be different because I'd have him all to myself.

Like old times.

A narrow rectangular shotgun house was across the street from the cemetery. The yard was dead and overgrown, and the faded paint on the house was peeling. A spray-painted cardboard sign on the front lawn advertised ROSES FOR SALE. I expected to see a street peddler, but no one was outside and I didn't see any roses. A faded neon sign in the window blinked FLORIST. Flowers had not crossed my mind until I reached the street where the cemetery was. I parked in the gravel driveway and walked up the front steps. Clay pots with crispy dead wilted things looking like they once were plants adorned the front porch. Maybe the florist had gone out of business.

A sign on the door said to ring the bell, and a large bell hung on a red rope around the door knob. I hesitated but rang it anyway. A tiny dog barked from behind the door and scratched at the threshold. After a few seconds, I turned to walk away and had just made it down a few of the steps when I heard the door creak open behind me.

"You wanna buy roses?" a slow child's voice asked behind me.

I turned to find a small black boy's face pushed out between the door and the frame. He had a finger in one nose and was holding a small dirty poodle back with his other hand. The poodle growled ferociously.

"I think I have the wrong house," I said, trying to dismiss myself as I continued backing away to my car.

"Who is it, Bud? Who's there?" a frog-like voice called from behind the boy.

Just then, a fat hand pulled the boy out of the way and pushed him behind the door. A small toothless woman whose skin resembled a burlap sack appeared. She was wearing a floral print dress that reminded me of bed sheets on a clothes line blowing in the breeze. The fabric pulled at every wrinkle in her fat little body hiding beneath it. Her hair was silvery white and pulled back in a bun. Her round eyes were distorted behind her thick coke-bottle glasses.

"You need somethin, sweetie?" she asked in a soothing grandmother tone.

"I saw your sign about the roses," I stuttered.

"Sho'nuff! C'mon in an' I'll fix ya right up!" she exclaimed.

Standing aside, she held the door open for me and welcomed me in with a gesture of her hand and a nod of the head. She instructed Bud to take the "damn poodle" in the back. The smell of sweet vanilla incense immediately filled my nostrils, covering me with a sense of pleasantry. A black pot-bellied stove in the middle of the room warmed the heavy air. I held my hands over it to feel its soothing love. The old wooden floor creaked beneath my feet like a haunted house or an old one-room church decaying in the backwoods somewhere.

The ambience of the old lady's shop was like an ornate dried flower arrangement with its brown, red, and orange flowers in various-sized vases all around the room. Faux pumpkins were nestled in shelves lining the wall next to colored glass trinkets and porcelain figurines. A tall freezer hummed behind the counter. Filled with large budding roses, it was an anomaly amongst the comforting décor of the little room. The old lady stepped behind the massive work counter and opened the freezer. She took out a dozen yellow roses and began wrapping them in cellophane.

"Boy, why you wear your heart on the outside today?" she asked.

"Excuse me?"

I stepped away from the stove and walked over to the station where she was working.

"You missing somebody?"

"Yes. Yes, I am, ma'am."

I felt like I was blushing, but it could have just been the heat from the stove. She didn't seem to take notice.

"They across the street?"

"Yes, ma'am."

"Ain't been there long."

I mistook this as a question.

"No, ma'am. Not too long. Their headstone was delivered today."

"I bet it's purty. You gonna be needing these then to dress it up a bit, eh?" she asked, handing me the yellow roses.

"I was thinking red."

"He say he don't want red."

"I'm sorry?"

"He say he want yellow roses."

I stood there for a moment studying what she had just said. It sent chills down my spine. The lady just looked at me kindly and grinned. Her cataract-glazed eyes looked through me.

"How do you know?" I asked.

"Red say you love him. He know dat already. Yellow rose be his favorite. You should know dat."

I did know it. Never taking my eyes off her, I reached for the flowers and took them from her slowly. I reached into my pocket with my other hand and retrieved a fifty-dollar bill and laid it on top of the counter. I felt her finger touch my hand gently as the flowers were exchanged between us. She took the money and tucked it into her pocket.

I stood there, unable to move. The little old lady walked back around the counter and touched me on the shoulder. She escorted me back to the front door.

"Thank you for the flowers," I managed to say to her as we stepped back out into the cold.

"Thank ya for stopping by today," she said.

"I'm glad I did."

I slowly walked down the stairs and had just made it to the car door when the old lady called out from behind me.

"Boy!" she yelled. I turned and glanced at her from over my shoulder. "JB say thank you. Thank you for everything."

Reluctantly, I turned and looked in my car. I looked at the front lawn of the little shop. I studied the cut-off broom sticks stuck in the ground to hold up the cardboard roses sign, expecting to find hidden cameras or someone crouching in the grass waiting to yell surprise. What joke was someone playing on me? How did anyone know I was here? There was no one there except for the wind. I looked back at the little woman standing on the porch with her hands folded across her belly. The look on her face read, "I told you so."

"Tell JB I love him," I said.

"You just did."

I nodded with a smile of contentment and got into the car. No one had ever known I called Justin "JB" except for the two of us. I leaned over to lay the roses on the passenger's seat. When I looked back up, the front porch of the tiny flower shack was empty. The old woman was gone. Tears made my eyelids feel heavy, so I closed them for a second or two before pulling out onto the highway and crossing to the cemetery entrance.

I was anxious and still overcome with shock from what had been said at the flower shop. I decided to stop by my father's grave first. I've always envisioned cemeteries like giant silent parties where I'm searching for someone I know amongst a bunch of faceless strangers. My father was surrounded by his parents. My grandfather went before I was born. He died from a black widow bite on his ass while going to the outhouse. Dad had a brother and a sister beside him, along with some uncles and aunts I'd never met. His brother fell into an empty well

165

when he was only three.

My father's headstone was a double stone with my mom's name and birth date already engraved on her side, an empty seat being held for her at the party. Our last name, WHITE, adorned the back side in deep block letters across the middle. Intricate crosses and roses bordered the corners where their names were. I wondered if they got those for free.

The fall arrangement fastened across the top of the stone today was bright and clean, large silk sunflowers with tufts of wheat under them and orange berries. They looked so new I wondered if Mom had already been here this morning before me.

As children, Mom sometimes brought us here on my grandparents' birthdays or for Mother or Father's Day. She'd let us help her hang an arrangement over the top of their stones. She'd kneel down and pull some of the plastic leaves and silk flowers out of the way so it didn't hide their name. If an old arrangement still hung there from our last visit, faded and wind-beaten, she removed it to take home with us.

Ellen would pick it up and hold it in front of her, pretending to be a bride. Sometimes she plucked the yellowed flowers out and gave them to us to stick behind our ears. Ellen called us Roman Soldiers and the flowers were our wreaths of honor.

A sword fight would ensue among the boys and our flowers would fall from our ears to the ground. Mom just stood there and ignored us for a moment or two, letting us be kids. Her eyes were focused on the graves and I knew now she was remembering the way things used to be. The beauty of those old flowers had weathered over time, but they still had possibilities thanks to a child's imagination.

I was always enamored by a small marker, almost the size of a brick, which sat on the edge of the neighboring families' lot. Mom said it was just a marker to divide up where the lots were, but I traced the word BABY across it with my finger. The word had been written across the stone when it was being cast from a mold. Someone probably used a nail while the cement was still wet. The letters were deep and perfect.

Dead grass had filled in the crevices from where a mower and come right up to the edge of it. I knew it was not a marker, but a grave, an infant at this party without a face or a name. I walked over a bit and found the stone still there today. The Y was covered by tall grass the careless mower had missed. I knelt and pulled the grass away.

Justin's grave was several lots away. It was quicker to get back in my car and drive over to it. In death, if I chose to be buried by my family, I'd still have to be apart from him. For now, the idea of being cremated and having my ashes scattered next to him sounded like a good idea. If I died tomorrow, or even next week or next month, that's what I would have done.

I knew if I lived to be eighty; by then there might have been other friends met and memories created which might determine a different place to go in the afterlife. Justin would have wanted me to meet someone else and be happy, but for now, my heart still belonged to him. I wanted to be near him if I did go.

The shiny black marble was like an oyster's glistening pearl. I could see it right away as I steadied the car down the narrow path to where Justin was buried. It was beautiful. Gravestones are such beautiful monuments, celebrations of those we loved. It's sad to think they never get to see it, but faith tells me they do see it. My heart told me now that Justin indeed liked his headstone.

JUSTIN "JB" BLACK
APRIL 20, 1976
JUNE 12, 2010

He hated his middle name, Oliver. He thought it was odd

because his initials spelled JOB. I left it off for him and put JB instead. I'm glad I had come so early; I had yet to see another car in the cemetery. Sometimes when we know we are alone, we are more likely to say the true things we need to say. I ignored the bitter wind and its attempt to chase me away. Instead, I sat down on the ground next to Justin. The rectangular patch of grass had grown back quickly over where he was laid, but it too was brown and gray from where an earlier frost had already fallen.

For a moment, I cleared my head of the loneliness and pictured Justin sitting on the ground across from me. The grass was green again and it was April. Both of us woke up and decided to call in sick to work. We had a late morning in bed before having our coffee. That afternoon we'd gone to the park for a picnic and to enjoy the first days of spring. It was Justin's birthday, and he wanted to go to the zoo afterwards. It was a simple day and we always made an effort to share many like them. I'm glad my head was filled with those days, and they weren't hard to grasp onto when I needed a memory of him.

The words I spoke in my head to him were not new ones. Like the flower lady said, Justin knew I loved him. We told each other everyday. The ten years we'd spent together seemed like a lifetime when we were living them. Now that he was gone, it seemed like it only lasted as long as the blink of an eye. I almost forgot about the roses I'd bought. Going back to the car to get them, I spotted a car over the hill entering the cemetery. It looked like Ellen's.

I watched her drive by Dad's grave and slow down, but she didn't stop. Maybe it wasn't her. The car turned toward the right and started in my direction but passed by me. It was Ellen behind the wheel. She never turned and looked in my direction. Her mind was somewhere else. She parked just down the hill and got out to approach another grave I was not familiar with. From where I stood I could look down the hill and see her. She wiped her eyes and I wondered whom she was crying for. She stood several feet from the marker as if unsure about getting any closer.

I guess I had stood there looking at her for too long, because eventually the feeling that someone was watching overcame her. She glanced over her shoulder, the wind whipping her hair in her face, and looked right at me. She turned away for a second unaware of anyone standing there besides a stranger, then she turned back again for a longer look, assuming her mind was playing a trick on her. It wasn't. I slowly raised a hand and waved, not moving my fingers, just a palm in the air like I knew the answer to our questions.

Although we were brother and sister, neither of us had words for each other that day. At any other place, any other time, we would have run to each other and embraced and at least said hello. Today, both of us just got back into our cars and drove away. Neither of us waited for the other to leave so we could drive by the grave and see whom the other had been looking at. She took the nearest crossroad which led to a side entrance where a grounds keeper had just opened the gate. I laid the roses down in front of Justin's stone and said my good-bye for the day. Back in the car, at the end of my path I turned to the left and went back the way I came.

At the entrance, I glanced back across the road to the old flower shop. The sign for the roses was gone, along with the neon sign in the window. The window had been broken out. There was no sign on the door, no bell on the knob. The yard still looked overgrown and the decaying plants still lingered in pots on the porch, but the house looked empty. And it probably was, or maybe I was just seeing things, imagining it all. I look back and think about that day now and can't remember.

It had already been a day that needed no explanation.

Martin

The kids were anxious to go to Grandma's to see their cousins, aunts, and uncles. Daniel was seven, the oldest of the four grandchildren. His sister, Nicole, was six. They both went to the grade school where I taught before. I loved my kids, but I think they enjoyed school more knowing their dad wasn't a teacher there. They had both always been very independent, and I don't know how they might react by the time they reached high school. There was another biology teacher besides myself, so neither of the kids would have to be in my class, unlike the way it would have been if I'd kept teaching junior high.

Like most kids their age, they had already picked jobs for when they grew up. I knew their answers well because every grown-up in town asked them when stopping us to talk at the grocery store or at the end of church. Daniel wanted to be a professional baseball player or a veterinarian. Nicole wanted to be a teacher like Daddy or some type of detective, maybe even a ballerina. I had those dreams too when I was their age. I wanted to be an acrobat or a teacher like Dad. The latter choice won since it was the easiest, and my parents paid for college tuition.

Marline was a bank teller at Citizens National, one of only four banks in this town. Her father was bank president, and his father before that. Thanks to some wise investing of our savings, and a cash gift from Grandpa, Daniel and Nicole could afford to go to college to be whatever they wanted. I prayed for the baseball player and the ballerina, any large dream that could shake the clutches this small town can have on people.

I was just a Biology teacher, but that didn't exempt me from the social status among students and teachers which determined how "cool" you were. Students all had their favorite classes and favorite teachers. The cool kids didn't like science of any kind, only the nerds. So, those students and the teachers who taught those classes were immediately at the bottom of the totem pole. Next came the jocks. These were the stupid ones who gave witty answers to questions in class to get a laugh, if they came to class at all. Behind closed doors, we were urged to pad their grades so they could play, if they were any good and the team couldn't win without them.

Next came the smart kids who were popular only because they were also cheerleaders or played on a team. They were the student council, the yearbook and newspaper editors, and the academic top ten. These kids had rich parents who bought them cars for their sixteenth birthday. Danyele Child fell into this category, so I had no idea what she saw in me. I'm sure her seduction was only a plan to insure a good grade, and I fell victim to it, putting my career and family in jeopardy.

The guilt had been unbearable at first. I stayed awake at night contemplating on going to the police. I wanted to come clean with Marline, but I knew the outcome would ruin our marriage. Danyele's disappearance was absurd, and it was even more absurd to blame myself for it. This all just had to be bad timing, or was it? I had to stop thinking and obsessing over it. There was nothing I could do to change the past. It was a secret I'd hopefully take to my grave.

I just knew there would be a knock at the door one day or a

photograph mailed to Marline at the bank. But the incriminating mail never came, and the police never showed up to ask questions. I eventually convinced myself to stop holding my breath. My wounded conscience would never be healed, but over time the weight of it had been lifted. We never forget the sins we commit against ourselves, the mistakes we make in life. We ask God to forgive us; maybe our loved ones forgive us over time if they even know what we've done. Being able to forgive yourself is what takes the longest, if it ever happens at all.

We raise our kids and teach them to hopefully *not* make the same mistakes we made in life, but there will always be a lesson we forget to teach them. In life, our loved ones are always the ones that hurt us the most. And yet, sometimes we don't even know it. Silence may keep them from the harm, but it doesn't keep us from hurting ourselves.

"Dad, can we walk to Grandma's?" Daniel asked.

Marline and I had just started letting the kids walk to Grandma's on their own. There was no fence separating us from what was left of the orchard between our yard and hers, so it was easy to make sure they stayed away from the road.

"I guess so. Are you ready to go now?"

"Yes," he elongated, afraid I would say he couldn't go yet.

"Go ask your sister if she wants to go too."

"Okay."

Daniel trotted off to the den where Nicole was helping her mother finish up some gift-wrapping. I followed. Nicole leapt to her feet from her place on the floor and ran to put on her shoes. Marline and I had intended on sending the kids shortly anyway so that we could play Santa Claus. We'd put out the kids' gifts while they were gone, so when we returned home tonight it would look as though Santa had come while we were just down the road.

"Kids, do you think Santa might come while we are gone?" I asked.

Their eyes lit up.

172

"Do you want to put out some milk and cookies just in case?" Marline asked.

"Yes!" they cried with joy.

In the kitchen, I helped Daniel pour the milk while Marline helped Nicole pick out some homemade cookies to leave on a saucer for Santa. We lifted each of them up so they could sit the milk and cookies on top of the mantel along with a Christmas card they both had signed in crayon print.

"Can I trust each of you to take a gift to Grandma's and not drop it on the way?" Marline asked.

"Yes, ma'am," they said in unison pulling on their coats.

I knelt to help Daniel with the buttons while Marline dug under the tree for what gifts to send with them. Marline knew that no matter whose gifts she sent with the kids, they would walk in the door and immediately run to that person and give them the gift right away instead of putting it under the tree like they were instructed to do. She gave them Clare and Sebastian's gifts from the kids, knowing they would not read the tag, but told them they were for Grandma.

Marline escorted them outside while I called Mom to tell her the kids were on their way. Mom would watch for them out her kitchen window even though it was just a few yards for them to walk. I told Mom they were bringing a few gifts with them. She said she would make sure they got under the tree.

"Are you guys coming down soon? Everyone else is here," Mom said.

"We are going to play Santa first, and then we'll be down," I said.

Hanging up the phone, I went outside and slipped an arm around Marline's waist. Daniel and Nicole were halfway across the yard. We waved to Mom who had stepped out her backdoor to welcome the kids. They ran to her and presented her with the two gifts. She hugged them for the gifts and then opened the door for them. She waved back to us as she followed them inside.

Back inside, we both went upstairs to our bedroom where

173

the kids' gifts were tucked secretly in the back of our walk-in closet. Marline had already wrapped most of the ones she bought back in November. Daniel's gifts were all wrapped in Santa Claus paper with a green background. Nicole's gifts were wrapped in hot pink ballerina paper. I helped Marline carry them downstairs and we sat them all on the sofa for now. We'd have to clear out all of the gifts to take to Mom's to make room under the tree first.

I grabbed two large plastic storage containers from the basement while she pulled the rest of the wrapped boxes out from under the tree. Loading the gifts into the containers carefully as to not rip the paper, both containers were soon full and we still had three more shirt-sized boxes we'd carry by themselves. I moved the containers of gifts out to the car. Marline waited for me to come back inside so together we could arrange Santa's gifts under the tree, Daniel's on one side and Nicole's on the other, with plenty of room in between for them to rip off the paper and play.

By now, we could load up the couple of dishes Marline had prepared to take and join the others at Mom's house for the holiday, but a quiet house with no kids is not something grown-ups take for granted. Marline winked at me with a shy laugh once we finished with Santa's gifts. Walking over to me, she slipped one hand around my waist and began unbuttoning my shirt with the other. I leaned down to kiss her on the neck. Rather than waste time going upstairs to the bedroom, we fell into each other on the sofa.

Our lovemaking was usually quick and quiet, for fear of waking the children. It was always in our bedroom in the middle of the night, and happened only if one of us had awoken from sleep and was possibly in the mood to wake the other. Chances like these where we were all alone were fully taken advantage of. It was like old times. We were loud and reckless. We laughed, and best of all, we took our time.

* * * *

An hour later, we were showering together, another romantic act which didn't take place often. The touch of Marline's body against mine was much more satisfying than Danyele's had been. I loved Marline. We dressed and put on our coats although the drive over to Mom's house took less than a minute.

Mom greeted us at the front door, having probably spied out the window at our car pulling out of our drive. Sebastian was waiting in the drive for us. Mom had more than likely asked him to go out and help us with the gifts and food we had brought. He waved to us as we pulled in.

"Merry Christmas," Mom said on the front porch, hugging both of our necks as if she had not seen either of us in months.

I followed Sebastian to the tree with the gifts, while Marline and Mom disappeared in the kitchen with the food. I heard Ellen greeting Marline from the kitchen. Travis and Clare stood up from their seat on the couch to greet me, each hugging my neck. Clare was holding Jake. I shook his little hand and said hello, giving his jaws a tickle to make him grin. Robbie and Rachel each clung to a leg, giving me a squeeze. They had been playing in the floor with Daniel and Nicole, surrounded by an array of action figures and dolls.

Out of all of my siblings, I felt the closest to Ellen and Sebastian. Ellen was closer to my age and had a family much like mine. We'd gone to the same college and both had professional jobs right here in our hometown. Sebastian and I were completely different, but I liked being the older brother he could look up to. He related to me much more than he did to Travis, and he knew he could come to me if he needed to. Since he had stayed here in town, I saw much more of him than I did Travis.

Although Clare lived here in Ruby Dregs too, the wall between us was one she had built between herself and every member of the family. She was the youngest, the rebel, the outsider, and I think she preferred being that way. Marline enjoyed helping her in ways that Clare might not want to seek out help from Mom, so Clare confided in Marline a lot and I liked that. A good role model was important for someone who was a young mother. The kids liked Clare too, and enjoyed playing with little Jake, so we liked having her as a babysitter sometimes.

Travis was more of an outsider than Clare. I imagined being gay had a lot to do with that. He moved away right out of high school, so he missed out on a lot of the daily activities that the rest of the family had lived through since we all lived here so close to one another. I didn't understand him, but mainly because I didn't know any other people like him. Gay people, that is. There were kids at school who got picked on and called "faggot," but they were feminine. Travis was never like them at all. I never once thought he was gay until he told all of us shortly after graduating from high school.

My relationship with Travis felt like a distant cousin you only see or speak to at holidays. Sure, I saw him several times a year when he came to visit. He always stopped by to say hello to the kids. He never missed a birthday. He had helped out with moving Sebastian into his new apartment, but he still felt like that far-away relative that never called or wrote. I loved him like a brother, but there was that detachment between us. The miles and the years between us didn't help either.

Once I had pried the twins from my legs and they went back to playing with their cousins, I walked into the kitchen to say hello to Ellen. She stood up from her barstool to hug me and kiss my cheek.

"How are things?" I asked her with the sincerity in my eyes that said she better not give me a canned answer.

"They're good," she said with a slight grin, looking away with a bit of embarrassment I had not intended.

I scratched her back lovingly and left it at that.

"Everything smells good, Mom," I said changing the subject to take the focus off Ellen.

"Thanks, sweetie. I stayed up all night slaving over the stove," she said with a wink.

She thanked Marline for the pumpkin cheesecake and pecan pie we had brought. The kitchen island was practically overflowing with food and steaming like a hot sauna. The side counter was a bakery and candy shop of colorful desserts. Never mind the gift-giving. I lived for the holidays just because of all the food.

"Let's eat," Mom called to everyone still in the living room. Those two words were a Christmas carol dear to my heart.

The four grandkids lined up first. Mom, Marline, and Ellen helped them with their plates and brought drinks to the kids' table for them. Sebastian was quick in line once the kids were out of the way. Clare and Travis followed, with Marline and I right behind them. Mom finally encouraged Ellen to go ahead of her. Once we were all seated, and Sebastian was up for seconds, Mom had finally fixed her own plate and sat down with us. She was always the last to sit after making sure everyone else was taken care of, refilling drinks and bringing second helpings to the kids so they didn't have to get up.

The White family holiday dinner was as down home as it could possibly get in this small town. We weren't a family who went out and hunted for holiday turkey in the fields, unless you count bargain shopping at the grocery story. We were a paper plate, plastic fork, and Styrofoam cup clan instead. Mom would never admit that half the side dishes were store-bought. We all knew Mr. Greer smoked the ham. Travis had even bought a fried turkey this year.

The days of a Norman Rockwell painting with a small family gathered around the candle-lit mahogany dinner table eagerly watching Dad carve and slice a ham or turkey were over. I don't remember us ever having a holiday dinner like that, as much as television commercials and postcards pictured it being, but it didn't matter. All of us being together for any meal was just as heartwarming.

Looking around the room at my family now, enjoying the company of each other, was a nice way to end the year. It was a single time and moment to forget the things outside of this house that hindered us. Marline asked Clare about work. Mom asked Ellen how the kids were doing in school. Sebastian and I talked about football. Ellen asked Travis how things were in Memphis. In the background, the kids shared their Christmas wishes, advertisements they'd seen for new toys, and what they asked Santa to bring. These were all conversations we could have at any time of the year. We had had them. But somehow it being Christmas changed the meaning of our words entirely tonight.

No weight on my shoulders from the stresses and worries of the day could take away the happiness and love I felt right now for my family. Not even the knock at the front door could fade the smile in my heart or on my face.

Lorraine

In 1963, I was sixteen and became a mother just a year later. I was still a baby myself. I remember times were hard back then, but I don't think kids these days have it any easier. We were much more appreciative of the few things we had then because Frank and I worked hard for them. Frank was a good man. He kept us fed and kept Martin in clean diapers. The electricity and the heat never got cut off. Outside of these needs, we did without.

My family grew up very poor. Daddy was a farmer and Mama was a housewife when she wasn't helping out on the farm too. She tended to the chickens, collecting their eggs, and would milk the cows and pick whichever vegetables were in season. She had no qualms about ringing a chicken's neck or slitting a hog's throat to put meat on the table. I had three brothers and three sisters, so large families in the house were quite comforting to me by the time I was raising kids of my own.

My brothers plowed the fields and picked cotton right beside Daddy. My sisters sold vegetables at our produce stand at the end of the street, when we weren't helping Mama with chores around the house. The farm claimed the life of one of my brothers. Jessie was sitting on top of the wheel guard of the tractor while Billy was driving and working soybeans. Jessie was going to turn around so he could look behind the tractor but he lost his footing. He fell forward and the large tractor wheel pulled him under. Billy reached for him but it was too late; the tractor rolled over him and crushed his rib cage. Billy never drove the tractor again after that day.

Christmases were small but special around the house that Daddy built. The boys got baseball cards with gum in the package. The girls got an apple, an orange, and a stick of peppermint candy. The very best year was when Mama got a new pair of shoes and the girls were given a chair. Just one chair, but it was special because Daddy and our brothers had whittled it from pieces of scrap wood using their very own pocket knives. One of my older sisters still has that chair today.

In the winter, Daddy worked down at the docks on the Mississippi River unloading steamboats for the mills. When Billy turned fifteen, he was old enough to work there too and went with him. The girls stayed home with Mama keeping the house warm and the barn clean. We fed the animals and learned how to sew, and played checkers with milk tops on a board we'd drawn on the floor with chalk. My younger brother Hank was not yet old enough to work the docks, so he stayed home and worked around the house.

One winter, Daddy was offered a job by one of the steamboat captains. His boat was low on men because of a bad case of influenza. He needed men to go down the Mississippi to Biloxi. A steel mill here and in Memphis was in dire need of a shipment that was too heavy for any other boat to haul. Daddy would be gone for twelve days, but he'd make twice what he made at the docks all winter long. My brother Billy was asked to go too and would be paid the same wage as Daddy. Hank would stay home with us to be "the man of the house" as Daddy called it.

"Takes three days to get down there. We'll spend three or

four days down there loading. Two days back to Memphis. We'll spend a day or two there unloading. One more day to get back here and a day to unload the rest down at the docks," Daddy told Mama.

She didn't want him to go. They'd never spent a night apart since the day they married, but she knew how important the money was to him. She knew what it meant to the family.

"With making this much money, I could take the rest of the winter off and be at home with you. We could put Billy's pay into savings," he said to allure her.

"Come back to me," she told him.

"I will. I'll come back to all of you," he said.

I remember all of us standing on the dock next to Mama waving good-bye to Daddy and Billy as the steamboat rolled away from land. Thankfully, it had been a mild winter and the river had not frozen across. Thin layers of fragile ice clung to the banks but broke apart when waves from the steamboat's paddle reached land. I took a small polished pebble from the banks of the river and slipped it into my pocket as a souvenir from that day.

Two or three days passed quietly, until one night Hank was out in the barn late. With four women in the house and him being the only man around, Mama didn't worry about him. She said he needed his time away from us and the house. Inside the house, we had all settled down to rest when there was a loud knock at the door. Mama did not call out because she thought it might have just been Hank locked outside. But then, the knock came again.

"Hank! Why are you knocking so loud? The door is unlocked," Mom called out, opening the door.

When the door opened, Hank rushed in carrying a young woman in his arms. He said he heard the dog barking at something at the end of the road and he walked down to the mailbox to investigate. He found the woman lying unconscious in the road that led up to our house. She was wearing a raggedy yellowed nightgown with holes in it. It was stained with fresh blood between her legs, and her stomach was swollen like a watermelon. She was about to give birth. Mama grabbed some extra bed sheets from the cupboard and covered our dining table so that Hank could put her down.

We did not own a telephone, so Mama gave Hank the keys to the truck and told him to drive to the sheriff's house, which was just a few miles down the road. She summoned us to start boiling large pots of water. I washed the woman's face with a cold rag while Mama gently slapped her face to get her to wake up. A burst of agony filled the air as the woman came to. She jerked and pulled under the weight of God because we could not see anything or anyone holding her down. Besides the vocal screams and grunts that escaped the woman's mouth, Mama determined the poor woman could not speak.

Mama hushed her and pulled the hair from her face, telling her to push gently. My sisters and I stood there in horror. We had never seen a woman give birth before. The limp and shiny body that appeared from between her legs glistened like a fat catalpa worm. Mama used her cutting shears to snip the slimy hose that kept the baby attached to the woman. She sent us away to pull the pots of water off the stove and to fill a dish pan to prepare a bath for the baby. I watched over my shoulder as Mama pulled mucous from the infant's mouth with her own hands. She held the baby over her shoulder and gave him a swift tap on the back. The baby cried. The woman on the table fainted.

By the time Hank had returned with the sheriff, we'd helped Mama wash the goo from the baby. It was a little girl. We were watching her sleep in Mama's arms while the woman on the table was sleeping too. The sheriff pointed to the woman and Mama called him over with her finger. She whispered in his ear and then he whispered to Hank. Hank and the sheriff wrapped the bed sheets up around the woman and carefully carried her outside. We never saw the woman again.

After asking everyone around town, the sheriff could not find anyone to identify the poor lady and claim the infant. She was buried in a pine box in the small cemetery that was lost in the woods down the road. Upon Daddy and Billy's return, to their surprise Daddy had a new daughter and Billy had a new sister. Daddy did not believe Mama when she told him the odd story of how the woman had come to us that night, but we all vouched for her.

"Another mouth to feed," Daddy groaned.

"I can't give her up to an orphanage, Paul. God sent that woman to our doorstep for a reason. I just know this baby is a blessing," Mama said.

Mama named her Benita, which meant "blessed one."

Benita was raised in our house never knowing she wasn't related to us by blood, and none of us ever treated her any differently. Her childhood was no different than ours. Mama and Daddy loved her like another daughter. We fought and made up with her like another sister. When Benita became a young girl, it was then that she turned very different toward the family.

She developed a habit of raising up her skirt or dress and exposing herself to Hank or to any male friend that was around. She laughed at it as being funny, but she wasn't usually wearing undergarments underneath so it could be quite embarrassing. A school nurse suggested that Benita was suffering from a psychiatric problem known as anasyrma. It was something neither Mama nor Daddy knew the meaning of, much less could pronounce correctly. The nurse explained that it was better known as "flashing." Daddy thought it was a bit funny, but the nurse took it quite seriously.

"Exhibitionism, or flashing, is exposing yourself for your own gratification. Anasyrma is doing it for the reaction from onlookers," the nurse explained.

Daddy did not take Benita's condition too seriously until he went into the barn one day and discovered Benita sitting on top of Hank in the hay loft. She'd pinned him down and was attempting to have sex with him. Daddy blamed Hank and gave him a beating, but Hank said he'd tried to get out from under her but when he pulled her off of him Benita would bite his fingers. By then, Benita was acting out at school and it was suggested that she stay home.

When she became loud and disrespectful toward Mama and Daddy, it was decided that she should be sent away to a special school for children who misbehaved. As oddly as Benita came into my family's life, she went out of it. Benita was only twelve years old, and I was jealous because she got to take a train ride. I'd never been on a train before. Mama accompanied her and was gone for four days, returning without Benita.

Mama and Daddy received letters in the mail notifying them of Benita's condition. It worsened, and medical tests confirmed Benita was slightly mentally retarded. I had written to Benita twice a month since the day she left, until after I met and married Frank. She never once wrote back. Daddy and Mama passed away within months of each other just after I turned twenty-one. My sister Sheila died less than a year later. She was hit by a car. My other two sisters and two brothers each married and started their own families. We all forgot about Benita, the unruly little girl with a one-way train ticket. It was easy to do since she wasn't our blood, but it was wrong of us because we were the only family she ever had. I tried hard not to forget her, although my letters to her eventually dropped to just one a month, and then maybe once or twice a year.

In 1980, at the age of thirty-three I gave birth to Sebastian. Travis was four years old. Ellen was ten, and Martin was sixteen. The kids loved having another baby in the house. Neither Frank nor I had thought about a fourth child, so Sebastian was a surprise. Sebastian would definitely be the last, but that all changed nine years later. In 1989, a letter came from Ringgold, Georgia. Ringgold is just across the state line, south of Chattanooga, Tennessee. The letter was from the assisted living home where Benita had been living after her stay at the psychiatric hospital in Summerville.

Benita was dead.

Like her mother so many years ago, Benita had died giving

birth to a daughter. An orderly had taken interest in Benita. The letter did not say if he had raped her, only that he had been fired when it was discovered she was pregnant. The baby was a girl and had been turned over to an orphanage in Savannah. In going through Benita's things when cleaning out her room, a nurse had found a large box of all my letters. She decided to take time to write to me to let me know what happened.

Frank knew of Benita, but I had never spoken about her to any of the kids. At the age of forty-two, I had long forgotten about raising another child but I could not leave that baby to possibly be raised in an orphanage. Weeks passed and I was riddled with guilt over having left Benita in institutional care for all these years. Frank and I decided to contact the orphanage about adopting the baby. It was the only way to make things right. I owed that much to Benita for not having been a presence in her life.

We flew into Chattanooga and rented a car. The drive across the Georgia state line was beautiful. Autumn had just set in across the countryside, turning the trees from green to fire red and burnt orange. It made me wonder what it had looked like so many years ago to Benita sitting on that train next to Mama, not knowing it was the last time she'd ever see Mama again. In Ringgold, I was impressed with the living facility. It was clean and the staff was friendly. It did not resemble a cold hospital or bleach-tainted retirement center as I had pictured. The rooms were carpeted and looked like small apartments filled with personal items, photos, and comfortable furniture to make the inhabitants feel more at home. Instead of bleach, the air was filled with the sweet fragrances of mint and honeysuckle.

"Who paid for this?" I asked a nurse, while waiting at the front desk for someone to collect Benita's things for us, in awe of how accommodating and relaxing the center was.

"Her parents did," the nurse said, in a heavy Georgian accent.

"What? I never knew of that."

"A lot of long-term patients live off donations given to us or government aid if they never worked or have no family, but Benita's parents left quite a bit of money to the facility for her care. She lived quite comfortably during the years she spent with us," the nurse explained.

I was amazed. Mama and Daddy had never talked about money for Benita, and there was no mention of her in either of their wills.

"Comfortably? What about the orderly and the pregnancy?" I asked.

"Mrs. White, Benita and that orderly were in love, but their relationship was against company policy. Since he was not related to her, he could not discharge her, and employees are forbidden to marry patients who live here. We all knew of their bond, but they kept it hidden as best they could. Her pregnancy was exciting, but also unfortunate for both of them."

"For both of them?"

"He lost his one true love, ma'am."

"Since he's the father, did he not want the child?" Frank asked.

"After losing Benita and being dismissed from his job, I'm afraid he took his life, sir. That's why the baby was turned over to the orphanage. There are no other living relatives besides you and Mrs. White."

There were just three boxes of Benita's belongings. Two were filled with my letters. She'd kept every single one. The center offered to ship them home to us. We thanked them for all of their generosity. Before leaving, I asked what had happened to Benita.

"Cremation. Would you like to have her ashes?" the nurse asked.

I thought about it and decided no. This had been her home for so many years, so I felt she belonged here among the people who knew her better than I did.

"We were going to spread her ashes next to him. He's buried in a cemetery not far from here," the nurse said.

"The orderly?"

"Yes."

"That sounds like a good idea to me. I'm sure they both would like that. By the way, what was his name?" I asked.

"Jeffrey Clare."

The drive to the orphanage in Savannah was long and tearful. I was ashamed of myself. How could I have gone all these years being absent from Benita's life?

"Are you sure you want to do this?" Frank asked.

"I have to," I answered.

Two days later, there were three of us on the plane leaving Savannah. We flew into Memphis, where Martin had driven everyone down to pick us up and to meet their new baby sister.

"What's her name?" Nine-year-old Sebastian asked when I held the pink bundle down so he could see her chubby face. Frank and I both had thought of the same perfect name when filling out the papers at the orphanage.

Clare.

Justin

I often marveled at the idea that had Travis and I been legally married and if two guys were as normal as any other couple in society, would more of his family have come to my funeral? Only his mother and youngest sister, Clare, came to the graveside. To the rest, although they had known me for ten years, I was just a close friend to Travis. I wasn't offended for my own sake, but I was for his. Had Martin or Ellen's spouse or God forbid one of their kids died, there would be no question about it. Travis would be there for them through it all. That's what families do. If I'd been a woman, would they have mourned me?

I never told Travis, but I never felt like part of his family. They all had time to accept their brother as he was. He came out in high school. There were boyfriends before me. Maybe they told him to his face that they were okay with it, and that was fine as long as they didn't have to see him with someone. I had never been introduced as the boyfriend. We were both approaching thirty, and Travis had always brought a "friend" for the holidays.

Lorraine tried her best to make me feel at home, but a

woman who purses her lips when she walks in on her son holding another man's hand while watching TV still has issues over his sexuality. When she got him alone, she told Travis she'd prefer no public displays of affection, just in case it made anyone uncomfortable. He sheepishly agreed, not knowing it was his own mother who was the most uncomfortable.

When I would come with him for an overnight stay, Lorraine put us in his old room despite there still being twin beds, and there being one other vacant room in the house with a double. Unbeknown to her, we locked the door and both slept in one of the tiny single beds anyway, crumpled into each other like overgrown kids. I always looked forward to the silent love making. We unmade the empty bed in the morning to make it look slept in just in case his mother walked by the room.

Such inconveniences on our relationship were the only exceptions to who we were. I never said anything because I knew how important Travis's family was to him, so I stomached it and pretended to be excited to take a trip home with him. That, and I never had a family of my own to be happy or upset about it. To at least get to sleep in the same room with Travis at his old house was a luxury.

At my parent's place, Travis would have been confined to the sofa with me upstairs in my single bed. Mom would have stayed awake just to listen for the sound of feet going up or down the stairs in the middle of the night. Knowing how much Travis would have been uncomfortable there, we would have been better off in a hotel. But, since his Mom lived less than two miles away we always stayed there.

I envied seeing him and his brothers and sisters together. Despite their flaws in life—and they all had them—at least he had a family to fall back on. I had an overbearing mother and father who still pinched my cheeks and said "good boy" when I got straight A's in college. No matter how much I hated it, I was the glue that held their loveless marriage together. I didn't know how they would get along without me, and while I was alive, I didn't care.

I blamed them for my small town misery where I was the piano-playing fag in school. I was the only boy who took piano lessons, and I only took them because my parents made me. Just like everything else, I excelled at the piano. I was the top pupil my music teacher had. She always had me go last at our recitals because I played the best. She said after all the wrong chords and slow keys they'd sat through, the parents deserved to hear something as good as Mozart or Beethoven. At eight years old, I ate up her praise like candy.

I wrote a paper in school about how I wanted to be the next Liberace. Kids laughed and called me a faggot right there in front of the teacher. I had never seen Liberace. I didn't know how he looked or dressed. I had only heard his name and his music when Mom played his records. He was magnificent at the piano, so I ranked him right up there with all the other great musicians I knew: Bach, Beethoven, and Mozart. Liberace's name sounded like it belonged right beside them. After the mockery over my paper, the next time Mom put on one of his records, I ran to the player and ripped the record right off the turntable and threw it across the room.

I was a smart student and a genius musician, at the mercy of my parents, stuck in a Mayberry town that sucked the life right out of its inhabitants. I dreamt of some Las Vegas scout sitting in at one of my recitals and coming up to my parents afterwards to offer them a great big check and my chance to become famous. He'd sweep me off to Hollywood to help sharpen my skills. I'd have an agent, a manager, a wardrobe specialist, and a ton of other important people standing by to cater to my needs. I'd never see my parents again, and the next time they saw me I'd be playing piano as a guest on *Johnny Carson*. Who knew dreaming could be so worthless?

Music is supposed to make people happy, but it didn't work that way for me. It usually made me miserable because it was something my parents encouraged, and anything that provided them with selfish delight was something I grew to hate. And so, I rarely played the piano ever again once I left Dogwood. I sat down from time to time at a piano in any room and searched for the feeling that brought joy to any other musician's face, but the feeling would not come. It was overshadowed in my head by the faces of my parents. The magic of the music had somehow missed me.

Travis came out to his family during his senior year. I doubt I would have ever come out to my parents at all had I never met Travis, but then again, who knows if I would have ever moved out. It wasn't easier living at home with them; it was convenient. I made enough money to support myself, but needed someone—or something—to push me out of the nest. I had never intended to stay with them as long as I did, but just like the small town we lived in, it seemed impossible to break out.

I don't like to think I used Travis as a means to escape. He would never see it that way either. His love life before me was almost nonexistent. He had only dated a handful of guys, nothing serious, but that's still more than I could own up to. I never knew anyone else in Ruby Dregs who was gay. If there was anyone, I guess they were closeted like me. We were all the "dregs of society," as rival schools liked to joke about the town name. Despite everyone in school knowing what I was— calling it out behind my back in the hallway everyday—I had never admitted it out loud to anyone until the day I met Travis.

I was a year behind him in high school. He didn't know who I was, but I knew him well. I think I had a crush on him when I was a junior and he was a senior because I drew a heart around his class photo in my yearbook that year. That was the year I signed up for track. I'd never played any sport before, but how hard could running be? I was tired of being the choir and orchestra nerd.

I was a pretty fast runner, always coming in first, second, or third in our meets. I quickly gained respect from my team members, the same kids who had called me names in the hallway the whole first two years of high school. Guys who ran track weren't like other jocks, though. We were smarter and did better in class. Travis was the same way, except he played tennis. We both wished we'd known each other in high school. Travis later told me he was never made fun of back then, but I knew he was. Massive torment from our peers would have ensued had we both been seen walking side by side between classes or sitting together at lunch. The teen angst and depression would have torn a fragile friendship apart for no real reason at all. Kids are so mean to each other, especially teens.

So, I liked to think it was meant for us to never meet back then. High school was soon over, and the name-calling had stopped. And like everyone else, we were shocked at a world full of nothing after high school. The possibilities were endless, and yet all those stupid jocks that taunted us now drove their trucks around town looking like zombies. The best part of their life was over. Now, they had to get jobs in factories or at burger joints and support their pregnant girlfriends, dreaming about the glory days growing farther and farther out of reach.

Five years after high school we were much more mature, Travis and I. We'd both been through college, Travis in Memphis and me with two years at the community college in Ruby Dregs. I still couldn't escape a dead-end retail job after that, pushing my way up the corporate ladder of being a salaried manager still working nights and weekends, still living at home with my parents. My days of dreaming about musician scouts were long over. I felt a lot like this God-forsaken town on a road map—easy to skip over, easy to forget. That all changed the night I met Travis.

Hello Dolly was playing that summer, a production being put on by the Stage Door Players. I'd played the piano for some of their musicals in the past, but not that year. It was the first time I'd seen Travis since he graduated. When our eyes met, we instantly knew the one thing about each other—the only thing—that mattered. I wanted so badly for him to come and speak to me during the intermission, but I'm glad he didn't. I was a nervous wreck, smoking half a pack of cigarettes during that fifteen-minute break. It was a bad habit I'd later give up just for him.

Somehow, I worked up enough nerve to wait for him in the back of the theater after the show. Not knowing what to say, I pretended to know him from high school and asked what year he graduated. Only I wasn't pretending. I did know him, and somehow I just knew to reach out to him that night. It was my one chance to finally connect with someone like me. Travis was glad I spoke up. We went for coffee after the show, nervously sitting across from one another like we were on a blind date. We spent almost every weekend together for the next few months. I took off from work early on Fridays if I had the weekend off and drove down to Memphis to stay with him. Six months later I was living with him.

I don't think I would have cared if neither of us ever went back to Ruby Dregs, but Travis's family was what kept drawing us back. My family was what kept me away. It's funny how that was the one thing that was opposite between us—besides out last names—growing up in the same town and having so much in common, but hating and loving home for completely different reasons.

So, I went with him and faked my excitement about the trip back to hell. I slept in his twin bed upstairs in his mother's house, but I still felt like a guest. I racked my brain over the thoughts in Lorraine's head and wished I could read her mind. I watched his siblings be just as distant to him as the preps were back in school. And Travis was blind to it all.

I couldn't make up stories and tell him my parents were going to be out of town because it was almost impossible to get to Lorraine's house without driving by my old house. So, Travis made me go see them when we were in town. I didn't always make him go with me, because I knew the thought of him being my boyfriend made my Mom uncomfortable. It was easier to cut the visit short when it was just me, but sometimes I let Travis go if he offered. I wanted Mom to see how happy I was now that I had someone, but even that happiness was hard to muster up in the misery of their presence.

My mom was usually always in a nightgown, which she had probably been wearing for days. Stray rollers were in her matted hair and she wore no make-up. The spacey look in her eyes was a sign her mind was absent. She spoke in a scratchy cigarette voice, another reason I quit smoking. When she was angry, she blamed a God who never listened to her anyway.

My dad was a bumbling whale whose eyebrows were constantly raised in question, causing his eyes to bug out. Scotch tape and super glue held his foggy glasses together because he was too cheap to buy new ones. His clothes were as pale and faded as his skin. He spoke in an effeminate voice like a female impersonator would. I swore I inherited my homosexuality from him, if such a thing could happen.

"You're too hard on your parents," Travis would say.

"You never lived with them," I bit back.

"How hard could it have been? Did they ever hit you?"

"No."

"Did they mistreat you?"

"Not really."

"Then I just don't understand."

"I don't expect you to understand because you grew up in a very different household. You had two loving parents and four brothers and sisters," I said.

"You're parents seem very nice," Travis said.

"Things aren't always what they seem."

"But you just said they weren't bad."

This was the one thing we usually disagreed upon, and one of the few things we ever argued about. I wasn't shutting myself off to him, but the only way for me to end the argument was to just be quiet and stop talking about them. My parents weren't bad people. They were just easy to blame for my miserable lonely existence from which Travis had saved me. I just couldn't bring myself to say that out loud to him without sounding like a sap.

The ten years we spent together were like playing catch up

with life. I experienced more joy and happiness during that time then I ever did growing up. I was like a kid all over again, out shopping with Travis in the malls or going to bars and restaurants. Every day there was something new in the city that our hometown could not offer.

And living with the first love of your life, waking up to him every day, being the center of his attention and he being the center of mine was better than any big-time Las Vegas dream of stardom. It just didn't last long enough. The cancer got in the way. It slapped us both in the face and made us slow down. It made us number our days and cherish all the memories we created together, because we both knew there wouldn't be any more.

All the trips to the hospital, the hours spent crouched over the toilet in the middle of the night during the chemo, the Frankenstein monster in the mirror, and the soiled bed sheets were not the days Travis would choose to remember.

They didn't exist.

I might as well have been a ten-year-old because all the days I spent in Ruby Dregs before meeting Travis and all the days I spent at the end of life battling cancer didn't exist. We both erased them from our heads, and so all that was left was the time we had together.

It was all that mattered.

Travis

I was sitting across from Martin at the dinner table when there was a knock at the door. With a mouthful of food, he swallowed hard with a painful expression as if the guest at the door was someone he knew, someone unwanted. Mom was accustomed to guests stopping by during the holiday months. They were usually members of her church or a friendly neighbor. The stack of store-bought fruitcakes in her pantry was a testimony to the number of guests she had already had this season.

Mom hated fruitcake. I don't think I had ever tasted it. As a traditional joke, she would unwrap one and slice it, then set it out on a decorative plate amongst the rest of the food just to see if anyone ate it. I think Robbie or Daniel ate a slice last year, having mistaken it for brownies or banana bread. They spit it into a napkin and never touched it again after that.

Fruitcakes were not the only neighborly gift that Mom ended up with duplicates of. For years, Mom had collected those doll-like angel tree toppers with satin or velvet gowns draped over a plastic or cardboard cone. One of us kids usually gave her one each year for Christmas, and she enjoyed displaying them throughout the house year after year on the hall table and the mantel. As the collection grew, she decided to leave them out all year and just move them into her sewing room until Christmas came around again.

After hosting a luncheon at the house for some church ladies one summer, Mom's fondness for the angel dolls quickly spread. The fruitcake count went down, and the doll collection mounted. Although Mom never frowned at any gift given to her, she was not always proud of the angels other acquaintances gave to her. Mom preferred the pricier angels with curly hair and real porcelain hands and face. What she got most of the time from the people who didn't know her quite well was a cheap knock-off you could find on the bargain aisle of any dollar store. These gifts quickly became known as the ugly angel collection.

Mom accepted these unsightly angels with a pleased look in her eyes and a smile on her face, but knew the angel would end up on display in her sewing room during the holidays. Only the more extravagant angels were brought out of the sewing room to be put on display through the main part of the house from after Thanksgiving to New Years. After the holidays, the ugly angel collection was packed away in the attic and the sewing room became the hibernation place for the ones she preferred to look at. But, year after year Mom dragged all the ugly angels back out again.

"What if someone who gave me one of them in the past stops by?" she'd say if you asked her why she put the unattractive ones back out at all.

Leave it to Mom to not take the chance of hurting anyone's feelings. She knew exactly who gave her each one. With a black marker, she would write the person's name and the year on the inside of the cone underneath the angel's garment on both the ugly and the pretty ones. Throughout the year, the door to her sewing room was usually kept open. During the holidays when the "good" angels had been moved out and the ugly angels moved in, that door stayed closed unless company came calling.

Mom had just sat down to eat when the knock at the door came. I stood up and offered to get the door for her. She stood too but I put my hands on her shoulders, gently pushing her back down into her seat. She sat back down to appease me.

"I'll get it, Mom, don't worry," I said.

"Will you open the door to the sewing room, dear?" she asked.

The knock came again. I unlatched the lock and opened the door to find a stout, bulky man in crisp blue overalls with a Kelly-green shirt underneath. His ears were bright pink from the cold weather, along with his fat round cheeks. His crew-cut hair was as white as the snow. He nodded and a dentured smile grew across his face when I appeared from behind the door.

"Hello," I said puzzled, thinking he must have been a deacon from the church, but he was dressed more like a farmer.

"Hello there. You must be Travis," he said with a deep booming voice like the bass singer in a choir. I found his tone oddly comforting.

"I'm sorry. You are?"

"Calvin. Calvin Baiter."

We shook hands. His handshake was warm and firm, and a bit greasy as if he had just put on lotion. I thought he might have come to drop off a gift for Mom, another fruitcake, but there were two large handle bags at his feet filled with wrapped boxes.

"I hope I'm not too late. I had some last-minute wrapping to do," Calvin said, looking down at the bags.

I was confused. Mom appeared over my shoulder.

"Travis, you've met Calvin. Hello dear, come inside out of the cold. Travis, will you get those bags for Calvin, please?"

"Hi Lorraine. I can manage these just fine," he said.

He lifted the bags and stepped inside the door, banging the snow from his boots on the threshold. I stepped aside as he entered, shutting the door behind him.

"Merry Christmas, dear," Calvin said taking off his coat

and kissing my Mom on the cheek, right there in front of me.

He hung his coat on the rack behind the door as if he'd been here before. Mom and Calvin ignored the stunned look on my face as she took him by the arm and led him into the dining room. I picked up his two bags of gifts and moved them over by the tree.

When I entered the dining room, Mom was fixing Calvin a plate. Sebastian and Martin stood to shake Calvin's hand like he was an old friend. I walked over to Mom and touched her hand. She looked at me, and I raised my eyebrows in question.

"Calvin and I met at church a while back," she said in a whisper as if that explained it all.

Mom served Calvin his plate of food as he sat down next to her place at the table. I sat back down too and aimlessly listened to Martin, and Sebastian laughing and talking with Calvin the way they once did with Dad. I watched Mom gazing at Calvin with that look in her eyes. She was in love, and she had failed to tell me. Even Ellen and Clare had got up to hug Calvin's neck like he was a favorite uncle. I was now a strange in-law in the room that no one likes to talk to.

I was lost.

I remained quiet through the rest of the meal. Mom asked everyone if they'd like to eat dessert in the living room before opening gifts. Calvin asked if it would be alright to light the fireplace, something Dad had always done right after dinner. Everything about him seemed so familiar, even rehearsed like a joke this strange man and my mother had planned out. I must have been the only one aware because everyone else acted as though they'd known this man for a long time and that his nice demeanor was quite usual.

Mom plated pie for us and loaded the kids up with cookies and brownies. They disappeared into the den to watch Calvin light the fire. I started clearing the table although Mom told me to just leave it for later. I had soon filled the trash can with our paper plates and cups. My intentions were to take out the trash, an excuse to step out of the house for a moment and get my thoughts together.

I stood at the edge of the house staring off into the darkening sky. The lazy sun had already disappeared behind the grove. I spotted Mom's cat hunting something out under the trees. He crouched low ready to pounce, a black shadow against the snow-covered ground. The air was cold and still. It was so quiet I could hear the squeal of a field mouse as the cat leapt upon it and pinned it down. The cat carried the poor vermin down the hill and disappeared into the woods.

I wanted to follow it and become lost in the woods myself. It was easy to do back when we were kids. Our imaginations transformed us to distant worlds every summer, far away from the confines of home. Too bad it was only pretend and couldn't work now for me. Once again, I felt like a complete stranger amongst my own family. I doubt they were even missing me now back inside. The screen door creaking open and knocking back against its frame several times, finally coming to a rest, broke my far-off gaze. Someone had stepped outside. I looked over my shoulder to see Ellen standing there.

"Mom didn't tell you she was seeing someone, did she?" Ellen asked.

With the sun now completely gone, she was a blurry haze of clothes in the distance with a ball of foggy white growing in front of her each time she breathed out.

"No, it appears I'm the last one to know."

"Shocked?"

"Yeah. Just a little."

"We were too at first, but Calvin's a nice guy. She really likes him. They met at church. His wife died a few years ago."

"Why couldn't she tell me all this? Why couldn't you? Why couldn't anyone?"

"I guess she forgot or we just assumed she had told you," Ellen said with a shrug.

"She forgot? She talks to me almost every other day on the phone. How long have they been seeing each other?"

"A couple of months now, I think."

I shook my head in disgust. I was so disappointed. There had been so many boring days in my apartment in Memphis cured by the simple ring of the telephone. When Mom called, I always had something to say. I liked to think we confided in one another. There was constantly something to talk about, even if I'd stayed in bed all day. She kept me up to date on my siblings and how everyone was. I would ask how she was doing after she got done talking about the family.

She had gone for a walk with Martin that morning, or skipped the walk to do the crossword in the newspaper. She went grocery shopping and ran into someone I went to high school with; they asked her how I was doing. Canned vegetables were on sale so she bought extra. Someone died or someone got married. I knew everything that went on in her daily life, or at least I thought I did. I realized our days are often filled with meaningless activities, and so we fill our conversations with meaningless words, but a conversation with Mom—no matter how insignificant—was never empty or worthless. She clung to every word we said. She was our audience, my audience.

I searched the black sky for a twinkling star like I had lost everything. Ellen came up behind me and wrapped an arm around my waist. Her hand on my chest was nice as she squeezed me close for a warm, consoling hug. My heart was still breaking, frail from the unclear punishment of my Mom keeping her happiness from me.

Had she not wanted me to know? Was she afraid of my reaction? My thoughts should have been the least of her worries since I did not live here, and she did not have to face me immediately. Maybe she just didn't want to tell me over the telephone. If so, then why had she not told me at all before Calvin arrived? Surely she knew he was coming over. Why leave the news to be born as a sudden surprise like this?

"Ellen? Travis? Are you out there?" Mom's voice called from the back porch.

"We were just taking out the garbage," I yelled.

"Hurry in. The kids are anxious to start opening gifts," she said closing the door.

I didn't move. Ellen let go.

"Are you going to be okay?" Ellen asked.

"Yeah. Yeah, I'll be fine." I still didn't move.

"Are you coming in?"

I turned and took her hand in mine and we walked back up onto the porch and into the kitchen.

As I entered the den, the heat from the fireplace chased the outdoor chills from my face. Robbie, Rachel, Daniel, and Nicole were all seated by the tree and giddy with excitement. Mom was leaning behind the tree digging through the gifts to start passing them out. She handed one to each of the kids to let them go first. Ellen sat on the sofa next to Clare and Sebastian. Martin and Marline were sitting on the hearth. Calvin was in Dad's old chair. I leaned against the doorway, still keeping my distance from everyone while Mom sorted gifts.

"Your Mom tells me you live in Memphis," Calvin said turning the recliner around to look up at me.

"Yes sir, I moved there right after high school to go to college," I answered nervously without looking back at him.

I was trying to sound polite.

"Bet there's lots of pretty girls down that way," Calvin said with a little laugh.

"I guess so."

"You should take your brother, Sebastian, with you and you two boys could double date. You'd like Travis to introduce you to them pretty Memphis women, wouldn't you?" he asked Sebastian jokingly.

Sebastian grinned and agreed with a nod, not really paying attention to the nonsense Calvin was speaking.

"I don't date women," I said unsympathetically.

"I beg your pardon," Calvin said, looking at me again.

"I said I don't date women."

"Oh son, I bet you got a whole black book full of pretty ladies' phone numbers, don't ya?"

"Calvin, why don't you pass out the gifts you brought?" Mom said, interrupting him.

"I'm gay," I said.

"What?" Calvin asked.

"Gay!"

"What?" he asked, again louder.

"I said I'm gay. I'm a homosexual. I don't like women. I like men. Men! I sleep with men." I had started to yell.

"Travis!" Mom yelled.

Martin and Ellen called out my name too.

"What? I don't understand," Calvin said again, looking at my Mom for an answer.

"I suck cock. I take it up the ass. I'm gay. I said I'm gay."

"Travis! Watch your mouth in front of the kids!" Mom shouted, coming towards me, but I was already walking out the front door.

"Mom! Stop!" Ellen called out.

Ellen followed me outside, putting a hand up to keep Mom inside. I was digging in my pocket for my keys, almost to my car. Ellen grabbed my shoulder.

"Don't go," she said.

"I can't do this, Ellen. Mom doesn't have the nerve to tell me she's dating someone, and she obviously can't bring herself to tell her boyfriend that she has a gay son either. I can't do this."

I shook her hand from my arm and opened the car door to get inside. She tried to hold the door open so I couldn't close it, but it slipped from her hand. Sebastian had come outside and was standing on the front lawn watching. I started the car and Ellen raced to the passenger's side to try to get in but the door was locked. Luckily, Clare had left enough room between my car and hers. I was able to maneuver the car sideways to turn around. I pulled my car into part of the yard adjacent to the driveway, knocking over a plastic lit snowman. I drove past everyone else's vehicles and onto the road, leaving Ellen and Sebastian standing in the yard. I spotted Mom on the porch crying on Martin's shoulder.

My own tears were now pouring down my face. I felt betrayed, not only by Mom, but by the whole family. I was too angry and confused to drive the hour and a half trip back to my apartment, but I didn't know where else to go. I drove past the cemetery expecting to somehow find the gate still open in my favor so I could visit Justin's grave, but the gate was closed. There was a sign on the fence that said the cemetery would be open tomorrow, Christmas Day.

The part of the city of Ruby Dregs where all the restaurants and commerce lie is to the north of old downtown, separated by an expansion of expensive brick homes, the high school, the community college, and the public park. It is a long stretch of highway with the shopping mall on one end, and the park on the other. For years, teenagers have driven the strip on Friday nights, circling the mall, riding down the road to the park, and either circling back again or congregating in the community pool parking lot. It's a shame small-town kids have nothing better to do than waste gas, but if there were other things to do besides go to the three-screen movie theater, who's to say they wouldn't still be bored with their simple lives?

Passing the public pool heading north, not a single car was parked there tonight and the strip was practically empty. Families and friends took traditional cues from holiday greeting cards and gathered at relatives' homes or at parties, where I should be right now instead. Young kids were already nestling into bed, unable to sleep with the anxiety that Santa was coming tonight.

I spotted a plane in the air. Its blinking red light way up above took me back to my own days of Santa Claus. Our grandparents would offer to take the five kids out looking at Christmas lights after dinner. Mom and Dad were supposedly in the car behind us following along. Grandmother would point out a blinking red light in the sky and tell us it was Rudolph the Red Nosed Reindeer. It's funny how the magic of a child's Christmas was built on little white lies.

Mom and Dad magically beat us back home and waited on the front porch for us to drive up, knowing we wanted to race inside to see if Santa had come. Boot tracks of snow were still fresh on the carpet. The cookies had been eaten; the milk glass was empty. And an array of toys and wrapped gifts, ones that had not been there when we left, were now nestled by the tree.

White lies. The thought of it made me laugh. The White Family lies. I didn't know what was worse, lying about something or not saying anything at all. No lies had been told about Calvin, but Mom's silence was as bad as a fib. At least, it was to me now.

I pulled into a gas station that was lit up like a casino. Sitting in my car at the pump, I waited a few seconds looking for an attendant to move around on the inside. I wanted to make sure they were open. Not seeing anyone, I got out of the car and walked up to the entrance. With hesitation, I pulled on the door expecting it to be locked but it opened. A curly-headed lady chewing gum stood up from her stool behind the counter. She was watching a black and white Christmas movie on a small ten-inch screen.

"Hey ya'll," she said, vaguely looking in my direction.

I turned to see if someone was coming in behind me who I had not spotted when I was outside, but there was no one.

"Hi. Just came in to see if you were open."

"Yep. Twenty-four, seven, three sixty-five," she said, signifying they were always open.

"You traveling through?" she asked, smacking her gum.

"I guess you could say that. Do you have any coffee?"

"Sure don't. Not too busy tonight, so I didn't make any. I didn't want it to sit and go stale. If you wanna wait, I'll make a pot."

"That's okay. I'll just fill up and be on my way. Can I use your restroom?"

She pointed to a door in the back corner. It whined on its heavy hinges as I pulled it open. It was dark inside, so I flipped on the light and expected to see the horror that is a public gas station toilet. Surprisingly, this one was as clean as my own and smelled of lemons. The floor shined from a nice wax job and there was no writing on the walls.

I didn't need to use the restroom. I just felt the need to splash some cool water on my face. The sink had cold and hot water, and both worked. There was one of those public restroom vending machines on the wall next to the mirror. I gazed at its contents: cough drops, aspirin, cheap cologne, and condoms. The advertisements for each were crude drawings of a stick man coughing or holding his head, except for the condoms. A bright-colored, scantily clad pinup girl stood above the crank to buy those. She towered over the stick men like a giant.

As a teenager I had always been intrigued by the tiny boxes these condoms came in. It was like those quarter machines outside the grocery store for gum or small toys, only for grown-ups. I dug in my pocket for two quarters to buy one now. I had not bought anything like this in years. Justin and I never practiced safe sex. We had an unopened box of condoms from the pharmacy in the nightstand that remained there for the whole ten years we were together.

I turned the crank and a tiny matchbox-size pack slid out into the tray at the bottom of the machine. I picked it up and admired the same pin upgirl on the machine also printed on the little box. I undid the flap at the top and checked inside to find the pinkish balloon rolled up and sealed in a small plastic bag. I closed the flap and tucked the box into my pocket. I don't know what kind of protection I thought it could give me now.

"If you got time, I know where you can go and get a nice cup of coffee, maybe a piece of pecan pie too," the woman said when I returned to the front counter.

"Lady, I got all night."

"Name's Peggy."

"I'm Travis."

"Hi, Travis. You know where Cozy's is?"

"I don't think so."

"It's downtown. Take the strip to the courthouse and it's on the south side, opposite the veteran's memorial. I can write it down for you if you want," she said, grabbing a pen and a napkin.

"I think I can find it. You sure they are open tonight?"

"Twenty-four, seven…"

"Three sixty-five," I finished.

"You got it!"

"Thanks for telling me. Merry Christmas, Peggy," I said, paying for the gas.

"Same to you, Travis, and you be careful out there. If you see Ricky down at Cozy's, tell him Peggy sent ya."

"I'll do that."

I pumped the gas and then drove downtown. All of the shops along the perimeter of the square were lit with strands of white lights bordering all of the windows. Cozy's was easy to find, as it was the only business lit up on the inside. A blue neon sign blinked OPEN in the window. A strand of large colored bulbs—red, orange, green, and blue—blinked around the door. There were two other cars and a truck parked in the front. I pulled in next to them and went inside. The clang of a cow bell announced my arrival. It reminded me of the bell Mr. Greer had hanging on the door at the grocery.

A large-bosomed lady was crocheting in one of the booths. She never looked up from her work, and seemed to be talking or singing to herself. An old man on a barstool at the counter feebly turned his stool to look at me. He was as skinny as a walking stick and raised his hand for a slow painful-like wave when I came in the door. His tobacco-stained grin was unusually reassuring.

A clean young man behind the counter gave a nod. He was skinny and pale with fire-red short hair peeking out from under a trucker's ball cap. He had a soul patch of hair down his pointy dimpled chin, and large almond-brown eyes. I had always had a strange attraction toward red heads.

"Sit anywhere you want to. I'll be right with ya," he said in a deep Southern twang, with a smile from ear to ear as if I had saved him from the misery of his geriatric customers.

Cozy's was a daisy yellow room with checkered picnic tablecloths and silk holly branches in fruit jars on the table next to disposable salt and pepper shakers. Faded newspaper clippings were framed on the walls next to copies of old menus signed by politicians and celebrities who had passed through over the years. Black and white photos of the courthouse and the days of horse drawn wagons and dirt roads hung haphazardly over each booth. The guy behind the counter brought a cup of coffee to me with a menu. I noticed the nametag on his bleached white apron said Tate.

"Cook's gone home to play Santa, but should be back in about fifteen if you want something from the kitchen."

"Coffee should be fine for now. Can I have some cream and sugar?"

"Sure," he said stepping behind the counter again. He filled a small pitcher with cream and brought it back to the table with a set of silverware and a bowl of packets of sugar and sweetener.

"Thanks," I said clearing my throat.

"How 'bout a piece of pie?"

"What kind do you have?"

"Pecan, cherry, apple, pumpkin, chess, chocolate, coconut, and banana cream," he recited. "Pecan is the best. My mom makes it."

"Pecan it is, then. Can you warm it up?"

"No problem. How 'bout a scoop of vanilla ice cream on the side or some whipped cream?"

"Ice cream sounds good right on the top so it melts."

"Coming right up. I eat mine the same way," he said with a wink.

Behind the counter again, he cut a slice from the pie chest and popped it into the microwave for thirty seconds, then dolloped it with a scoop of ice cream.

"Is that Ricky?" I asked in a whisper, pointing to the old

man propped on the counter, when Tate returned with my pie.

"I'm Ricky," the young man said.

I took a second look at his nametag. He followed my eyes.

"Ricky Tatum. Friends and family always call me Tate," he explained. "Who are you?"

"Travis White," I said, sounding like some sort of trespasser.

"Nice to meet you, Travis. How did you know my name?"

"Peggy sent me," I said, more like a question as if it were some type of secret password.

He laughed.

"You know who Peggy is?" I asked. "From the gas station?"

"She's my mom," he said.

"Too bad both of you have to work tonight."

"Nah, we don't mind. We'll spend Christmas together tomorrow. It's just me and her anyways."

"You live at home?"

"Hell no! She'd drive me crazy. I have an apartment above the men's store next door. Mama's got a house over on Hillcrest."

I liked the way he said hill; he drew it out and it sounded like *he-el*. I liked the lazy drawl of people in town. No one in my family had it, so I swore up and down we were northern transplants. Mom said we were all born and raised right here though, her and Dad both. She blamed the thick-tongued accents of locals on the lack of education. I blamed our lack of the sound on too much education.

"My sister has an apartment here on the square somewhere," I said for no reason at all but to prolong the conversation with Ricky Tatum.

I found myself attracted to his friendly demeanor and would have invited him to sit down if he wasn't working.

"What's your sister's name?" Tate asked.

"Clare."

"She got a baby. Jake. Yeah, I know Clare. Her apartment

is down on the corner. She works here part time."

"She does?"

"Yep. She's worked here a long time."

"I never knew that." I knew that Clare worked in a diner, but had no idea it was this one. "How long have you worked here, Tate?"

"All my life. Worked in that kitchen back there and as a bus boy since I was fifteen. Moved up front during my junior year of high school."

"Where did you go to high school?" This was my way of hopefully finding out how old Tate was.

"Ruby Dregs, of course. Class of 1998. What about you?"

"Class of 1993." I could see him doing the math in his head. "I'm 35," I said.

"Seems weird, don't it? That means you was born in '76. I's born in 1980. I was four years behind you all through school 'n stuff, but after that out in the real world everybody's equal. Age don't matter no more. Nothing really don't."

I liked what Tate had to say. Nothing really did matter. The lines were drawn by what grade you were in and how tall you were. Schoolyard teams were divided by how good you were at playing sports. You rode the bus or drove the car your parents bought you. You were a jock or a prep. You were college bound or destined to be a high school dropout. After you threw your mortar board and tassel in the air, it was all down *he-el* from there. You had to go to college or struggle to find a job. No matter how you earned your living, it was time to start learning the lessons they couldn't teach you in school.

"Tate, can I get my check, please?" the old man at the counter groaned.

"Leaving already, Mr. Griffin?" Tate called out. "He's been here since three this afternoon. I'll be right back," he turned and said to me.

Tate tended to her then handed Mr. Griffin a handwritten tab. Mr. Griffin didn't look at it. He put two twenty-dollar bills on the counter, and told Tate to keep the change. Then, he looked over at me and nodded and said Merry Christmas. I said the same back with a cordial smile and watched him walk out into the snow. The cowbell gave a clang when the door closed behind him. It woke the napping knitting lady. She shook awake and asked Tate for a last cup of coffee and her check.

Tate took Mr. Griffin's plate and cup to the kitchen and wiped the counter with a damp rag. He rang up the sale on the old manual cash register, making change for his tip, which he tucked in his apron. The old cash register's bell and the slam of the till drawer was so loud it drowned out the carol playing on the radio somewhere in the background. The phone rang. It was the cook. Tate told him Mr. Griffin just left and that there was no one here.

The fat lady heaved herself out of her booth after finishing off her coffee. She gathered up her yarn and things and threw them into a bright-pink shoulder bag. Leaving her money and ticket on the counter while Tate was on the phone, I watched her walk out the door. The beam from the headlights of her car glared off the front windows of the diner and then faded as she pulled away.

"Looks like it's just you and me," Tate said hanging up the phone.

"I should go if I'm keeping you."

"My shift don't end till six in the morning," he said pointing to the clock on the wall. There was still about three hours left to Christmas Eve.

"Who owns this place?" I asked with curiosity.

"Peggy," Tate answered.

"Your Mom? And she won't even close this place for Christmas Eve?"

"Nah. Where else would Mr. Griffin go? He's in here almost every other day, but been coming in on Christmas Eve for well over twenty years. Spends less than ten bucks each time, but leaves a thirty-dollar tip."

"And you accept it?"

"He'd be offended if I don't. Ask your sister sometime

about ole Griffin. Sometimes she gets thirty-five."

"He has no family?"

"Not a one. Neither does Ms. Rose who just left. Never married. No kids. I always wonder who she's knitting for. She'll be back in here tomorrow."

"So, Cozy's is the refuge for the lonely and desolate, the *dregs*, who are just trying to get through the holidays, huh?"

"Is that why you're here?" Tate asked.

I swallowed the sip of coffee I had just taken. It stung my throat like the truth. I paused and looked down at my ice cream pooling in the saucer around the brown nutty pie, a sweet glazed mess of holiday confusion that I was going to eat anyway.

"Indeed it is," I answered.

Sebastian

I parked across the court square, opposite the Cozy Kitchen and turned off my headlights. After Travis rushed off from Mom's, I stuck around for about an hour and then said my good-byes.

"Where ya headed, bro?" Martin asked.

"Oh, just back to my place. Me and a buddy are gonna hang out."

Martin just looked at me. I knew that look too. Inside his head, he was asking what I was really going to do. I saved him the breath from having to ask out loud.

"You don't have to worry. We're probably just gonna share a bottle of wine at my place. Nothing else," I told him.

He nodded and smiled with satisfaction, giving me a pat on the shoulder.

"Merry Christmas, man. I love ya," he said.

"You too."

I kissed Mom on the cheek, told her I loved her and that I'd see her tomorrow. After saying my good-byes and giving hugs to everyone else, I pulled out of the drive and headed back to my place. Oh the way, I thought about Travis and couldn't really understand what the big deal was. So what if Mom hadn't told him about Calvin, or that she hadn't told Calvin about him. I doubt she'd told Calvin about my problems, or anyone else's in the family for that matter. Hell, if those were the first things out of her mouth, she'd probably never find a man who wanted to keep seeing her. I was just happy she'd found someone. My Mom was a good lady and she didn't deserve to be alone.

Yeah, I have to admit it felt strange at first seeing her with someone who wasn't Dad, but I was cool with it. I was happy for her, and Mom deserved happiness. Dad would have wanted her to be happy too.

Mom and Dad both had spent so much of their time worrying about us kids, and rightfully so. We all gave them plenty to worry about. Now that we were coming out of those phases in life and finally getting our shit together, it was our time to worry about Mom and her well-being. Sure, we didn't have to fret about her roaming the streets or doing drugs, unlike her kids—unlike me who'd fucked up as a rebellious teen. But more than anything, I didn't want to have to worry about Mom being unhappy or alone. As long as Calvin was good to her and gave her happiness, that was all that mattered.

I had not intended on following Travis, but it was sort of fun. It reminded me of when we played hide-and-go-seek out behind the house as kids and I used to climb up in the loft of the barn and peek out and my siblings running around looking for me. It was like eavesdropping on a pretty girl at the bar while working. She'd be at a table with her friends and I'd watch her just long enough for her to feel the weight of my eyes on her. I'd look away before she caught me. The intensity caused by getting caught at anything—good or bad—had always been a rush for me.

It was Christmas Eve and there weren't a lot of cars on the road, so I figured he'd be easy to find. I knew him well enough to know he wouldn't go back to Memphis without going to Justin's grave first, so I drove passed the cemetery. It was locked, so I drove on into downtown to cruise the strip. That's when I saw him filling up at the gas station. I pulled into a parking lot across the highway, watching and waiting.

Through the windows, I could see him going to the restroom. After a few minutes of talking to the attendant, he walked out and got in his car and headed for the court square. He parked outside Cozy Kitchen and went inside. He didn't ramble around or circle the square a few times as if searching for something to do, some place to go. It was as if someone had told him Cozy's would be open. He drove right to it.

I almost went inside, but decided against it. First, I didn't want it to look like I'd followed him. Second, I didn't want to sit down and either have an argument or some heart to heart with my gay brother. Sure, I loved Travis and he'd been good to me when I needed him. He'd helped me out when all the shit with Lind went down, but all that was over now. I'd gotten my life back on track, and he knew I appreciated what he'd done for me.

There was another reason why I didn't want to go inside, but Travis didn't know about that. No one in my family did, and I wasn't about to tell them.

Travis was inside for at least a good thirty minutes. At one point, his was the only car still parked outside. I saw Mr. Griffin waddle out, then some old lady came out and drove away. I was about to just go to my apartment and forget about this, but curiosity got the best of me. I stayed there, across the court square and waited.

Travis finally came out, got in his car and drove away. I wanted to follow him but half-expected him to just head back to Mom's. Instead, I started my car and drove around the block and parked in front of Cozy's. Clare had been working here for a while. I came in to see her once but she wasn't here. I'd sat down to eat a burger and that's how I met Tate. We'd become pretty good friends over time, and for some reason, I'd managed to keep it from Clare. Tate was kind of feminine, not someone I'd usually hang around. I knew Clare, of all my siblings, wouldn't care who I hung around, but I still liked keeping Tate a secret. As far as I knew, Tate didn't even know Clare and I were related.

"Hey there," I said as I came inside, the bell jangling on the door as it closed behind me.

"Hey man, what's up?" Tate said, coming over and giving me a high-five.

"Just left my Mom's house. Thought I'd stop by and see if you still wanted to hang out after you got off work."

"Sure. Things are pretty quiet here right now. I don't expect them to pick up."

"You think you might be able to leave early?"

"I'm sure I can work something out once the cook comes back."

"Who was that guy that just left?" I asked just because I wanted to see what Tate would say.

"Some guy named Travis. He's from here but lives in Memphis. In town visiting his family. Seemed a bit upset, but didn't really say much."

Tate walked over to a booth and picked up a plate and cup, pocketing a tip that lay on the table probably from Travis. He put them in the sink behind the counter. When he turned around, I was right behind him.

"Shit, man, you scared me. What are you doing?" he asked looking up at me. I was at least a foot taller than him.

I was nervous as I put my hands on his hips and pulled him closer to me. He let me. I hesitated as I looked into his eyes. He just smiled and blinked. Then, I planted my lips hard against his. He opened his mouth to reciprocate. Just as he was about to slip me his tongue, I broke away.

"What was that?" he asked with a huge smile.

"Nothing. Just wanted to kiss you."

"I liked it."

I turned and walked away and sat in one of the booths. Tate followed and sat down opposite me. He reached across the table and tried to take my hand but I wouldn't let him. I pulled them away and put them in my lap.

I didn't consider myself to be gay, and would probably never label myself as that either. I didn't even want to say I was bisexual. With Tate I just felt different on the inside. It was almost the way I'd felt with Lind.

I'd loved her.

I never would have guessed I'd feel that way toward a guy, the way Travis felt toward Justin, I guess. Up until now, I'd been holding back. I wanted to tell Tate how I felt, and I had an inkling he was attracted to me too.

I contemplated what I had just done and decided it was okay. It just felt right.

"Merry Christmas," I said with a nod, and I put my hand back on the table with my palm up. I waved my fingers, indicating for him to give me his hand.

"You just gave me the best gift ever," Tate said, putting his hand in mine.

Ellen

"I feel like this is my fault," Calvin said to me outside.

Mom and Sebastian had gone back inside shortly after Travis left. I picked up the snowman he had knocked over. Its bulb was blown. Then, I just stood there in the yard amongst the nativity and the waving Santa staring down the road as if expecting for Travis to circle back. I stood so still I almost felt like one of the ornaments on the lawn, staring blankly out at the black road cutting through the frosty white, and seeing nothing.

A car driving by slowed down to look at Mom's light display. The passenger, a young girl I recognized from Rachel's class, waved at me. I waved back, then crossed my arms to keep warm. Calvin came outside. He said the tension in the house was still pretty thick. Mom wouldn't stop crying, and he felt he was to blame.

"It's not your fault. Travis has been different ever since Justin died. Justin was his partner. They were together for about ten years. I just don't know why Mom didn't tell him about you," I said.

"She tried to tell him, but he wouldn't listen," Calvin

explained.

"What?"

"One night about a week ago, he had called while I was here. Your Mom and I were watching television. She'd got up to go to the bathroom and the phone rang. She called out for me to go ahead and answer it, so I did. It was Travis. He didn't ask who I was, only that he'd hold for Lorraine."

"What did he say?"

"Nothing. I said it would be just a minute. I tried to say hello but he wouldn't talk back, so I laid the phone down."

"Did Mom say anything?"

"She tried, but he interrupted her and said he had to go and he'd call her back the next day."

"If that was just a week ago, he probably didn't call back. I bet they haven't spoken again until today."

"I'm sorry, Ellen. Do you know where he might have gone?"

"No. He doesn't really know anyone here except Justin's parents. He might have gone there, but I doubt it. Maybe he's driving back to Memphis."

"I hope not. I hate that I ruined the holiday for everyone."

"It's not ruined. Don't worry about it," I said patting him on the shoulder.

"You knew he was—," Calvin paused, searching for the right word.

"Gay? Yeah, we all knew."

"When did he tell you?"

"Right at the end of his senior year of high school, I think."

"And you were okay with it—*are* okay with it?"

"Yeah, but I've been exposed to a lot more than Mom has, so it didn't bother me as much."

The truth was Travis had told Mom way before any of us knew. She had refused to accept it, and forbidden him to talk about it. She didn't want anyone else in the family to know. She must have been too overwhelmed with the pain, and with blaming herself, so she eventually told me. To be fair, I took

Travis to lunch one weekend while he was in town and I told him that I knew. He asked how, and so I told him Mom had told me. She needed someone to talk to about it, so she came to me.

Travis was relieved that she was finally opening up about it. She eventually told Martin, who had no qualms about it at all. Martin told Sebastian and Clare. They both had suspected it all along, and thought it was cool to have a gay brother.

"Don't you worry about him being around your children?" Calvin asked.

"Who? Travis? No, he's their uncle. He's gay, Calvin. He's not a pedophile. He'd never harm the kids."

"What about those things he said inside the house?"

"Well, he was angry and he lost his temper. He didn't mean it, and he'll probably apologize for it later. Besides, I think the kids were too caught up in their gifts to be paying attention to what was being said," I explained.

Calvin was older and set in his ways. I couldn't blame him for not knowing about such things. Mom was the same way. She didn't have email, and refused to learn how to even use a computer. The world was moving faster and faster these days, with or without them. I wondered what Calvin thought of Jake being biracial. If he knew about my marital problems and Sebastian's stint with drugs, he would probably have second thoughts about wanting to see Mom with such a messed-up family.

"Maybe I should go," Calvin said.

"No, you don't have to leave. Let's go back inside and cheer Mom up and try to enjoy what's left of the holiday."

Like Calvin, I believed the holiday was ruined. For the kids' sake, I hoped the rest of the evening was quiet, with or without Travis. I was angry, but at no one in particular and I certainly wasn't mad at Travis. Back inside, Sebastian and Clare were sitting on the sofa with the television on. The sound was turned down really low almost as if they were eavesdropping on Mom. She was in the kitchen, still crying, with Martin. The kids were in the floor, playing with the new toy each of them had opened. Calvin was right about the apprehension. We went into the kitchen.

I hugged Mom. She dried her tears with a damp paper towel. Calvin kept his distance and stood in the doorway like a nervous guest.

"I don't know why I didn't tell him," Mom cracked through sobbing breaths.

"Mom, it's okay. What's done is done," I said.

Martin lovingly scratched her back.

"Do you know where he went?" she asked.

"I don't really know. He might have gone to see the Blacks."

"Maybe. Calvin, are you okay, honey?" Mom asked looking over at him.

"I'm a little rattled, but I'll be alright. Sorry to have upset everybody," he said with a little bit of embarrassment, like a shy child who had just come into a room full of adults.

"Oh, what's a White family Christmas without a little excitement?" Mom managed to say with a laugh.

Martin and I grinned and nodded with agreement. Calvin looked confused.

"So, you aren't mad?" he asked.

"Mad? Why should I be mad? Mad at myself, maybe, because this is really my fault. I should have been more open with both of you."

Inside, I knew Mom's heart was breaking. I don't think there had ever been a peaceful holiday with all the kids together since we were kids. Since then, Martin or I were having Christmas with the in-laws usually. Sebastian and Clare often worked on Christmas Eve. Travis stayed in Memphis to have a quiet holiday with Justin a few years back. Justin was sick during Christmas another year. Then, Mark and I were having troubles.

Mark.

I'd forgotten about calling him. He wasn't expecting me to

call, but it was growing late. I convinced Mom to go ahead and open a few gifts without Travis. Calvin and Martin led her back into the living room where Sebastian and Clare stood up to greet her as if they'd been sitting in a hospital waiting room. The four grandchildren raced to her and surrounded her with hugs, each thanking her for their gift and asking if they could open another.

"Ellen, are you coming?" Mom called out.

"I'll be right there. I'm going to step out and make a phone call real quick."

I put on my coat and stepped out the back door. A blinking glare from the Christmas lights lit the back yard with a yellowed glow. I looked over at the trash can and expected to see Travis still standing there and watching the horizon, as if these last couple of hours had just been a quirky dream. I sat down on a stiff wicker chair on the back porch and dialed the number. The chair creaked with the warmth and weight of a human. It felt wet beneath me. I rubbed my hands along my pants, but they were only cold to the touch, not damp.

"Hello?" Mark said with a bit of harshness.

He must not have looked at the caller ID to see who was calling.

"Mark?"

"Yeah."

"It's me."

"Hey there. Where are you?"

"I'm at Mom's."

"Is everything okay?"

"Yeah, things are fine. How are your parents?"

"Fine. They asked about you."

"That's nice."

This was the point in the conversation where we normally just said I love you and good-bye, or Mark asked what was for dinner. It was one of our typical small talks where I always knew what to say and what he said was very little. Tonight, I was using the small talk to buy time while inside my head, I was rehearsing what I really wanted to say to him.

"Do you think you can get away for a second?" he asked.

"Umm…probably. Is something wrong?" I asked.

My heart started racing.

"No. Nothing's wrong. I'd just like to see you is all," he said, choosing his words slowly.

"Where are you?"

"I came home. I was hoping you might call. If you didn't, I was going to call you later to see if you wanted to come back and help with the kids' gifts."

I was silent, and must have been for too long.

"Ellen? Are you still there?"

"Yeah, I'm here."

"Do you think you can leave for a little while?"

"Sure. I'll be right there."

I hung up the phone and sat there for a moment. It was Christmas Eve; surely he wasn't going to spring bad news on me tonight. Was he seeing someone else? Was he moving out now instead of in January? Did he want to fight me for full custody of the kids? My mind ached with all these questions. I wanted to cry, but knew I needed to hold it back until after I'd gone inside to tell Mom I was leaving for a little while.

"Mom, can you come back to the kitchen for a minute?" I said when I came in the back door.

"Be right there!" She seemed to be in better spirits now. "Are you going to join us to open your gifts? Ellen, honey, what's wrong?" she asked walking into the kitchen.

She rushed over to me and put a hand on my shoulder, concerned with the worried look on my face.

"It's Mark. I called him and he wants to see me," I said, still holding back.

"Right now?"

I told her that he had left his parents' house and gone back home to put out the kids' gifts. I'd called him to tell him I still love him and I didn't want a divorce, but I never got a chance to say any of that. Instead, he asked me to come home and talk to him.

"Are you sure about this?"

"Mom, its Christmas Eve. I don't think he would make me come all the way home tonight just so we could argue. I hope not, at least, but I need to go. Can the kids stay here?"

"Of course, do you have your purse? Go out the back door. Go now, and I'll tell them you ran to the store for me. Call me if you need me."

"Are you alright?"

"I'm okay. I'm worried about Travis, but don't let Mark spoil your Christmas. You get out of there if he wants to argue. I don't want to have to be worrying about you too."

"Thank you, Mom," I said kissing her on the cheek.

I said good-bye and quietly snuck out the back door. I left the lights on the car off until I was able to pull out of the drive and onto the road. Back at home, Mark's truck was in the driveway. I could see the tree lit in the window and the downstairs lights were on. When I opened the door, Mark was lying in the floor putting together an action figure command center for Robbie.

"Hi," he said looking up from his project.

"Hi," I answered in a quick short breath.

"I got all the gifts out of the attic. There are still a few to put together, and Rachel's dollhouse. I thought you might want to help arrange everything around the tree," he said, filling the air with nervous words.

I was nervous too, but I didn't know why. I took off my coat and sat my purse down at the bottom of the stairs. I walked over and sat down in the floor next to Mark to admire his work.

"So, this is what Robbie wanted so badly?"

"Yep, it's pretty cool. Wish I had one when I was his age. All of these lights really work, and if he pushes these buttons it makes sounds. Here's the control center, here's the arsenal. There's even a little jail where he can lock up the bad guys," Mark explained, while pointing out all the features with just as much excitement in his eyes as Robbie would have when he saw it in the morning.

"Where are all the little men we bought?" I asked.

"In that bag on the sofa. Want to grab them and we can set them up? I'm done with the command center."

I took the bag and emptied its contents onto the floor. There must have been at least twenty or thirty different action figures. I tore them from their plastic and cardboard packaging and put them all in a pile. Each came with a little gun or accessory. Mark took those and hung them in the command center on tiny hooks and clips to stock the miniature arsenal.

"These will all be lost in a few days," Mark said holding up a tiny pistol.

"Yep. And these must be the bad guys," I said holding up a boy and a girl action figure.

They were dressed in punk rocker clothes. The boy had bright orange hair, and the girl had pink hair. Their sleeveless shirts revealed arms filled with tattoos. Their little plastic cheeks had scars.

"I want to be him," Mark said taking the male figure from me and examining him up closely.

He scrunched his eyebrows at the little man's tattoos.

"I guess I'll be her," I said. "What now?"

"Well, we have the command center all to ourselves."

"Great. Let's order a pizza," I said in my play voice, which I used when playing dolls with Rachel.

I somehow doubted this chick figurine sounded like that.

"There are twin beds in the holding cell," Mark said in his playful voice, walking his figurine through the roofless halls of the center.

"These beds are too hard," I said.

I reached down and tapped one of the hard molded plastic beds. The sheets and pillow were painted on in the dull gray, which was the same color as the walls and the floor of the giant toy, far from the soft, elaborate setup of Rachel's doll house. But then again, I don't think boys were worried about the sleeping conditions of the action figures they locked up as prisoners.

"Okay, Goldilocks, the three little bears don't live here," Mark joked. "How 'bout a kiss?" he asked, walking his figurine up to mine.

"Fresh!" I teased.

With the magic of pretend and a little human intervention, I held my figurine up above the command center in midair as if she were flying. Mark held his up too, extending the stiff arms for a hug. Our little figures met in the sky above the command center and kissed, their hard plastic faces barely touching. It was sweet.

"You do know these two are brother and sister, don't you?"

"Oh no, we're perverts," I said pulling her away and laying her down on the bed in the prison. "They should be locked away."

I started sitting the other figurines up in various parts of the command center, sitting in chairs and standing at the control panels. They were frozen in position, waiting for Robbie's much healthier imagination to bring them to life. Mark watched with his knees pulled up to his chest. He was still a kid at heart, and I knew he couldn't wait to see the look in Robbie's eyes when he saw his new toys. I caught him watching me.

"What? Am I putting them in the wrong places?"

"No, you're doing great. I was just...watching."

"Stop it! You are making me nervous."

"When's the last time I told you how beautiful you were?" he asked.

I froze like one of the action figures, thinking about what he just said. It was not a question he would want me to answer truthfully.

"I dunno," I said like a silly blonde school-girl.

I felt like he should be admiring my breasts and I should be twirling my hair. Maybe he was.

"Well...I'm sorry because I don't know either. I really should have been telling you that everyday we've had together."

"Mark—"

"Shhh," he whispered.

He put a finger to my mouth to keep me from talking.

As if some imaginary kid was standing over us and we were his command center toys, Mark held his arms out stiffly pretending to be a little action figure giving a hug. It made me laugh. Then, Mark leaned into me and planted his lips on mine. His face was warm and gentle, not the machine-molded parts of a little plastic toy. It was familiar, but sent chills up my back because it had been a long time since he kissed me like this. He stood up and took my hand to help me to my feet.

"What about Rachel's dollhouse and the rest of the toys?"

"It can wait. We have all night," he said.

And with that, he led me upstairs to the soft double bed with real sheets and pillows, in our bedroom where no make-believe was needed.

Mr. Black

An overdose would be easy, planting too many of her pills in a pot of coffee, but Helen didn't trust me to make a pot of coffee right or to even pour a cup for her. She'd take one sip and pour it out, saying it was too strong or too weak, even if I measured it exactly the way she did. She would stomp into the kitchen and pour the whole pot down the drain and remake it her way just to be spiteful.

I could strangle or suffocate her, but that would require sneaking up on her and touching her while she was still living. I abhorred the thought of having to touch her right before killing her. Plus, she had more energy than me and might be able to fight me off and escape.

An ax or large butcher knife would suffice, but it would be awfully messy. I'm accustomed to cleaning up her messes, but all the blood would require bleach water and soap. Depending on what room it happened in, the carpet might have to be removed or the walls scraped and repainted. Such activity might draw suspicion to the house because I'd have to haul away the old carpet and buy supplies. As much as I dreamed of hacking her to pieces, it would be too risky.

Fortunately, there was an old box of arsenic powder at the school used to lace rat traps in the boiler room. I scooped a few spoons of it into a bag several weeks ago and hid it in the basement inside one of the small model homes on the train set. Helen never went down there. I was hoping to taint her food with it, or possibly sprinkle some in her pill bottles.

Helen had just gone upstairs. I'd slept downstairs on the sofa or in the spare bedroom for years now. I was still sitting on the sofa contemplating Christmas when there was a knock at the door.

"Helen? There's someone at the door," I called out, forgetting for a moment that there was no way she could hear me upstairs with her door closed.

I lugged myself off of the sofa just as the knock came again. My knees popped from the agony of standing. I grabbed the arm of the sofa for support to turn myself around and go toward the door. I had no idea who would be knocking on the door at this hour, much less visiting us at all. To my surprise, it was Travis.

"Travis? I thought we wouldn't see you till tomorrow." I stood aside so he could come in.

"Sorry it's so late. I hope I'm not intruding. I knew that you and Mrs. Black kept late hours and I saw all the lights on. So, I thought I'd stop by since I was out," Travis explained.

"Oh, you aren't intruding at all. It's always good to see you. Helen just went upstairs to bed a few minutes ago."

"Don't wake her just for me. I could come back tomorrow if that would be better," he said.

"No, no, please come in."

I gently tugged at the sleeve of his coat to urge him to come in. Some friendly company and conversation would be nice. This house had not seen any in several years. I knew that Helen had just locked herself in her bedroom and would be reading for several hours, but I chose not to disturb her to tell her Travis was here. If she overheard us talking, she'd mistaken it for the television anyway. Besides, it would be nice having a guest all to myself for a little while.

Although I was blatantly looking Travis up and down and admiring his lean physique, I would have to try hard to control myself and not look too eager in front of him. Just barely touching the back of his hand when I pulled at his coat would have to be sufficient. There was so much I would love to talk to him about concerning the love of men but given the circumstances, Travis was not the person I could confide in.

"Thanks, Mr. Black," Travis said as I took his coat and scarf and hung them on the back of the door.

"So, how's the family?" I asked.

"Fine."

"You don't sound so sure."

"Well, you know how the White family is. It's a never-ending soap opera."

"I've seen your siblings' names in the paper a time or two, but it's no different than anyone else in this town."

"Oh really?"

"Sure. Town Secure Bank's president was just arrested on charges of credit card fraud and embezzlement. That tells you how secure they are! The bank will probably close because of the number of accounts that have pulled out. About thirty people will lose their jobs. Most of their employees have already relocated. And one of the private practitioners just skipped town. Did you read about that? He was being investigated for some huge pharmaceutical drug deal that went down on the Internet."

"Things never get boring in this town, do they?"

"The Dreg's dirty laundry sure keeps the newspaper in business. And the dry cleaners too, I guess." I laughed a little too loud at my own joke. I stopped when I saw the expression on Travis's face. He looked like he was wincing in pain. "Is everything okay, Travis?"

"My mother is seeing someone," he said.

"Oh yeah. What's his name, from church?"

"Calvin," he said in a sigh.

"That's it. Calvin. He's a real nice fellow, crazy about your mom too. I take it you aren't too crazy about him."

"It's not that I don't like him. I don't know the man; I just met him for the first time tonight. As long as he's good to Mom, it shouldn't matter what I think, but she didn't tell him about me."

"Tell him what about you?" I asked. Travis gave me a hard stare with his eyebrows raised as if I should already know. It finally registered with me. "About that—if your life could be any easier…would you—"

"Do you consider your life to be easy?" Travis asked.

"Fair enough."

I didn't consider my life to be any easier. As a matter of fact, it was probably a lot more difficult. At least Travis had experienced true love with the type of person his heart really desired. Just for that, I was jealous of him. Despite any small joys masked by my own ignorance in life, I still always longed to be somebody else.

"Have you been to Justin's grave any?" Travis asked, changing the subject.

"No, I haven't." I looked down at my feet in shame.

Travis kept quiet and just nodded. His silence was punishment enough. I don't really know why I had not gone to visit Justin's grave. I don't think Helen had gone to the cemetery since the day we buried him. Time just slips away from us. It keeps moving, and often we forget to stop and take time for the things in our life that aren't going anywhere.

"I'm going to go tomorrow, and then head back to Memphis," Travis said after a long break of awkward silence.

"You're not going back to your Mom's?"

"No. I made quite a fool of myself back there, said some things I shouldn't have and then stormed out. I'm pretty embarrassed about it."

"What did you say?"

"A few things I'd be more embarrassed to repeat. Calvin was making some friendly jokes about pretty girls and such,

231

and so I told him I don't like girls. I said it right there in front of everyone. It had already been pretty obvious that everyone had met him before. They all knew about him, but Mom never told me. "

"So your Mom kept both of you a secret from each other, huh?"

"I guess. He knew who I was, but he didn't know everything about me that he should have probably known."

Travis's words made me think of Justin and how hard it must have been for him to carry the burden of his secret for as long as he did. How long did he know he was gay before he told us? All of his life, perhaps? I wondered if he would have ever chosen to tell us at all had he never met Travis. Helen and I both admitted that we never suspected anything about Justin. Neither of us had a clue until he told us. It broke Helen's heart. She really wanted grandchildren. It didn't bother me as much, but it was as if suddenly Justin was a completely different person whom I'd never known at all.

"And you blame your Mom for not telling him?" I asked.

"Well, I don't blame her."

"Think about how hard it must have been back when she first found out about you."

"She forbade me to tell anyone else."

"But eventually she came around, right? I mean, the rest of your family knows now, don't they?"

"Yeah, eventually her embarrassment subsided and she was ready to talk about it. She even let me bring someone home one Christmas for everyone to meet."

"I wouldn't call it embarrassment, Travis. It was probably more like anger. As a parent, we do our best to raise our children the best way we can. Finding out one of them is gay all of a sudden makes us think we did something wrong. We think it's our fault."

"Is that how you felt about Justin?" Travis asked.

I paused and gave it some thought.

"Yeah, I think it was how we felt. You think you know a

232

person, Travis, your own flesh and blood. Finding out something like that doesn't make you love them any less—it shouldn't—but it sure makes you wonder what else there might be that you don't know about them. You blame yourself for having missed out on who they really are."

"It still doesn't explain why Mom didn't tell Calvin that I was gay."

"Sure it does. Think about it. You have an advantage over your Mom. You come home to visit her as much as you can, but then you get to leave. You get to go back to Memphis where you are more comfortable being yourself, where it's more accepted in a big city, I bet. You can forget all about the hold this small town had on you once. You broke free long ago. Your Mom isn't so lucky."

"I don't think I understand what you are getting at, Mr. Black."

"Well, look at it from your younger sister's point of view. No offense at all toward her little baby. He's as cute as a button, but people talk. I don't know what they say to her face, if anything, but I do know what they say behind her back. It's just like that gossip in the paper. Now, you think your sister would be talked about if she lived off somewhere in a big city?"

"No, probably not. Things like that are just more accepted."

"Now, think about it from your Mom's point of view. She has a gay son. No big deal, really. She still loves ya with all of her heart, I'm sure of that. But she lives here too, just like your sister, and—"

"And when I'm not around she can pretend I don't exist?"

"Travis, that's a bit harsh. Let's just say your Mom would never parade around town screaming at the top of her lungs that she has a gay son, but in a town like this there's nothing wrong with being reserved about such things."

"Is that how you were with Justin?"

"No. We never knew about Justin till after he met you. He moved away right after that."

"I'm always the one to blame."

"I'm not blaming you, son, please don't look at it like that."

I wanted to slap some sense into him. I just couldn't get the words to come out right. I wanted to tell him how he should respect his mother for not wanting to necessarily discuss her son's sexual preference when he's not around. She was a loyal and well-known citizen of this community, and she'd been through enough with her other kids.

She had a mixed grandbaby, a druggie son, a daughter who got raped by her boss, and a son who cheats on his wife with his student who she probably doesn't even know about. A gay son was just the icing on the cake. Sometimes I was glad Helen and I didn't have any other children. Raising Justin was hard enough. I could only imagine the hardships of raising five in the White house, had their sufferings not already been quite publicly known.

Travis had gone quiet again, and I was out of words trying my best to prevent an argument with him. The stairs behind me creaked. I knew it was Helen.

"Manny, you should have told me we had company," she said, standing there on the stairs in her heavy pink housecoat and fuzzy house shoes.

"Sorry, dear. I thought you might be asleep." I lied.

It was also the first time I had called her dear in ages.

"Travis, how are you?" Helen said, coming down the last of the stairs.

Travis stood to give her a hug.

"I haven't been here long. Maybe thirty minutes," he said looking back at me with a shrug.

"How are things with you in Memphis?" she asked.

"Fine. Lonely at times, but everything is fine."

"I bet, and how's your Mom?"

"She's good."

I laughed to myself inside my head finding joy in how Travis opened up and talked to me, but gave Helen the generic "how are you" answers. No one ever says how they really feel anymore.

"That's good. Manny tells me he sees her in church quite a bit," she said taking a seat on the sofa next to me but leaving at least a foot of space between us.

Travis sat back down in the armchair.

"I was just telling Mr. Black about my plans to go see Justin tomorrow," Travis said.

I really wished he would have refrained from talking about Justin at least for a few more minutes. The truth was there was nothing else to talk about between us. Much like Justin, we barely knew Travis at all. His link to our son was the only bond we had to Travis, so it seemed only fitting for it to be the first thing—and probably the only thing—we'd talk about now that Helen had entered the room.

"Manny, what don't you make us some hot tea? I'm sure Travis would like something to drink," Helen said, looking at me.

I looked at Travis, assuming he probably didn't want anything. I rose to my feet and waited there like some butler.

"Thank you, Mrs. Black, that would be nice," Travis said.

He and Helen both looked at me, waiting for me to step away, as if I had interrupted their conversation. I turned and went into the kitchen.

I retrieved three mugs from the cupboard: a black one, a blue one, and a red one. I filled the kettle with water and lit the stove. After placing a tea bag in each mug, I retrieved a tray from the pantry. I put the sugar and honey on it. That's when I remembered the arsenic. I raced out the back door as quickly and quietly as I could. There was an outdoor entrance to the basement. I unlocked the door and raced down the stairs, pulling a chain overhead to turn on the light.

Standing over the train set, I reached down to our house and gently lifted the roof, which I'd purposely put on a hinge. Down inside, a tiny Helen and I were gathered in the living room around a miniature Christmas tree with Justin, a diorama-like memory from years ago. I twiddled my fingers at them, waving. I gave Justin a wink, plucking the tiny bag of white powder out of the little kitchen.

I held a finger to my mouth, pretending to shush them as I closed the roof back. I looked over at the White's house and noticed it was missing. Just gone, like a black hole had swallowed it up. But the only black hole in this house was Helen. Not for long. I turned out the light and raced back upstairs and into the kitchen. The kettle had just begun to whistle.

"Did you know Justin had his first piano recital when he was in the fifth grade?" she asked out loud, and not particularly to anyone.

Travis didn't answer, knowing this was just a prelude to a story Helen was about to tell to fill the time. She cleared her throat and began to stare blankly across the room as she spoke.

"He hated piano at first. All the other kids were playing trumpet or saxophone, a smaller instrument they could carry in a case on the bus. Justin had wanted to play clarinet, but we couldn't afford one. We already had a piano, so I made him play that. He was so mad because he couldn't carry his instrument on the bus for all the other kids to see.

"Years later he was glad for that because the high school kids teased the musically talented kids with their large black instrument cases in hand. Justin said they called them band nerds or asked if they were selling cosmetics. Cosmetics? Can you believe that? The lady who used to stop by here selling door to door didn't even carry a case resembling any musical instrument I'd ever seen. So, Justin never got teased on the bus. He said he felt like an undercover musical spy because no one knew he was taking lessons too. He always did enjoy a bit of mystery in his life, didn't he?"

"I guess so. He never really talked about that before," Travis said with the tone of a classroom kid answering a question out loud to which he didn't know the right answer.

Helen went quiet with a limp smile on her face, the kind she smiles when she's lost deep in her thoughts and memories.

She was probably also smiling for knowing something about Justin that Travis didn't know. At least, he led her to believe he didn't know.

I sat the tray down on the coffee table and immediately indicated the blue mug for Travis. I picked up the black one, leaving the red one for Helen.

"Justin played the Winter Waltz at that first recital. He was the best out of twenty-something other students. Most of them were older than him too. He took home the first place medal in his division. It was the first time he had ever won anything."

I looked at Travis and could tell he was searching his brain for a sliver of that story from where Justin had already told him. He was probing the boxes in his brain for what the Winter Waltz sounded like. Had Justin ever played it again for him? Did he have that medal at his apartment with Justin's other things? I saw anger in his face because all of this escaped him. In the confines of his recollections, he couldn't find this one. I couldn't find it either. I barely remembered yesterday, much less that many years ago. Justin had probably lost the medal because Helen allowed him to play with it, or another kid had stolen it.

"Justin was so proud of that medal. It was a heavy gold coin with a piano engraved on it, hanging from a silk yellow ribbon. He complained about how heavy it was around his neck, but he was really bragging. I hung it over a trophy he won later which we placed on the mantel. You remember, don't you, Manny?"

I agreed with a nod. The mantel was once cluttered with trophies and framed award certificates. It was hard to keep track of what Justin won them for.

Helen reached into the pocket of her house coat and pulled out a small flat square box. It was worn at the edges, like an old jewelry box intended for antique costume jewelry. She leaned over and handed it to Travis.

"I found this today and I want you to have it," she explained.

Justin took the box from her, carefully opening the lid to reveal a bed of soft white cotton that glistened like snow. Justin's medal was lying inside, probably just as shiny as the day he'd won it. Its yellow ribbon was frayed at the edges, but just as bright as a lemon. He picked it up by the ribbon and took it out of the box, letting it dangle in front of us.

"Thank you so much, Mrs. Black. You don't know how much this means to me," he said with honesty.

"Justin would have wanted you to have it," Helen said.

Her voice cracked as if she might tear up, but she held back. She reached down and poured a packet of sugar into her tea and began to stir it. She raised it to her lips and took a sip. I looked at her anxiously, awaiting her approval. She licked her lips and instead, concentrated on Travis who was still admiring the medal.

I wanted to ask to see it. I wanted to hold it in my hand and feel the weight of its value. It was just a child's piano recital medal, but it might have been worth enough at the pawn shop to put a tank of gas in the car one week or to pay the water bill. If it was in Justin's old room or in the basement, I can't believe I never found it before. I couldn't believe Helen's generosity and willingness to part with it.

I refrained from asking Travis to take a look. It was too late. It was his now, but just another reason to hate Helen. I faked a smile for Travis's appreciation of the gift, but on the inside I was smiling diabolically for myself.

And for Helen.

Mrs. Black

After destroying the miniature of the White's house, I
turned to go back upstairs. I took a quick look around the
basement because I had not been down here in years. It was as
if I had discovered a secret room behind a bookcase and was
seeing it now for the first time. I couldn't remember what the
basement looked like, nor could I remember it ever looking so
clean.

Manny spent so much time down here so I expected it to be
dusty and littered with fast food wrappers and trash. Instead, it
was immaculately clean with no trash at all. The storage boxes
in the corner were stacked neatly and labeled. For a moment, I
thought they were train parts until I paused to read some of the
writing on the boxes. A few of the boxes had JUSTIN written
on the side of them in neat black letters. I could not remember
packing these boxes after Justin died. It was because I didn't.
These were boxes that had accumulated while he was still
living at home.

I walked over to the boxes and lifted the lid off the top one.
Inside was a stack of piano sheet music, along with some of his
very first books of piano lessons. His name was written in

faded blue ink at the top of each piece, some in my handwriting when he was young and some in his own. I managed to lift the heavy box and scoot it to the edge of its stack. Its weight pulled my arms downward as I moved it to the floor so that I could look inside the next box underneath.

The second box was full of framed awards. They were cheap black diploma frames I'd always found at the dollar store every time Justin had received a certificate for the Straight A Gold Club or for perfect attendance. Each year I had neatly framed his awards and hung them above his bed. When he passed to be in the next grade and received a consecutive award for the same thing the following semester, he'd take down the one from the year prior and hang up the new one in its place. I should have recycled the frames and scrap-booked the past awards, but I never did.

I counted twelve frames for Straight A grades, one for every year of school all the way through high school. He had at least eight perfect attendance awards. He was a healthy child and missed less than two weeks of school all together. The awards from high school became more plentiful as he became involved in other activities like debate team, science club, and the foreign language union. There were two plaques for his wins in track.

I thought the next box might be full of his recital trophies, but most of those were packed in boxes in his room. I'd kept them displayed on the mantel long after he moved to Memphis, removing them only a few months after his funeral. I don't know why I took them down, besides them being mementos of when Justin was growing up. For some reason, I felt the need to pack them away like all the other memories I'd filed over the years.

Instead, the next box was actually a file itself. Credit card account statements, paycheck stubs, and random receipts were all filed by the month and year. Justin had always been meticulous about keeping his life organized, a trait that had since failed both of his parents. I pulled out one of his paycheck records and looked at the date. It was from fifteen years ago when he was working at the wicker store but had not yet been promoted to manager.

A heap of small receipts in an envelope revealed gas fill-ups for his car and fast food purchases over a few months. I quickly sifted through the small pieces of paper which all looked the same, some printed in purple ink, some in black, and some on yellow carbon copy paper. I don't know why he kept them, but it was a jarring feeling to know I could put them in order by the date and time and track my son's life for months—maybe years—from so long ago.

Amongst the pile was a small envelope. I held it up to the light only to find what looked like another receipt inside. Despite feeling like a prying mother, I opened it. It was a receipt for coffee at a diner from almost twelve years ago. Although it had been protected inside the envelope, it had still yellowed a bit. Nothing in particular would have made it stand out from all the other pieces of proof of payment, except that Justin had written Travis's name at the top of it and circled the date.

There was no explanation on the back. There didn't need to be. Justin had wanted to remember this trip to the diner for some reason and it had involved Travis. The exact reason was tucked away in his head. Had he known Travis then? Maybe this receipt was from the first time they met or their first date. I put it back in the envelope and tucked it into my pocket.

The file box was lighter than the other boxes I had sifted through. I pushed it to the side and decided to take a peek into one more box. My trip down memory lane had become sad and tired, although I had yet to shed a tear. Upon opening another box, I discovered a treasure chest of multiple items, some of which might not have even belonged to Justin. There was an old wallet with a dollar in it, some keys, small empty gift bags and boxes, cat toys, ink pens, a few birthday cards, a couple of books, and a half-burnt candle that had faded over time.

I shuffled through the contents quickly and found nothing

of real importance until I came across a small jewelry-sized box at the very bottom. Curious, I retrieved it from the mess and opened it to take a look. I knew what it was as soon as I put my eyes on it. With its shiny engraved surface and frayed yellow ribbon, it was a medal. This was another one of Justin's awards that I was surprised to find stored away in a box like this with such a hodge-podge of other unimportant items.

The medal was significant because Justin had won it at his very first piano recital. He had been so proud of it and wore it around the house for days. It eventually found a place on the mantel hanging around the neck of one of his trophies. I had no idea how it ended up down here. I took it out of its box and held it by the ribbon, letting it fall to the length of it like a pendant. The medal dangled and spun at the end of its rope, a shiny golden coin that had filled a child's heart with such riches. I felt a tear of happiness slide down my cheek because the look on his face back then had filled my heart also.

I put the medal back in its box and into my pocket with the receipt and restacked the boxes back as they were, neatly on top of each other with the lids closed. I took another last look around the basement hoping to find more forgotten boxes from our past. There was only the hot water heater and the furnace. Going back up the stairs, I turned out the light on the memories of who my son was to me, stored in boxes next to the mini replica of this town we lived in.

Manny was still on the sofa where I had seen him last, slumped over into a growling nap. I went up the stairs to the bedroom and closed the door. Locking it was just a habit and to keep Manny out, although he had not come upstairs to sleep in the bed in years. I could count on one hand the number of times we had made love since Justin was conceived. It didn't matter, especially now. I had known for some time that Manny preferred the company of other men, just like his son.

I wanted to blame Manny for some disease Justin had inherited from him, but the cancer he inherited from me was much worse. Besides, I didn't believe that homosexuality was hereditary—I still don't—no matter how much Justin preached it to me. Instead, I chose to convince myself that I never knew. Justin had never told me. It was all an odd dream, the kind you don't remember five minutes after waking up.

I felt the same way about Manny, but it was easier to pretend I didn't know about him because he'd never told me. I'd wasted my whole life married to the man out of convenience, really. He kept us fed and clothed and kept the bills paid, by the skin of his teeth sometimes, but he managed. I never worked a day in my life, and maybe I was selfish for standing by him all this time but we all reach a point in our life where we stop thinking about the better things. We stop dreaming of tomorrow because we've opened our eyes to too many days of the harsh boring reality of the fruitless life we've been living. We accept the fact it is not going to get any better.

The headlights of a car crossed the window. It was someone pulling into the drive. I had no idea who would be visiting us at this hour, or visiting here at all. I hoped it wasn't carolers. I went to the window to look out and saw Travis getting out of his car and walking up the sidewalk. If Manny did not wake up to go to the door, I was not going to go down and answer it either. I stood at the window, hidden behind the drapes, waiting to see if Travis would be walking back to his car and driving away. He knocked and then knocked again. Then, I heard Manny's voice and all went quiet outside as he let Travis in.

I waited there for a minute or two like an eavesdropping parent, listening for their voices from downstairs to rise through a vent in the ceiling. I thought about getting down on my knees and putting my ear against the floor to try to listen, but it seemed silly. And it was silly for me to think their muffled conversation was intentional so that I couldn't hear it. I hesitated for a few minutes, unsure if I should go downstairs or not.

I stood at the door to the bedroom with my hand on the knob, rehearsing a conversation in my head that I knew would never take place. Too much time had passed for me to change my mind and still blame Travis for taking Justin away from me. No matter how many questions I had about the last ten years of Justin's life away from this home, the answers wouldn't bring him back. No matter how Travis might answer, I knew his words would not appease me.

I opened the door slowly, expecting it to creak on its hinges. It didn't. I slid into the hallway up against the wall like some sort of burglar or spy. Cocking my head to one side, I strained to hear their voices rising up the stairs. I could only make out an occasional word or two, nothing that signified they were talking about Justin. I stuck my hand into my pocket and felt the medal's box and the piece of receipt paper. I had almost forgotten them there tucked into the warm folds of my housecoat. I took them out and opened the small box. I took out the medal and the cotton it lay on and placed the receipt in the bottom of the box. I covered it with the cotton and laid the medal back inside. Closing the lid, I slipped the box back into my pocket and then descended the stairs.

Manny said he thought I was asleep. It was a lie I'd expect from him. Travis could have been here for several hours and Manny would have kept him all to himself if he could. Dying to flirt with him and unable to keep his hands to himself, he'd practically drool over Travis. He'd keep calm just because of who Travis was, but inside his head he'd be committing unthinkable acts. Travis would leave and Manny would rush to the bathroom to lock the door and abuse himself.

Travis stood up to hug me. It was a distant hug with a light pat on the back, not the presumable warm bear hug he'd given his Mom when greeting her at the door. I was not going to be the first to bring up Justin, despite us really having nothing else to talk about. It was Travis who mentioned him first, though, when he said he was going to visit Justin's grave tomorrow. I knew he would ask us to come along, and I wouldn't go with him anyway. Neither of us would be able to say the things out loud we'd want to say to Justin if we were standing there alone.

At the top of the stairs, I had decided to give the medal to Travis. I didn't want it to seem like a last-minute Christmas gift I pulled out of a closet or drawer, so I started talking about Justin's first recital. I liked watching Travis squirm when he didn't know the name of the tune Justin played. The Winter Waltz. I made Justin play it for me from time to time all the way through high school, and especially during the holidays. I doubted he ever mentioned it to Travis because I had made him play it for me so much. It was still nice to have a memory of Justin without Travis in it.

There were many. After all, Justin didn't meet Travis until after high school and after two years at the community college. But, since he'd been gone from our lives long before his death, those memories had grown harder to find. Letting go of one more of them was not as hard as I thought it would be.

I sent Manny to get tea because I wanted to give Travis the medal while we were alone, but something kept me from giving it up. Instead, we sat in silence and waited for Manny to return. I decided the look of horror on Manny's face, when I gave Travis the medal, would be worth the wait.

I took the box out of my coat pocket and handed it to Travis. He opened the lid and admired the medal in front of us. The look in his eyes was of sincere appreciation. I meant it when I told him Justin would have wanted him to have it. Manny fidgeted next to me like a jealous kid brother who had wanted the shiny coin instead. I realized this was the closest I'd sat next to Manny in years. I wanted to get up and move to the chair across from him, but kept my seat on the sofa to avoid embarrassing him in front of our guest.

Instead, I took a sip of the tea although I knew Manny could barely boil water without making a mess of it. It was bitter and stale, probably because our tea bags were so old.

Travis put the medal back in its box, not lifting the cotton to find the receipt. I knew he wouldn't throw the box away, so I decided not to tell him about it. Some day, sooner or later, he'd find it and I knew it would be a pleasant surprise for him.

He'd wonder if I had put it there. Or maybe he'd think I never knew the receipt was there at all. He would remove the piece of paper and unfold it, and his mind would race with an array of memories from that night with Justin at the coffee shop.

Travis would imagine Justin had put the receipt there in its safe place. I found solace in knowing that although Travis would never suspect I put the receipt there for him, it would be me who was ultimately responsible for his fond reminiscence, just as I had felt when I found Justin's awards in the basement.

Perhaps he'd place the receipt in a frame or in a memory album, or maybe he'd put it back in the box under the medal and tuck it away in a special place. Travis might not ever remove the complete contents at all to find the receipt.

It didn't matter.

That minuscule piece of paper, which had obviously been important to Justin for some reason, was now with Travis. And as I told him when I gave it to him, Justin would have wanted him to have it.

The tea was making me sleepy and I suddenly felt ill. I wanted to believe it was just from parting with Justin's medal. It was hard giving it up, but I didn't regret it. I finished off the tea and excused myself to go up to bed. Travis said he needed to be going anyway and walked with me to the door. I didn't blame him. The less time spent alone with Manny the better.

Manny got up and followed behind us. He handed Travis his coat and they shook hands. Manny awkwardly tried to hug Travis but ended up just patting him on the shoulder. Travis thanked me again for Justin's medal. His good-byes were quick, but sincere.

The medal was my gift now to the both of them—Travis and Justin. It still hurt. As soon as the door shut, I ran up the stairs to the bathroom. I was going to be physically ill. I leaned over the toilet, crying, waiting for the pain to escape. But it felt like it didn't want to leave this time.

Manny just stood at the front door, even after Travis had driven away. Lost in thought, some perverted trance. And just smiling.

Lorraine

A holiday, especially Christmas, makes it easier to forget about the problems in life from the day before. We celebrate the birth of Christ, and yet we also celebrate the birth of our family traditions. A smoked ham, a pecan pie, a strand of colored lights on the outside of the house, stockings on the mantel, greeting cards adorning the doorway, or a tree for each of the kids' rooms are all things we hold close. They are all physical things, but unlike people, they are the things that have been there year after year. They help us to remember.

Having all of my kids here was most important of all. It rarely happens at any time of the year, much less during the holidays. To think this year could have been the best year of all was just selfish of me. There has always been a broken toy, tears to dry, fights to break up, or in-laws to visit instead. Then, Frank left us and I never thought another Christmas could feel complete without him. I wondered if things might have been any different had I already told the kids about the cancer.

Ellen called and told me she and Mark had made amends. Who could ask for a better gift for her and her family than that? They came and got Robbie and Rachel a few hours after she had left. Santa had already come to their house, so the kids were anxious to get home. I was almost jealous that Ellen got to spend the night with her family tonight.

Sebastian kissed me good-bye on the cheek, eager to go back to his apartment or wherever young men go after visiting with their family on Christmas. Martin and Marline eventually retired to their home up the street with the kids. Calvin said his good-bye and wished me a Merry Christmas, thanking me and apologizing for the evening. I told him no apology was necessary.

I expected Clare to leave too, but she and Jake stayed. I was glad because I wasn't ready to be all alone again. We sat down in the floor beneath the amber glow of the lights on the tree and entertained Jake with his new toys. He soon grew tired and was ready for bed. Clare took him upstairs and decided to turn in too.

I tidied the kitchen, storing away the leftovers and taking out the trash. A mother can never relax until the kitchen is clean. Marcus greeted me at the back porch, hoping for a plate of scraps. I didn't want to disappoint twice in one evening, so I fixed him a plate.

"Merry Christmas, Kitty," I said as I stroked the back of his neck.

He purred loudly, devouring the bits of ham on the plate in front of him.

Back inside, I retrieved a large black plastic bag from under the kitchen sink and took it into the living room. I filled it with the torn paper and ribbon from the opened gifts. Like a hobo digging through a dumpster, I salvaged gift bags and bows from the paper which I could store away and use again next year. I found a sparkly gold gift bag that had been used again and again for at least three or four years, nearly another tradition of my own that no one else was aware of. It was now torn down one side. I hesitated, but placed it in the bag with the other trash anyway. Everyone had offered to help clean up before they left, but I urged them to just leave it. By now I was quite accustomed to picking up the pieces of the holiday at the end of the night.

Satisfied with the living room, I carried the trash bag full of paper outside. Marcus's plate was empty so I picked it up and slid it into the dishwasher when I came back inside. Marcus ran under my feet to come inside too. He didn't usually like to come inside much, but I guess he had had enough of the snow. I sat down to rest my feet and admire the tree. It looked so bare without any gifts under it. It was like coming home and finding a piece of furniture someone has moved across the room. Your mind refuses to settle on the changes that have been made.

With the cat on my lap, I guess I had dozed off for a bit. I was dreaming of Travis. He was in his car and headed back to Memphis. I could see him as if I was a passenger sitting next to him, but he didn't know I was there. He looked like he was crying. I called out to him, but he couldn't hear me. I was not really there.

Suddenly, a small knock at the door woke me from the dream. I checked my watch and it was just thirty minutes before midnight. I stood up to go to the door, picking up Marcus from my lap and putting him in the chair behind me. I checked the peep hole to see who could possibly be at the door this late. It was Travis. I quickly unlocked the door and opened it for him as if he was a long lost relative who'd come home at last.

"Sorry, couldn't find my key," he said with a shrug.

"It's okay. Want to come in?" I asked.

"I thought maybe you'd want to go looking at Christmas lights," he said in a stutter.

"Now? It's late. Do you think people will still have their lights on?"

"Yours are on."

"Only because I fell asleep and forgot to turn them off."

"Well, if we don't see any, we'll just keep driving around the block and going by your house."

"Let me get my coat."

Travis stayed at the door like some polite delivery person who was just dropping something off; even the smile on his face seemed a bit unnatural. I thought he might still be mad at me, but when I returned to the door with my coat on he offered me his arm. I took it and let him lead me outside and down the steps of the porch. He opened the passenger's door to his car for me and closed it once I was in. It was still warm inside from his drive back from wherever he'd gone. I watched him walk around and get in behind the wheel. He looked at me and smiled. I raised my eyebrows and smiled back, still unsure of his true intentions. He started the car and turned down the radio.

"I guess I owe you an apology, don't I?"

"I think I owe you one too," I said.

"No, it was all my fault. I blew up at Calvin for no reason at all."

"Well, it was my fault for not telling you about Calvin before today."

"I would have liked to have known you were seeing someone. Everyone else knew, didn't they?"

"Yes, everyone knew," I said after some hesitation.

"Why didn't you tell him about me?" Travis asked.

"I guess I forgot."

"Forgot?"

"Well, I didn't forget, and I didn't intentionally forget to tell Calvin about you, Travis. It's just one of those things I felt didn't matter. I didn't feel the need to explain to him the personal lives of all my children before inviting him over."

It broke my heart to hear Travis ask if I was ashamed of him. He stared blankly across the steering wheel as if waiting for something or someone to appear in the distance, when actually both of us were just facing the back of my car parked in front of him as we sat there in the driveway. Yet, I knew his mind was looking at something else. I wasn't ashamed of him. I wasn't ashamed of any of my children. I had yet to explain most of my own faults to Calvin in the little time I had known him much less those of my kids, but I knew Travis wouldn't understand that.

"I'm not ashamed of you Travis. I'm proud of you because of who you are. Not just *that*. That's just a part of you that doesn't make me feel any different about you as a person."

"It just seems like you were hiding it, even hiding him from me," he said.

"I barely know Calvin. Do you think he sat down the first day we met and told me all about his life? Your sexuality shouldn't be an instigator on who I choose to see, just like Jake, or your brother's drug use, or what happened to Ellen shouldn't be either. Those things are all just a part of life. And as far as hiding Calvin from you, that's not why I hadn't told you about him. Your opinion means the most to me, so I wanted him to be a surprise, I guess."

"A surprise?"

"Yeah, after you met him tonight I couldn't wait to sit down with you after everyone was gone and hear what you thought about him. That would have meant a lot to me."

"I'm sorry I ruined it for you."

"Oh, Travis, you didn't ruin anything. It was my fault for thinking the outcome of all of this could never possibly be *unpleasant*."

You think you know your kids. You raise them and try not to make the same mistakes your parents made. You think you've taught them right from wrong, and you pray as they grow older that they were listening. But none of that can change who they become. None of it changes the path they choose when you aren't standing there next to them. Travis always said this was never a choice for him; he was born that way. I blamed myself for the longest, wondering what I had done wrong.

Those types of wounds never heal completely, but time helps to fix the things we can't change. If I could have Travis any other way, of course, I'd want him to be different than he is now. But who's to say he'd be any happier? Who's to say I would be? There are things I'd like to go back and change about all my kids, but I know I can't. So, as a mother, I have to accept it. Getting Travis to believe in my acceptance is the hard part.

After both speaking our apologies and working things out as only a mom and her son can, I reached across the seat to hug him. He turned off the car, and we got out to go back inside the house.

"I'll apologize to Calvin if you'd like," Travis said pausing on the steps.

"Don't worry about it for now. Let it all blow over. Besides, I think your choice of words on what you do in the bedroom was quite an eye-opener for him," I said with a laugh.

Travis blushed.

"Did Clare spend the night?" he asked, quickly changing the subject.

"Yes, she and Jake went up to bed a few hours ago," I said opening the front door.

"Mom?"

"Yes, Travis."

"If it means anything to you, I think you and Calvin make a nice couple."

"Thanks, Travis. That actually means a lot to me."

Just as we stepped back into the house, the grandfather clock chimed midnight. Christmas had arrived. Travis and I hugged again and wished each other Merry Christmas. Then, he went up the stairs to take a hot bath before bed. I hung my coat on the wall and then wandered through the house looking for things to pass the time. I almost asked Travis if he felt like staying downstairs to sit and chat with me for a while, but I knew he was tired. Besides, I liked the idea of having the first hours of the birth to Christmas morn all to myself while two of my beloved children and one grandchild were sleeping soundly upstairs in their beds.

After finding nothing else to clean or pick up, I decided to sit down again in the recliner and talk to Frank. He had always been a good listener. And although I considered myself a quiet woman, always willing to lend an ear to those who needed it, I always had gentle words to share with my husband at the end of each day, in life and in death.

"Frank, honey? Merry Christmas, dear. I can't say it was the best one ever, but it sure would have been better had you been here, love. Frank, I've decided to tell the kids. About the cancer. We've wasted too much time in this house keeping secrets. I'm not going to keep this one any longer. I'll see you soon, my love. I'll see you soon…"

Travis

I arrived at the cemetery just as the caretaker was unlocking the gate. He was a wobbly old man that limped out of my way as I pulled my car in. Last night at the gas station, I had spotted fresh flowers for sale sticking out of tubs on a stand near the front. They were sprays of white lilies, holly branches, and red roses. Happy to find any filling station even open, I stopped in this morning and bought two of the bouquets, one for my father's grave and one for Justin's. Peggy was already gone. A small bubbly blonde girl greeted me from behind the counter with a friendly smile, despite being at work on Christmas Day.

"Did you forget somebody special today?" she asked out of politeness.

"Nah, I didn't forget."

I never liked fake silk flowers. I looked across the highway at the small flower shop where I thought I'd bought flowers from the mysterious old lady before. The windows were boarded up and the tiny house still looked deserted. There were black patches on the shingles where the snow had encircled holes in the roof. The quaint little shop looked like it had been condemned for quite some time, as if no one had lived there in years. I could remember being inside the warm cottage, inhaling its sweet candle aromas, and talking to the kind black woman. It was all quite vivid to me, but the illumination of my memory told me it might have just been a brilliant dream.

I stopped first at my father's stone. With no disrespect to my father, I hoped the spot next to him stayed vacant for a long time. I felt like I needed to say something but kept all my words inside. I knelt and laid one of the bouquets in front of the headstone.

When I turned to walk back to the car, I stepped carefully back through the footprints I'd made in the snow. From the car, I looked back out at my tracks that led to Dad's grave and stopped like some person had been standing there and then just disappeared. The cellophane wrapped around the flowers reflected the dancing light against the snow.

I drove deeper into the yard to Justin's marker. I pulled up behind it. The flecks in the marble glistened like diamonds. I was stunned to find a set of snow prints already there, as if someone had just been here before me to visit him. It is possible they were left from someone visiting yesterday. I wondered who it could have been. Seeing the snow disturbed around his headstone bothered me for some strange reason. I wanted to be the first one traipsing through the clean frosty blanket of white to visit him. I walked around to the front of his headstone, leaving my own set of prints.

"JB," I whispered under my breath.

The wind answered and I turned around to see if anyone was watching. I was all alone in the garden of granite and marble, slabs of stone jutting out of the white hills like the teeth of sleeping giants. Brushing the cap of snow from the top of the stone, I laid the bunch of flowers across the top. The petals of one of the roses got lost in the wind, pouring across the frosty snow like droplets of blood. My nose started to run and I couldn't tell if it was from tears or from the chillful air.

I knelt for a moment close to the ground, steadying myself with a hand on the rim of Justin's headstone. There were no words I could speak out loud that he had not heard before, so I let my mind wander to every picnic we'd taken in the park, every movie night at home with microwave popcorn, every late night kiss in bed we shared, every early cup of coffee on the balcony. Those were the most meaningful things I kept close to me now. And so, I reached into my pocket and took out the small box that Helen had given to me last night. I opened it, revealing the yellow ribbon like a ray of sunshine. I took the medal from its pillow of cotton and draped the ribbon around the edge of the stone, crowning my hero.

I stood up, slipping the empty box back into my coat pocket, and stepped back to admire the ornament hanging there. It clanged against his stone like a wind chime. I smiled and thought I heard angels singing. Someone was singing. A chorale of holiday music was coming from behind me. I turned to see Mom's car pulling up behind me. Clare and Jake were in the back seat. She had the window down and I could hear her radio playing.

"Mind if we join you?" Mom called out.

I shook my head no and smiled, waving at them like they were on a float in a parade passing by. Clare held Jake up to the window and waved his tiny hand back at me as she pulled the hood of his coat up over his head. They both got out of the car, pulling their boots through the snow to come stand next to me.

"I've never seen Justin's stone before. It's nice," Clare said.

"Thanks, Sis."

Another car pulled up behind Mom's. Martin, Ellen, and Sebastian all stepped out of the car. Ellen was carrying a bouquet of red and white roses.

"Merry Christmas, Bub," Sebastian said walking up to me and hugging my neck.

"What are all of you guys doing here?" I asked.

"Mom invited us," Ellen said, kneeling to place her flowers next to Justin's stone.

She reached for the medal and turned it around in her hand

to read its engraving.

"Have you been to Dad's grave yet?" Martin asked.

"I stopped there first, but we can go back there if you guys haven't been," I answered.

"You done here?" Mom asked, winking at me.

"Yeah. I think I am done here."

We all got back into our cars and drove back to Dad's marker. Ellen rode with me and quickly told me how she and Mark had made up last night. I told her how happy I was for her, and I really was. Each of us had had enough tragedy in our lives. It was nice to hear that at least one of us had one less obstacle to overcome. She'd no longer have to find that odd middle-aged balance in life of trying to start over after you've spent a better part of your life with someone, but woke up suddenly to find them gone. I was tired of denying myself the opportunity to start over. I was going to have to do it whether I wanted to or not. It might as well be now.

Mom shed a few tears at Dad's grave. Martin and Sebastian comforted her with their arms wrapped around her. Clare rested her head on my shoulder while holding Jake. He was the innocent one, too little to understand, too young to know of the loving man he'd never met long enough to remember. Clare was a beautiful mother though and I knew she'd tell him all about his Grandpa some day.

"Is there anyone else we need to see while we are here, kids?" Mom asked, looking over her shoulder right at Ellen.

"Not today," Ellen said, shaking her head.

"Are you coming back to the house?" Mom asked me with an eager grin.

"No, I put my bags in the car this morning. I think I'll leave from here and head back to Memphis if that's okay."

"You go ahead if you need to. Call me when you get back to let me know you made it in okay," she said.

"It's less than two hours away. You should come back and stay a while," Martin said with a gentle punch on my shoulder.

"Oh, I'm sure he's got things to attend to back at his place,"

Mom said in my defense.

"Merry Christmas, Mom," I said wrapping my arms around her neck.

"Merry Christmas to you too, Son."

I said my good-byes to each of my siblings and Jake. I waved to my other nieces and nephews, who had remained in the car keeping warm, enjoying handheld video games Santa had brought. Martin, Ellen, and Sebastian left first. Then, Mom, Clare, and Jake drove away. I stood there for a second admiring the bright morning sun sparkling across the powdery snow. When their two cars were out of the gate and down the road out of sight, I turned and walked back to my own car.

Back down Highway 55, I pulled into Four Points Grocery for a cold drink. I was shocked to find the glass door locked. I stuck my face up to the glass, but did not see Mr. Greer inside. The butcher counter was clean; the small convenience store was dark. A sign in the window indicated he was not open today: CLOSED FOR CHRISTMAS, REMEMBER THE REASON FOR THE SEASON.

I sat in the idling car for a moment to contemplate the two directions I could take from here. One was a boring stretch of highway that led back to my lonely apartment in the city, and the other was just a few blocks away leading home.

I chose home.

A NOTE FROM THE AUTHOR:

Although writing is an extremely lonely and personal task, there are still a few people I'd like to thank who played some integral part in making this book possible, whether they knew it or not. First, thank you to Kathy Lindsey for reading the manuscript in its infant stages and letting me know it was my best yet. Big hugs to Cheryl Anne Gardner for her formatting assistance, and for just "getting me." An emoticon smiley ☺ to R. J. Keller for her help in making a big difference in "the end." To LK Gardner-Griffie, my online partner in crime, for her advice and honesty; this book wouldn't have a name without you. To photographer Sally Ashbrook for her generosity in giving my book a face. All my love goes out to Tress and Tami, two of my biggest fans. The book is finally done, girls! Lots of love to John for believing in me and this book even when I didn't. And to my own Mom, my true audience, thank you for the standing ovation.

A NOTE ABOUT THE AUTHOR:

Shannon Yarbrough is the author of two books, *The Other Side of What*, first published in 2003, and *Stealing Wishes*, first published in 2008. He lives in St. Louis, Missouri, with his partner, John, and their many pets. He is always at work on another novel. Visit him online at www.shannonyarbrough.com.